"YOU PLANNED THIS,"
SHE SAID IN TONES THICK WITH
ACCUSATION.

Rhea's disgruntled snarl didn't deter him in the least. Steve simply reached for her hand and pulled her next to him. "If it makes you feel any better, we'll do our warm-up exercises in tandem today."

Her frown faded. Her interest was piqued. He turned her toward him, standing so close, his toes nearly touched hers.

"This is an exercise?" She eyed him warily as he set his hands on each side of her head. From the blinding blue of his eyes to the set of his strongly sculpted jaw, she clearly read his intent. And still she asked, "W-what are you doing?"

"Another exercise," he murmured. "For the lips."

He lowered his mouth to hers, slowly, surely. A quivery surprise rippled through her. Yearning dizzied her. At some vague level she wondered at the intensity of need pulsing through her, but the reasons *why* she felt were quickly overshadowed by *what* she felt. . . .

A CANDLELIGHT ECSTASY SUPREME

NO STRINGS ATTACHED

Prudence Martin

A CANDLELIGHT ECSTASY SUPREME

Published by
Dell Publishing Co., Inc.
1 Dag Hammarskjold Plaza
New York, New York 10017

Dell ® TM 681510, Dell Publishing Co., Inc.

Candlelight Ecstasy Supreme is a trademark of
Dell Publishing Co., Inc.

Candlelight Ecstasy Romance®, 1,203,540, is a registered trademark
of Dell Publishing Co., Inc.

ISBN: 0-440-16416-8

Printed in the United States of America
First printing—December 1983

For Carin, with thanks.

To Our Readers:

Candlelight Ecstasy is delighted to announce the start of a brand-new series—Ecstasy Supremes! Now you can enjoy a romance series unlike all the others—longer and more exciting, filled with more passion, adventure, and intrigue—the stories you've been waiting for.

In months to come we look forward to presenting books by many of your favorite authors and the very finest work from new authors of romantic fiction as well. As always, we are striving to present the unique, absorbing love stories that you enjoy most—the very best love has to offer.

Breathtaking and unforgettable, Ecstasy Supremes will follow in the great romantic tradition you've come to expect *only* from Candlelight Ecstasy.

Your suggestions and comments are always welcome. Please let us hear from you.

Sincerely,

The Editors
Candlelight Romances
1 Dag Hammarskjold Plaza
New York, New York 10017

CHAPTER ONE

The crunch of metal meeting metal echoed into the frost-filled air with a sickening grind.

Rhea's seat belt clicked as it tightened against her chest; her body jolted even as her fingers clenched the steering wheel. The jarring of impact, the shattering of glass, the screeching of brakes, seemed to last a lifetime. But in seconds the car stilled.

She sat stiffly, as if afraid to discover she was hurt. She looked out the windshield. The crumpled hood obscured her view of the other car.

"Damn," she muttered in a voice oddly unlike her own.

Shaking, she turned off the ignition, undid the seat belt, and opened the door. A brisk draft chilled her cheeks and tingled her nose. She heard the sound of purposeful footsteps ringing over the pavement of the parking lot. Gulping a chunk of cold air, Rhea forced herself to stand. As her lungs filled, reality seeped in. She reluctantly turned toward the front of her car and saw the back of a dark wool trench coat as a man bent to examine the damage. On legs still quivering from the unexpected fright, she moved to join him.

"You must have taken that turn at a tidy clip," he said without looking at her.

Gray puffs of his breath hovered a moment, then dispelled. Rhea watched them waft away, then clasped her gloved hands together. "I'm sorry—"

11

"Not as much as I am," he interrupted. He straightened and confronted her.

To her immense surprise, she found herself looking up into a face more filled with resignation than rage. A pair of astonishingly blue eyes studied her without the scowl she'd expected. A brown moustache curved over a pair of finely drawn lips. The nose was strongly sculpted, as was the jaw. It was, on the whole, a comforting face. Rhea began breathing more normally.

"I've only had the MG two days," he said.

She ran her eyes over his car. It was small and sat low to the ground, with a black canvas top and fancy hubcaps. The front displayed its mint condition in a glossy dark green. The right rear side wrinkled and puckered like an aging beauty queen, the shiny green mangled beyond recognition.

"Oh, I am sorry," she repeated, the inadequacy of her apology resounding in her ears. "I didn't see you. . . ."

"That much is obvious," he said with gentle sarcasm.

Shards of glass snapped beneath his feet as the man moved between the two cars. Though the sky was overcast, occasional glints of bronze streaked through his hair. She focused on the various shades of reds and sable brown mingling through his hair. That way she avoided seeing the dented metal and the broken lights.

Finally he hunched his shoulders and asked, "Is your car operable?"

"I don't know."

"Try driving it into a vacant slot."

"But aren't we supposed to wait until the police come?"

"This is a private parking lot. They don't have jurisdiction over accidents on private lots."

Another car turned into the lot and eased past them, the driver wrenching his neck to survey the remains of the accident. The man glanced at her with a hint of impatience. "Go see if you can move your car."

He strode away and Rhea returned to her damaged Chevette. Her hands were still trembling, but she managed to turn the key. The ignition fired instantly. Relieved, she shifted into reverse and slowly backed. Though the front end shimmied wildly, she was able to maneuver into one of the parking slots. She sat rigidly, gripping the steering wheel and watching the man drive into the slot he'd been backing from when she'd smashed into his car.

She shivered with the memory of the lurching impact and the harsh grating of metals and brittle shattering of glass. She remembered turning from the street into the lot; she remembered angrily thinking of all the things she should have said and didn't during her visit home. The anger had pulsed through her veins. It had pulsed right down to her foot on the gas pedal, sending her plowing into the MG.

Sighing, Rhea once again got out of her car. She met the man beside his corrugated bumper. He was scribbling over the back of a wrinkled envelope, but spoke as she drew near.

"Do you live here in the complex, or are you just visiting?" he inquired.

"I live here." She paused, then held out her hand. "I'm Rhea Nichols, apartment two fifteen."

His brief clasp was firmly confident. He thrust the envelope at her. "Steve Bradley. Three forty-six. I've got an appointment to go to, but here's the name of my insurance agent. He's listed in the book. Have your agent contact him to work out the details."

She glanced down at the bold scrawl on the envelope, then back up at him. Those blue eyes of his actually smiled at her. It was too much. Had he yelled at her, blamed her, cursed her, Rhea could have met it all with an indifference as frosty as the late November air. His kindness, however,

13

undid her. To her horror, instead of calmly thanking him, she burst into tears.

Through the blur of her watery gaze, she saw surprise, consternation, compassion, flit over his features. She lifted her balled fist to her mouth and tried unsuccessfully to stop acting like an hysterical fool. He did not even hesitate. He wrapped her in his arms, pressing her into the soothing support of his shoulder.

A piquant aroma blended with the wool to tickle her nostrils. A subdued strength emanated from the arms securely enfolded about her. Steam fogged her glasses; tears clumped her lashes together. She burrowed farther into the warmth he offered and tried to mumble an apology. Her sobs smothered the words.

He pulled her closer and gently rubbed the back of her quilted down jacket. "Hey, hey, don't worry. It's just the shock. Go ahead and cry it out."

She followed this advice to the letter. She cried until there wasn't a tear left in her system. At intervals she feebly attempted to pull away from him, but each time, he firmly tightened his hold on her and she soon ceased to resist at all. He continued to murmur words she didn't hear in a low, pleasant voice that tranquilized her. Sobs gradually gave way to sniffles, and he loosened his hold. Feeling utterly foolish, Rhea took the handkerchief he held out, blew her nose, and hiccuped.

"I—I'm sorry. You've p-probably m-m-missed your appointment," she stuttered around another frame-shuddering hiccup.

"Ah, well, these things happen."

Too embarrassed to look at him, she fluttered the handkerchief in his direction. He did not take it. Instead, he reached out and removed her glasses. Her head whipped up and she squinted to watch myopically as with measured movements he unbuttoned his coat, freed the tail of his shirt from the waistband of gray cord slacks, and

14

wiped the lenses clear. She looked from the indistinct blur of his hands to the indistinct blur of his face and felt the intensity of the searching gaze she could not see.

"Thank you," she managed when he returned her glasses to her nose. She looked down, unable to meet the kindness in his gaze. She felt awful. Her eyes were puffy and she knew her face was blotched. Her face always blotched when she cried.

"You okay?" he asked as he pocketed his soggy handkerchief.

Rhea hiccuped and nodded, then said insanely, "It wasn't this. It was my mother."

Those penetrating eyes narrowed just a fraction. She wished she'd kept her mouth shut. Those eyes saw far too much. But he merely smiled and turned to leave. She also turned and took a step. His hand tapped her shoulder. She slowly faced him.

"Here," he said, extending a business card toward her. "If you ever feel you need to talk to somebody."

She hesitated, not moving. "Oh, great," she muttered beneath her breath. "The guy probably thinks I'm a grade-A loony."

The card flapped impatiently before her nose. Anxious to beat a retreat from her embarrassment, Rhea accepted the card and jammed it into the pocket of her jacket. With another sniffling hiccup, she scurried away. As she reached her battered car, she abruptly yanked the card back out. In black block letters the card read simply STEVE BRADLEY, and below that, a phone number. Her gaze lingered on it a moment before raising to glance quizzically in the direction of the MG.

Steve Bradley had gone.

Shrugging out of her cranberry down jacket, Rhea eyed with disinterest the stack of mail waiting on the hall stand. She hung the jacket in the closet, then scooped the pile up in one hand as she hefted her leather suitcase with the other. She gave a cursory glance to the havoc that spilled from the tiny kitchen to the living room, then trudged down the narrow hall to the tidy refuge of her bedroom. There she dropped the valise to the sand-toned carpet, dumped the mail onto the neatly made bed, and sat wearily on the edge.

The envelope with the name boldly written over it lay within her grasp. His insurance agent. She'd have to call her own insurance agent and relay the name along with the bad news. Could she reach her agent on a Sunday?

On a dreary hiccup she decided to wait until the morning to contact her agent. She simply didn't feel up to talking claims. She didn't feel up to anything. The accident had capped what had been a perfectly depressing week and all Rhea wanted to do was soak in a hot bath and pretend none of it had happened.

She shook herself, then rose to begin unpacking. She tossed a week's worth of dirty laundry into the hamper and put away the home-canned jams her mother had sent back with her. She prepared a bath and by the time she slid into the steaming water, had overcome both her hiccups and her lack of interest in her accumulated mail. She flipped through the letters and bills as she soaked, discarding them on the floor one by one, until she came to the last—a square vellum envelope. She extracted the gilt-edged card and held it between her finger and thumb.

"Be prepared for the time of your life—"

Rhea sighed. She had no doubt whatsoever that the annual Chambers, Chambers, Whitson and Company Christmas party would not be the time of her life. She flicked the card open and skimmed the scripted details. It wasn't printed in that fine curlicued script, but she read the hidden message clearly. *Be there.* She gave up sighing and turned to groaning.

She was still groaning long after she'd returned a semblance of order to the apartment, clearing away pyramids of dirty dishes from the kitchen and scattered hillocks of discarded clothes from the living room. Groaning, however, hadn't helped. She'd still have to go to the party. She plopped onto the foamy cushions of a U-shaped armchair. Planting her bare feet in the plush pile of the carpet, she vented yet another sigh laden with gloom.

"Hey, what's the matter? You sound about as cheery as a beached whale."

Rhea looked up from her contemplation of her toes digging into the carpet. "Oh, hi," she said with a notable lack of enthusiasm. "I didn't hear you come in."

"You were too busy caterwauling to hear a little thing like the door slamming," retorted Laurey brightly.

Despite her desire to wallow in self-pity, Rhea couldn't help responding to her roommate's sparkling display of teeth. She couldn't even get angry with the cyclonic clutter that swept in with the younger woman, the clutter Rhea knew she'd be cleaning up later as always. Carelessly dropping her fur jacket onto one end table and her purse onto another, Laurey kicked off her shoes, discarding them like crumbs to mark her whirling progress across the living room. Her hose were peeled and dangled over the branch of a pole lamp just before she spun to a stop.

"I take it the holiday at home was a flop," she said.

"Less than successful," admitted Rhea. "I knew I was in for trouble when the first words out of my mother's mouth were 'My dear, you've gained weight, haven't you?' "

Frowning at her reflection in a chrome ball on the pole lamp, Laurey thrust her thick mane of honey-blond hair upward, then let it drop to her shoulders. "Well . . ." She let the word roll out meaningfully before revolving to face Rhea.

"Oh, not you too! Now I know just how Caesar felt."

Laurey's smile faded. "Sorry. Sore spot, huh?"

17

Rhea met this observation with a sigh that heaved a wealth of dejection. She spread her fingers and ticked them off. "That and my hair and my clothes and most horrendous of all, my naked ring finger."

"Oh, is *that* all? I hear that lecture from my folks weekly, like clockwork. Noon on Sundays. I think it's a law or something that parents have to pressure unmarried daughters over the age of twenty about their lack of husbands-to-be."

An unwilling smile settled on Rhea's lips, indenting each side of her mouth with a pair of symmetrical dimples. "What about big brothers?"

"Don't you know it's mandatory for big brothers? They can be worse than parents. And if you've got aunts and uncles, you're really in trouble. It's the whole family, except for younger sisters, who'll generally tell you to hang in there." She threw one last glance at her distorted reflection in the lamp and added, "Well, anyway, I'm glad you're back. I've missed you."

"I'd noticed," said Rhea dryly, remembering the mess she'd come home to.

Laurey had the grace to look sheepish. "I meant to get the dishes into the washer, but, well . . ." She shrugged and grinned. "So anyway, you're back now. There's no need for you to be down."

"No, not if I forget the mere fact that I mashed my front end into the back end of another tenant's sports car."

"You what? What happened? You weren't hurt or anything, were you?"

"Only my pride. I've never even pinged a car before." She grimaced. "But when I do it, boy, do I do it. You should see the dents I put in both cars."

"Your fault then?"

"Definitely my fault. I wasn't paying attention, tore into the lot too fast, and *bang.*"

18

"No wonder you were looking so bummed out. How'd the other tenant take it?"

Rhea shifted restlessly. She didn't want to discuss the aftermath of the accident. Her hysterical outburst had been too disturbing; she simply wanted to forget the entire incident. Tonelessly she replied, "Surprisingly well. He didn't even get mad."

"He? Was he a looker?"

"Doesn't your mind ever run on any other track?"

"Was he?" Laurey's brows rose teasingly. "You're blushing. He must've been quite a hunk."

"Well, he wasn't. He was . . . comfortable-looking," she said slowly, recalling the kindness, the strength in the man's face. No, though he was good-looking, she wouldn't have called him handsome. Certainly not handsome by Laurey's definition. Friendly, calm, nice, but not a "hunk." Only his eyes had lacked the composure displayed in the rest of his features. His eyes were so piercingly blue.

She shook herself, dispelling the image, and heard Laurey say cheerily, "Well, speaking of men, I've gotta rush, a dinner date with Cal."

"Cal? I thought you were dating that disc jockey, Bobby or Billy or something."

"Billy Bob," Laurey corrected her. "I gave him up ages ago. Too possessive. Like Mac. Remember Mac, the stockbroker? He couldn't understand that women need some freedom too. Men. They're just so smothering sometimes."

She should have such problems, thought Rhea as she sighed and slowly got out of the chair. She'd love to be smothered by a man, any man. She caught herself up short at that. That sounded like something her mother would say. There wasn't the remotest chance that she'd ever have to worry about problems like Laurey's anyway. She was neither slim and statuesque nor stylish and supremely lovely.

Though they'd been sharing the apartment for well over a year, she and Laurey Wellman were more companions than friends. Their relationship remained casual, due as much to Rhea's reticence as to their differing life-styles. Rhea found it difficult to open up to other people; she felt vulnerable enough without exposing all her insecurities. Tonight, however, she felt an overwhelming need to confide in someone, anyone, and so she trailed behind Laurey, not really certain what she should say, if she should say anything at all.

Rhea leaned in the frame of the door to watch Laurey step over colorful piles of discarded clothes, delicate little heaps of frilly lingerie, tangled lumps of cast-off shoes. She looked on with interest as the blonde began riffling through the hangers in her closet. "Don't you ever get tired of being constantly on the go? Of all the men?" she asked after a time.

Laurey glanced over her shoulder, her enormous eyes wide, dominating her narrow face. "No," she said, sounding surprised that anyone should ever consider such a thing.

She yanked a teal wool jersey dress from its hanger. Even before the hanger stopped swinging on the bar, she dropped the garment behind her in a forgotten puddle. Finally she selected a black-lace-trimmed dress of glazed cotton lawn. She drew it on and as her head emerged through the stand-up collar, said, "I won't always look like this, you know. Someday I'll get wrinkles and cellulite and gray hair. I'm just making the most of what I've got while I've got it. I want to have memories to look back on when I'm old. That's what each affair I have is, a memory for my future."

Such logic was unique, to say the least. A smile played

20

over Rhea's lips. "Your personal retirement fund," she murmured dryly.

"Exactly," agreed Laurey with a grin. She bent toward the mirror above her dresser and shadowed her eyes.

It never ceased to amaze Rhea how makeup transformed Laurey's thin, narrow face into a work of art. She wished she knew the secret. When she put on makeup, the only noticeable changes were the brighter lips and cheeks, darker lashes and eyebrows. No matter what, she still looked like plain ol' Rhea Marie. . . .

With short, quick strokes, Laurey brushed on blusher, then eyed herself critically. She carefully blended the blusher with a powder puff. "So what exactly happened at home?"

"Oh, nothing really." Rhea came into the room, nudging a swirl of scarves and belts with her toe. Laurey worked with her hair, clipping a handful of honey-streaked curls casually to the side. Rhea thought how ridiculous she'd look if she tried that with her limp, mousy brown hair. The mental image she saw elicited another profound sigh and Laurey looked briefly at her.

"Well, something's sure under your skin," she observed before returning her attention to her reflection.

"Ummm. Everything and nothing. A combination of things."

Now that they'd gotten to the point, Rhea really didn't know what to say. She wasn't even sure herself just what had her feeling so blue. She knew only that it had begun before her Thanksgiving vacation at home. This odd discontent she felt had been simmering within her for months. The week at home amidst the loving banter and affectionate criticisms had only exacerbated a dissatisfaction she'd been trying to ignore for weeks, for months.

Laurey drew on smoky gray hose. Rhea imagined the unknown Cal's eyes bugging out when he set sight on those long legs, and failed to suppress yet another sigh.

21

Shooting her a sharp look, Laurey said, "There must be something definite eating at you."

Without meaning to, Rhea abruptly blurted out, "There's the office Christmas party, for one thing."

Puzzlement flicked through Laurey's wide eyes. "What's the problem with that?"

"I don't want to go."

"Don't want to go?"

"I don't want to go."

After staring at her with the look of one confronting a three-eyed alien, Laurey shrugged. "So don't go."

"I have to. It's required. They take a head count and the next day they lob off the absentees." A tide of gloom flowed into each word. Rhea dug her toes more firmly into the mound of scarves and studied the furrows she made. "I hate things like that. I'm not like you, Laurey. I don't have fun in a crowd. Everyone around me will be having a great time and they'll expect me to have a great time too. I'll have to pin a smile into place and pretend all night. I'm lousy at pretending."

The doorbell jangled. Laurey grabbed a small evening clutch, but paused before dancing off. An unfamiliar severity sat oddly on her lovely features. "You know what your problem is? You've gotten so used to being down, you've forgotten how to enjoy yourself. Rather than trying to have any fun, you walk around here with your chin on the ground, feeling sorry for yourself."

On the second jarring note of the bell, Laurey said a hurried 'bye and raced down the hall. Rhea could practically hear Cal's eyes bugging out when her roommate opened the door. Laurey's animated laughter sounded just before the door clicked shut.

That elation echoed into the quiet, winding its way down the hall and into Rhea's ears.

Is that what I'm like? she wondered. *Down all the time?* She looked at the gaily colored clumps speckling the carpet, then up at the contrast of her pale, plain face in the mirror.

Well, she amended, maybe not plain. Unremarkable. That was it. She had a pleasant, nondescript, rounded face noted only for the unforgivable tilt to the end of the short nose. The thick fringe of lashes were, to her view, lamentably pale, as were the nicely curved eyebrows. Faint freckles spattered the peach-toned cheeks and speckled the bridge of her nose. The mouth was neither full nor thin, but simply as unexceptional as the rest of her features. Her eyes might have been her one claim to beauty, being perfectly almond-shaped and of a distinct, gold-flecked green, but hidden behind the gigantic square lenses, their beauty was lost.

She lifted a handful of the hair she called mousy brown, but which others more generally termed caramel, and held it to the side for several seconds. Not quite the effect Laurey had achieved. For work she usually twisted her fine hair into a no-nonsense chignon. At home she simply ignored it. With a deprecatory smile she let her hair fall limply over her ears. As she smiled her dimples put in an appearance, her round cheeks shot upward. Chipmunk cheeks, she thought, and looked downward. Her smile slithered off her face.

Excess poundage was clearly visible on the thighs, hips, and waist. To her horror, she could see the start of a tummy bulge. Where had all this flab come from? Now that she looked at herself, Rhea remembered how her favorite pair of wool slacks had been uncomfortably snug the last time she'd worn them.

How had she let this happen?

And when was the last time she'd felt happy, really happy? When was her last evening out with a man? Her brow wrinkled. Last year she and Dave Pritchett had been a steady thing. Gradually they'd drifted apart. There'd been no final farewell parting scene. Their relationship had simply faded away. Since then, Rhea now realized, her social life had dwindled to occasional nights out with secretaries from the firm. She hated the singles scene, and more and more, she'd cocooned herself in the apartment. And apparently in about ten pounds too many.

Rhea stared at herself in dismay, then spun and hurried from the room, from the condemning mirror. She'd rather be glum and alone than stuck with a man just to be with a man. Why should she feel less of a woman without a man? The notion upset her. She didn't want to analyze the reasons why. Like Scarlett O'Hara, she'd rather think about it tomorrow.

CHAPTER TWO

She thought of him a little over two weeks later.

Standing by a long trestle laden with hors d'oeuvres, dips, two enormous punch bowls, and an ice sculpture of a Christmas tree, Rhea strove to look as if she *were* having the time of her life. It wasn't easy. Her jaws ached with the effort of keeping a smile bolted in place. She wondered if her dimples had cemented into permanent notches.

"Great party, eh . . . eh . . ."

Rhea let Peter Stockard struggle to remember her name for a fraction of a moment before nodding, murmuring her agreement that it was a great party and taking a sip of her drink. She tried not to shudder as rum and cola burned its way down to her stomach. She wasn't much of a drinker, never having developed the taste for alcohol, but she'd accepted the first glass thrust into her hands, glad to have something to hold on to, something to keep her occupied in the midst of the cheery babble surrounding her.

The junior associate slid away. She heard him saying "Great party, eh, Neva?" to the firm's head bookkeeper and turned toward the table. Selecting a small sausage wrapped in pastry, Rhea nibbled on it and hoped no one would dream of speaking to someone with such a mouthful. She lifted her wrist and surreptitiously checked her watch. Her hors d'oeuvre stuck in her throat. She'd only been here thirty minutes!

Someone jostled her elbow. The dark liquid in her plastic glass sloshed against the sides but didn't spill over the rim. The sausage shot down her esophagus.

"Sorry," said Pat. The receptionist offered an apologetic smile. "I was anxious to get at all this food. Great party, huh?"

"Great," said Rhea. She moved down the length of the table, pausing at the tray of steaming Swedish meatballs. Red velvet rustled as Pat sidled down beside her.

"Have you met my husband, George?"

"No," she answered, and bobbed her head toward the man past Pat's right shoulder. George briefly beamed at her before riveting his attention on the meatballs. Rhea hurriedly picked up a celery stick stuffed with pimiento cheese and slid into the corner shadows. She watched smoke drift through dim red and green lights to swirl over the melting ice tree. Time crawled forward. She vowed to leave the instant she received her bonus check.

She wouldn't have come at all if Laurey hadn't been so persistent. Since Rhea had returned from her vacation, Laurey had been like a missionary consumed by her cause. She forcibly dragged Rhea through Denver's most exclusive stores, pressing her into fitting rooms with dresses that scandalized her in both cost and cut. They eventually compromised on a cocktail-length bronze chiffon with long, puffy sleeves and a discreetly plunging neckline. The fabric belt had an imitation pearl buckle that added an old-fashioned touch, and Laurey had lent her pearl drop earrings to match.

Whoever said clothes made the person? This dress was the most romantic thing Rhea had ever owned, and she didn't feel the least bit romantic. She felt dumpy. She couldn't forget that she was wearing a full size larger than the last dress she'd bought. Not even the makeup Laurey had applied or the clever topknot Laurey had wrought from Rhea's stubborn hair helped. She still felt uncomfortably out of place.

She surveyed the raucous activity surrounding her, feeling as if she'd wandered onto Noah's Ark by mistake. Everyone else seemed to have come with someone. The lights spilled over pairs sharing laughter, over couples exchanging quips with other couples, while she stood in the shadows, alone, munching on a stuffed celery stick.

If this were indeed the time of her life, she wryly surmised, she was in big trouble. . . .

A man she didn't recognize bumped into her. "Pardon," he said, then paused. "It's a great party, isn't it?"

"Ummm," she murmured while longing to deny it. He glided out of her sphere and she decided the next person who mentioned what a great party it was would receive a well-deserved kick in the shins. Didn't anyone have anything more original to say?

"So when do you think Big Ben is gonna show up with the moola?" inquired a pert voice behind her.

Rhea spun round. A genuine smile enlivened her face. "Janice! Don't, for God's sake, please don't tell me what a great party it is."

A soft laugh sang with understanding. Janice rolled her eyes until her eyebrows disappeared beneath a fluff of auburn bangs. "Have no fear. As far as I'm concerned, it'll be great only when I have my bonus in hand. So how long till Big Ben pays up?"

"He'll come as late as possible. It's his way of keeping us here and promoting the myth that"—Rhea deepened her whisper to a rough rasp—"this firm isn't a firm, it's a family."

"And a family gathers together to celebrate the holidays," Janice added in a grating growl. She grinned and said in her normal, distinctly feminine voice, "What d'ya say we fortify ourselves for the wait?"

They threaded their way through the growing crowd toward one of the bars at either end of the extensive banquet room. Rhea felt measurably cheered. Janice had that effect on most people. She was short, sexy, and sweet. She had curves that men followed with wishful eyes and a smile that erased other women's envy. Although they'd never socialized outside of the firm, she and Rhea shared lunch and office gossip often enough to consider themselves friends as well as coworkers.

At the bar they spoke briefly to Catherine Young, the associate who shared Janice's secretarial duties with Peter Stockard. Catherine drew their attention to a graying gentleman with crinkled eyes. "Mike, I'd like you to meet my secretary, Janice Ekland and the firm's legal librarian, Rhea Nichols. I couldn't get along without either one of them. Ladies, my fiancé, Michael Hilliard."

"A legal librarian," he said, and the crinkles beside his friendly eyes deepened. "Now, that I find interesting. Tell me, just what is a legal librarian?"

"A glorified gofer," answered Rhea with a dimpled grin. "Actually, we have a library of all federal and state legal cases, as well as those handled by the firm itself. Besides maintaining a semblance of order in the library, whenever an attorney needs to cite specific cases, my job is to help locate it."

Mike appeared impressed and asked several questions. Rhea's dimples flashed more often, and without knowing it, she began to relax. The four continued to exchange the necessary social chitchat while awaiting refills on their drinks. When they had glasses in hand, Rhea and Janice moved to a circular table occupied by secretaries, their husbands, and dates.

"I bet ol' Cathy's glad to see you go," remarked Janice as they took the only vacant chairs.

"Why? What do you mean?"

"Oh, come on. There you were, charming the socks off her fiancé. She must have been thrilled."

"Charming? Me?" squeaked Rhea in astonishment. She gaped at her friend, who merely clicked her tongue in a knowing fashion. Rhea twisted to look back at Mike Hilliard. He was standing intimately close to Catherine, gazing at her with absorption. Rhea decided Janice had inhaled too many fumes while standing at the bar. She turned back in her seat and caught the other's arch smile. She briskly changed the subject by asking, "Didn't you come with a date?"

"Bring a date to this? Are you kidding? The only man I'd bring to an affair this dull would be one I was trying to lose," Janice replied with a sparkling grin. "If Big Ben didn't make it mandatory, I wouldn't be here at all."

"Neither," said Rhea with feeling, "would I. But when Big Ben speaks—"

"We listen," finished Janice.

"Or else," Rhea added, and they laughed.

Bennett Chambers was the founder and driving force behind the prestigious law firm that he claimed was successful because it was "not just a firm, it was a family." Though everyone from the file clerks to the accountants to the attorneys called him Big Ben behind his back, it was done affectionately and with underlying respect. Like the clock from which they drew the name, Ben towered above other men. He was traditional and seemingly timeless.

At precisely ten o'clock, the double doors of the banquet room swung open and Bennett Chambers swooped in. He was greeted with sincere applause and cheers. He received them with a benevolent nod of his silvered head and the charming smile for which he was famous. He charged forward to clap Samuel Whitson on the shoulder. The double doors yawned, wavered, then flew wide a second time.

A soft murmuring ripple passed through the women in the room. With every bit as much grace and a great deal more polish, Addison Chambers sauntered in behind his father. He looked, Janice had once irreverently said to Rhea, as if he'd been created for the sole purpose of touching a woman. He breathed sensuality, and women responded to it like dandelion puffs, floating away on his mere presence. The dimmed, colored lights played over his iridescent blond hair, making it appear transparently fine, and sharpened the classical profile that made breathing a disconcerting task for the female population.

Clinging possessively to his arm was a dishy brunette encased in the tightest garment seen since the demise of the whalebone corset. Her satisfied smile skimmed the room as she triumphantly eyed the countenances of the less fortunate women around her.

Rhea quickly averted her gaze. She lifted her glass and gulped deeply. It was ridiculous, this tingling she felt whenever she set eyes on Addison. It was foolish and stupid and inevitable. She was hopelessly, helplessly, infatuated with him. But then, every female in the firm had a crush on the swinging bachelor who was regularly rated as one of the city's most eligible men.

With her glass pressed to her lips, she glanced at Addison over the rim. What would it feel like to have those long, slim hands of his run over her? What would those full lips of his taste like?

Blood rushed into her face. She swallowed, then swallowed again. Looking at Addison was an activity that should be restricted to women with strong hearts. And hers, she instantly decided, was getting weaker by the moment. She pulled her gaze away from the beauty of him to glance at the shimmery second skin adhering to the voluptuous form beside him. The tight sheath was a dark, sequined green that reminded Rhea of a lizard's skin. She looked at the rapacious face above the dress and decided it was appropriate.

Rhea pictured her own face, her figure inside that sleeve of a dress. Her arm wrapped within his. Her hip pressed into his thigh. Her breast so close to his long fingers.

The blood that had settled in Rhea's face now galloped

everywhere. Her veins rocketed with the charge. She downed her rum and Coke and thumped the empty glass to the table. What, she silently demanded of herself, was she doing? She was really going off the deep end if she thought there was the slightest hope a man like Addison Chambers would look twice at her. Even Peter Stockard couldn't remember who she was half the time. Addison Chambers probably didn't realize she existed. What was the matter with her, sitting here mooning like a teenager over a man like that?

She gripped her hands together in her lap and wished she could talk to Janice about it. To Laurey. To her mother. To anyone. But she couldn't bear the knowing pity she was certain they'd feel for her. No matter how sympathetic they'd be, their eyes would be saying, "Poor Rhea, drooling over Addison Chambers like a lovesick adolescent. Poor Rhea, lost without a man." No, she couldn't bear to face that. She couldn't talk to any of them. She stared at her knuckles as they whitened and into her mind came a low, pleasant voice.

"If you need somebody to talk to . . ."

Rhea slowly unclenched her hands. That guy. The one whose sports car she'd tried to demolish. The one with the soothing voice and kindly face. What was his name? Like she did with all unpleasant things, she'd put the incident out of her mind as quickly and as thoroughly as possible. Knitting her brow, she sought her memory for his name, his apartment number. Well, she could always call her insurance agent and find out his name.

"It looks like we're finally getting around to the reason we all dressed up and came," whispered Janice into her ear.

Startled, she glanced up and saw Big Ben and his son at the main table, a stack of white envelopes between them. Ben was speaking and had been, she now realized, for some time. It was his annual we've-come-through-

31

another-year-together speech and judging from the rest-less anticipation stirring through his audience, he was nearing the end of it. The bonus checks were about to be awarded.

Rhea pushed her eyeglasses up the bridge of her nose and straightened in her chair. She would grab her check and her coat and be out the door in one motion. Big Ben's gravelly voice ground to a halt. Amid the applause he gestured toward his son, who palmed the envelopes and stood.

Her glasses slid back down her nose. She stared raptly at Addison as he slowly swept his gaze over them all. A very sharp attorney, Addison played particularly well to women on juries; it came as naturally to him as breathing did to other men. As he looked over them now, he paused several times, always on a woman. His eyes lingered on Janice, and Rhea felt her heart skitter from simply being near the object of his attention.

"As my father said, this year has been another year of prosperity for Chambers and company—" A stunning smile spread over his lips as he acknowledged the outburst of applause with a raised hand. "—and we'd like to share the success with those who made it possible, with each of you."

Cheers and whistles rang in Rhea's ears, but she heard only the lazy charm of Addison's words. His voice had none of the raspy depth of Ben's, but was instead filled with a melodic allure. He exhorted everyone to enjoy themselves as long as the food lasted and the bar remained open. Handing the envelopes to two of the firm's file clerks, he sat down. Even in the hazy shadow the sculpture of his profile was breathtaking.

Rhea found her resolve to leave weakening. Just to stay and look at him a little longer . . .

It was well past midnight when Rhea unlocked the door

to her apartment. When she entered she slipped the safety chain into place, then leaned against the door with her eyes closed.

A five-piece ensemble in matching emerald velvet coats and ruffled shirts had played old standards like "Stardust" and "Moonlight Melody" interspersed with the occasional Christmas carol. Listening with an unconsciously tapping foot, Rhea had finally relaxed. She'd been humming beneath her breath when Addison had stopped by their table. Flickers of light streaked through the soft, fine layers of his hair. The tune lodged in her throat. After a general greeting that encompassed the entire table, he had bent toward Janice.

"I've heard a very nasty rumor, Ms. Ekland, that you won't dance with anyone tonight. Tell me it isn't true." His smile had spread from his sensual mouth to his radiant eyes.

"Well, it's almost true," Janice had replied with a saucy grin. "I won't dance with anyone but you tonight."

He laughed and the sound of it melted every bone in Rhea's body. Black envy pervaded her heart as she watched him escort Janice to the dance area, as she watched his arms enfold the other woman's body. Her only consolation had been the knowledge that throughout the room, other eyes were just as enviously following his progress as he danced with Janice. Addison's date hadn't been happy about it either. The brunette had exhaled so harshly, for a moment Rhea feared the sequined sheath would split at the seams.

Now, with her eyes closed, her mind filled with the image of Addison bending toward her, speaking to her, smiling for her. She recalled the resonance of his laughter and imagined it had been for her ears alone. She pictured him taking her into his arms and slowly drawing her against him. Her body swayed forward to meet his.

She snapped to a rigid line. Her eyes flew open. She saw

the empty hall, the cluttered living room. She saw her own utterly ridiculous behavior.

"What on earth are you doing, Rhea Nichols?" she demanded of herself. "Maybe Fletch is right. Maybe big brother knows best. Maybe I do need a man in my life. This teenage fantasizing is sick. And so is talking to myself," she observed with wry self-reproach.

She shook herself into action, and without bothering to take off her coat strode into the kitchen. She lay her borrowed evening bag atop an opened box of crackers lying on its side on the counter. Empty cans and dirtied pots spread from the sink to the stove. Remnants of Laurey's dinner had congealed to a plate; Rhea wrinkled her nose in distaste.

"One of these days," she muttered through her teeth, "that girl is actually going to have to wash a plate, and I want to be there to see it."

She flung the leather coat, also borrowed, over the back of a dining chair, kicked off her heels at the doorway separating the kitchen from the small dining area, and shoved her puffy sleeves over her elbows. Rhea ran water into the sink and began clearing the counter. While she set the dishes to soak, she filled the coffeemaker with water. She reached for the coffee tin and grasped air. An exasperated sigh shuddered through her. On the rare occasions Laurey did think to put something away, she invariably put it away in a never-to-be-discovered cache.

After searching through cupboards and slamming the doors with ever-increasing resentment, Rhea yanked open the refrigerator. The coffee wasn't there either, but a bottle of rosé stood waiting. She grabbed it.

"What the heck," she said as she poured a glassful. "I'm not driving anywhere else tonight. And who cares what they say about people who drink alone? Could it be any worse than talking to myself?"

Comforted by that bit of rationalization, she happily

downed the wine and washed the dishes. She finished a second glass while drying them and was into her third by the time she had them all put away.

"That wasn't such a bad job," she said, and her voice sounded oddly high-pitched. She giggled and that sounded odd too. It made her want to giggle again, so she did. "Boy, oh, boy, oh, boy. You'd better hit the brakes, kiddo, your train is leaving the track. Whoooh-whoooh."

She picked up Laurey's coat, and with a shake of her head she wove to the closet to hang it up. "You really are losing your marbles, kiddo. I think you've been diving into a pool without water. What you need, Rhea Marie," she finished up emphatically as she wrenched open the closet door, "is somebody to talk to."

The phrase seemed to reverberate around her, expanding within the silence. She stood stock-still. All the giddiness of wine atop rum drained out of her. Was she truly facing a problem? Was this depression of hers escalating into something far more serious than a little case of year-end blues?

She listlessly settled the coat onto a hanger and wondered what she should do. The cranberry sleeve of her quilted jacket caught her eye. She stopped in midmotion in the act of closing the closet. She very clearly visualized her hand jamming a card into the pocket. Throwing open the door, she plunged her hands into both pockets at once. From amid worn tissues and old movie ticket stubs, she extracted a bent business card.

BRADLEY. That was it. She stared at the lettering and heard the echo of that pleasant voice saying, "Steve Bradley. Three forty-six." As she had earlier that evening, Rhea remembered the reassuring warmth of the man. She stared at the number printed on the card. She could call him in the morning.

She wandered back to the kitchen and propped the card against the stem of her wineglass. She pictured herself dialing that number, saying hello, pouring out her tale of misery. The image shattered into fragments of reality.

She'd never be able to do it. Even her lingering wine buzz couldn't deceive her on that note. No matter how kindly he'd been, Steve Bradley was still a stranger and the notion of baring her soul to a complete stranger was thoroughly unthinkable. It was hard enough for her to open up with friends and family, much less a man who'd offered his sympathy in passing.

In all likelihood, he hadn't actually meant for her to ever call him anyway. It was just the sort of thing people said to soothe, never expecting to be taken seriously. He probably didn't even remember her.

Sighing, she picked up the card and deliberately tore it in half, then in half again. Tossing the shreds into the trash beneath the sink, she turned off the light and headed for bed. Steve Bradley and his card were forgotten as she anticipated dreaming of Addison Chambers.

CHAPTER THREE

The white tip of an envelope caught her eye as Rhea passed her mailbox. She hesitated, then hurried on through the concrete tunnel where walls of narrow metal mailboxes loomed on either side of her. A low rough wood-and-glass building hunched over the snowy lawn beyond the tunnel. She turned to a door on the left marked Manager. A middle-aged woman with an overabundance of garish makeup glanced up as Rhea entered.

"Ah, Miss Nichols," observed the woman in cool tones. "How are you today?"

"Fine, thank you, Gladys," murmured Rhea as she laid a check on the desk. "Here's December's rent."

Gladys picked it up, thinned her lips, and said pointedly, "You mean the rent that was due on the first?"

"Yes, well, sorry we're late," she responded, backing out the door. "I was out of town and Laurey forgot, and I only just found out it hadn't been paid. I'll see it's on time next month."

An acerbic "That would be gratifying" echoed in Rhea's ears as she retraced her steps through the mail tunnel. "Old bat," she muttered, then stopped by her box. She could plainly see an envelope through the narrow slot at the top, but she didn't have her mail key. As soon as she'd realized Laurey hadn't paid the rent, she'd dashed out of the apartment at a gallop. Well, she'd just have to go back to the apartment and get the key.

She took a step, paused, and took another, then halted altogether. On the other hand, she was expecting that Christmas check from her parents. She turned around and examined the slot. Maybe she could fish the envelope out. Rummaging through the pockets of her down jacket, she came up with her apartment key. She poked it through the slot and jabbed at the edge of the envelope. Several times she caught the corner and almost succeeded in pulling enough of it to the slot to grab hold of. Almost. Each time it maddeningly slipped away from her, Rhea became more determined to get it out.

Steam filmed her glasses. Other tenants cast her odd looks as they passed by. Footsteps slowed behind her. She ignored them all and again turned the key flat, trying to catch the flap of the envelope.

"Tampering with the mails is a federal offense," said a voice disconcertingly close to her ear.

Rhea jumped. Her hand flew back. Her apartment key disappeared down the slot. The clunk as it hit the bottom of her mailbox tolled in her ears. She gaped in horror at the box and slowly pivoted to face Steve Bradley.

"Do you know what you've just done?" she demanded.

"Tell me," he invited her with interest.

Not even the fog covering her lenses could disguise the amusement on his face. Rhea would have enjoyed scraping it off with a snowplow. She wasn't feeling the least bit amused.

"That clunk you heard," she said witheringly, "was my apartment key. It is now locked inside my mailbox."

He rearranged his expression to one of proper solemnity. The ends of his moustache, however, tilted suspiciously, marring the effect. "This is your box," he said.

"My box," she confirmed.

"And your mailbox key . . ."

"Is locked within my apartment."

"The key to which—"

"Just dropped into the locked box," she cut in on a bite.

Pursing his lips in a soundless whistle, he glanced from her to the box and back again to her. "I'm sorry," he said sincerely. "I didn't mean to startle you."

The smile he offered was apologetic. It was also as thoroughly pleasant as she'd remembered it. Her flare of annoyance faded. It really hadn't been his fault and he was, she decided, much too nice to dislike. She shrugged and presented him with a self-effacing display of her dimples.

"It's okay. I know you didn't mean to do it. It was a stupid thing for me to be doing. I just thought I'd save myself the effort of walking back to my apartment and down again. It wouldn't even matter, except that my roommate is gone for the day."

"So you're locked out?"

She ran a finger over the cold metal of the box, pressing the pad of it into the keyhole. "Yup, I'm locked out."

Concern darkened his eyes. Seeing it, she hastily added, "The manager can let me in with her passkey."

Without realizing it, her distaste clouded her features. Gladys Tulley ran the complex with an iron fist, and Rhea was more than a little intimidated by her. But however much she disliked the thought of it, she would just have to march back to the manager's office and face the dragon lady. If she humbled herself abjectly, Gladys would no doubt let her into her apartment. So immersed was she in steeling herself for this, it was a moment before Rhea realized Steve was speaking. She pressed the bridge of her clearing glasses with her forefinger and half smiled at him.

"Pardon? I'm afraid I've not been listening."

Tilting his head to the side, he studied her with an intensity that disconcerted her. "Should I be insulted or relieved?"

"Relieved?"

"To know that you weren't looking so cross on my account."

Before she could gather her wits to respond to that, he'd taken her arm in his hand and twirled her around. "I was saying," he explained, "that you can come up to my apartment to wait until your roommate returns."

"Oh, that's kind of you, but—"

"No, buts. I insist. You wouldn't have lost your key if it hadn't been for me."

She dug in her heels and twisted to look up at him. "But really, the manager can—"

"If you can actually go in there and tell Gladys Tulley what you've done with your keys, you, Miss Nichols, are a far braver soul than I."

They exchanged grins. She decided his was definitely the nicest smile she'd ever seen. "Actually, the mere thought of it makes me quiver," she confessed.

"Then it's settled," he said as he regained possession of her arm. This time she made no protest. As they walked across the landscaped complex, he remarked casually, "I've been hoping to see you again, you know. I've wondered why you never called."

She shot him a look of surprise mingled with suspicion. "Oh, well, there was no need," she said warily. "The insurance agents handled it all between them."

That wasn't what he'd been referring to, and she knew it. But he let it pass, simply inquiring, "How's your car?"

"Still in the shop. And yours?"

"Still in the shop," he replied, and they laughed together. "You should do that more often," he said. "You shine when you laugh."

Rhea looked away, unaccountably discomfited. She wasn't sure how to respond to such a compliment. She opted for silence. He lived in the far end building. They made their way along artfully winding sidewalks lined with low, snow-mantled shrubbery. Her oversize boots clomped noisily on the shoveled pavement. She began to think this wasn't such a good idea after all. What did she know about this man?

Steve held the door to his building. She paused, then entered. The door clanged and she jerked. He appeared not to notice her nervousness, but took her elbow and led her toward the stairs. Her glasses fogged over, obscuring her vision and heightening her apprehension. Upstairs he steered her down the hallway. Her boots slapped her feet. She halted. The insistence of his palm on the flat of her back nudged her forward. He stopped before a door whose brass numbers she could mistily read as 346. She removed her glasses, swiped the film off on her sleeve, and shoved them back on her nose. It was definitely his apartment.

He unlocked it and gestured her into the void. A dim halo of light from the hall lapped at the dark cavity of the living room. She stopped again.

"Uh, maybe I just better go," she said in a wavering voice.

"And maybe you just better take off your coat and sit down."

He brushed past her. A tangy, nutlike aroma momentarily teased her. A light came on, chasing away the obscure shadows. Rhea blinked. The room was vibrantly warm, cozy, and inviting. Books crowded each other in mahogany bookcases covering the far end wall. Small wooden carvings stood upon some shelves, primitive figures of some ancient art she couldn't identify. An abstractly patterned woven rug in brick red and gray spread over the sand carpet. Intent on not looking at Steve as he moved to turn on a second stoneware lamp, she gazed fixedly at a grouping of stylishly painted wood masks that hung above the burnt umber couch. The savage geometric expressions ranged from fierce to frightening. She began to wonder just what she'd gotten herself into.

"Like them?"

She started. He was beside her. She squinted at the masks. They leered at her. "Oh, well, they're, um, unusual."

"African," he said, and smiled.

"Oh," she said, and managed a quirk of her lips.

"From Mali, Bambara and Bobo tribal art," he explained.

"Oh," she repeated, feeling worse by the second. What was she doing here?

He nodded toward the couch. "Take off your coat and have a seat. I'll get some coffee brewing."

When he was gone, she perched on the edge of the couch, protectively clutching the front of her jacket as if to ward off evil spells. She divided her time between rehearsing a departing speech of apology and inspecting her surroundings. Two barrel-shaped wicker chairs with cinnamon cushions stood at opposite ends of the bookcases. A tower of fat file folders tottered on the floor. Open books and magazines were on the tables. A pipe lay in a ceramic ashtray. A sleeping cat curled in a colorful mound of plump pillows stacked in the corner.

Unlike Laurey's messy disarray, the haphazard clutter in this room seemed comfortable. The intimate ambience of it all disturbed her. She shifted nervously. The edge of the smoked-glass coffee table grazed her knee, snagging her hose. She pulled back, which was a mistake. The couch was one of those spongy lounges that sucked the unwary into its depths.

Caught off-guard, legs awkwardly bent, she tried vainly to scoot forward. A resonant chuckle froze her. She gaped over her raised knees at Steve's amused face.

"I should've warned you about that. My friends call this couch the Venus's-flytrap." He grasped both her hands in one of his and lifted her to her feet with ease. His hands were warm and firm. He'd discarded his wool coat and his cobalt blue cashmere sweater crackled with electricity.

She tugged once. His fingers tightened slightly. He lowered his gaze slowly over her and slowly raised it again. He shook his head.

"Are you always this intractable?"

"What?" she said blankly.

He released her hands and began unsnapping her jacket. "I distinctly recall telling you to take off your coat."

More certain every minute that she'd made an enormous mistake in coming here, Rhea feebly resisted his efforts to divest her of her coat.

He whisked the jacket off. "Those too," he added with a nod toward her boots.

Rhea recognized the voice of authority when she heard it. She also recognized that he had the kindest voice she'd ever heard. She pulled her feet from the boots. He instantly scooped them up and set them beside the nearest wicker chair. He lay the coat atop the cushion. Rhea busily smoothed the skirt of her dress, though the jade knit didn't need smoothing. She looked up to find his moustache tilting at her.

"The coffee ought to be ready in a minute," he said. "Why don't you sit down and relax?"

She glanced toward the couch. "In that?" she said in a voice throbbing with doubt.

He laughed. It certainly wasn't the bone-melting melody of Addison's laugh, but it was very nice. For the first time, Rhea began to relax. He dropped into a chair and said, "If you ease into it, you'll find it's really quite comfortable."

Inching into the couch slowly, she managed to maintain her dignity and upright position. An awkward silence sagged in the air between them. Some of her tension returned. She cleared her throat and glanced wildly at everything but Steve.

"So you've been to Africa," she said abruptly.

"No, though I'd like to go someday. I just collect the art."

She attempted a furtive glance. He was regarding her steadily. "Uh, the, um, the rug," she mumbled. "Is it African too?" Lord, how inane could she get?

"No. The rug is Navajo. I picked it up in New Mexico a couple of years ago."

"It's nice," she said, then stopped. This was dismal. Making conversation with strangers was one of the things she'd never been able to do. She ought to go before she made a complete fool of herself. The stirring of the cat caught her eye. As it stroked its tongue down the length of one gray paw, she chirped, "What a lovely cat. Quite . . . fluffy and—and . . . lovely."

As if understanding her, the cat ceased its licking and turned a pair of enormous yellow eyes upon her. After staring a moment, it obviously found her lacking. It yawned widely, then resumed its bath.

Steve chuckled. "Socrates is part Angora and no matter how often I try to prove otherwise, he's convinced *he* owns *me.*"

Socrates paused, glanced disdainfully at them, and looked away. Steve stretched his legs out, crossed them at the ankles, and looked at her. Rhea pressed against the arm of the couch and looked at her feet.

"Well," she said. "Well, it's surprising that you should have a cat."

"Is it? Why?"

"Oh, well, men don't usually have cats, do they? I mean, they tend to have dogs, don't they?" She cast a sidelong glance, saw his open grin, and thought of ripping her tongue out. This was the most awkward, ridiculously stupid—

"Haven't you ever heard that a woman who doesn't like dogs doesn't like men and a man who doesn't like cats

44

doesn't like women?" He touched a fingertip to his moustache.

"Um, no, I haven't heard that," she replied.

"I like cats," he said.

She nervously crumpled a handful of her skirt. What on earth did he mean by *that*? She flicked her eyes toward the hall.

"Coffee should be ready. How do you like yours?"

He'd risen; she had to bend her neck to look up at him. "With cream and sugar."

She couldn't be certain, but she thought she heard a *tsk* as he nodded and left. For one brief second she considered grabbing her coat and making a run for it. But it was a mere flash. She may be feeling uncomfortably awkward, but he was exactly as she'd remembered. He was kind and soothing and actually quite nice.

Besides, she really had nowhere else to go. By now the manager's office was closed. As it was, she was lucky she'd found Laurey's note directly after arriving home from work. She'd barely made it to the office in time to pay the rent. And there was no sense in returning to the apartment. Having gone out with Cal, Laurey probably wouldn't be home for hours. If at all tonight. That thought struck Rhea with the force of a lead pipe. She might be locked out all night!

Her body tensed. Steve Bradley might be kind and soothing and nice, but he was still a stranger. What was she to do?

Steve returned with two mugs. Rhea slid her eyes from the thin wale of his gray cords to the mugs. His was white with blue sea gulls on it. Hers was blue with white sea gulls. He set hers on the table and smiled down at her.

"Hope you'll be able to drink this. It looks pretty strong. Even with a brewer, I'm the world's worst at making coffee. I can measure it out exactly the same, but it

45

never comes out the same two times in a row."

She lifted the mug, sipped, and gazed up at him over the blue rim. "It's fine, thank you. In fact, I want to thank you for taking me in like this. You're being very kind to a stranger."

"Stranger? How can we be strangers?" he asked. He ruffled his brown hair in apparent puzzlement. "After the way we've already bumped into each other?"

As she opened her mouth to sputter, she caught the teasing glint in his eyes and found herself smiling instead. His smile altered imperceptibly. She glanced down into her coffee. His cord slacks rustled as he moved to take his seat.

"You know, I've thought of you several times since our accident."

"You have?" Did that voice belong to her?

"I've wondered what had you so upset."

It was a statement, but she perceived the question in it. With anyone else she'd have evaded that question. With him she inexplicably stumbled into speech. But after she'd started the same sentence three times, he cut in, asking, "Would you mind if I smoked my pipe?"

She looked up from watching her toes twine with the fringe of his Navajo rug. Distress faded from her eyes, replaced by a relieved smile. "No, not at all."

Methodically he knocked the old ashes from his pipe, filled it with fresh tobacco, and lit it. Rhea sipped her coffee and watched him, studying the way his hand curved around the bowl of the pipe. Even his smallest actions had an assured composure about them.

A plume of smoke floated into the air and slowly drifted over to tantalize her. She recognized the pungent, nutlike scent. It had clung to his coat the day they met. . . .

"So you'd just come back from a visit with your family," he remarked casually.

46

She inhaled and said with surprising calm, "Yes. Basically we're a pretty close-knit family; I've always had a good relationship with my parents and with my older brother, too, and usually I love going home. But that whole week went wrong from the beginning. It wasn't anything specific, just little things adding up that had me feeling angry and depressed when I left."

He drew in deeply on his pipe, then examined her through the furling smoke. "You don't have to tell me anything, of course, but I'd be willing to listen if you want to talk it out."

Unconsciously she tucked her feet up under her and settled into the corner of the couch. "I'm not sure I can explain, but"—she shrugged—"the visit was a . . . focus, a focus on feelings I've had for a long time. Negative feelings about myself. The moment I arrived, Mom pointed out I'd gained weight. Dad said I wasn't smiling like I used to. Fletcher told me three different times I needed a man."

"Do you?" he asked.

She shot him a sharp look, but eased at the obvious sympathy in his eyes. "I don't think so. The last man I had was enough for me. But the point is, they made me face my dissatisfaction with myself. I resented them for it and came home totally depressed. Which is why I sobbed all over your shoulder," she finished with a lopsided smile that bespoke an apology.

"I can't think of a better use for my shoulder," he said, then flashed a wicked grin. "Well, maybe I can, but I'd let you soak your tears there anytime."

"I'll keep that in mind."

"You do that." He puffed silently on his pipe while she finished her coffee. As her empty mug reached the table, he inquired, "So why aren't you smiling like you used to? The last man leave you feeling bitter?"

47

Surprise flicked over her features. She hadn't expected him to delve any further into her problems and she certainly hadn't expected him to evidence any interest in her nonexistent lovelife. She fumbled around for a proper reply and finally said, "No, I don't feel bitter about Dave. We just drifted apart. He was one of those guys who expects his women to fall into line with whatever he wants, and when I didn't, our relationship withered. But there was no animosity or bitterness."

He studied her until she felt unnerved by the intensity of his gaze. She uncoiled her legs and buried her toes beneath the rug fringe. "So why have you been unhappy?" he asked quietly.

She thought of not answering. She wasn't sure she had the answer. But one glance at him and she was saying slowly, "I'm not sure. There's no reason really. I like my work. I'm a legal librarian for Chambers, Chambers, Whitson and Company. It's just . . . well, it's me. I've been feeling . . . incomplete, but I'm not sure why."

A small silence seemed to echo in her ears. She waited, but still he said nothing. Hesitantly at first, but with gathering momentum, she went on to tell him of the growing discontent she'd felt with herself and her life over the past few months, of how her social life had dwindled to nothing, of how she'd spent more and more of her free time alone and feeling sorry for herself.

He methodically tapped his pipe against the ashtray, then arched his arms over his head. "It sounds to me like you lack direction. You ought to decide what it is you want, and then go after it. Do you have any idea what it is you want?"

"I want Addison Chambers," she blurted out without hesitation, then gaped at him in astonishment.

His features were perfectly blank. He prompted her to go on by asking who Addison Chambers was. Still feeling stunned by her admission, Rhea explained and even confessed her hopeless crush on the handsome attorney, then instantly wished she hadn't. She felt one part relieved, but three parts foolish. Certain he must be laughing at her, unable to meet the amusement she knew would be in his eyes, she fixed her gaze firmly on her lap.

"Well, it seems simple enough to me," said Steve calmly, so calmly that she instantly looked up at him. He wasn't laughing. He appeared composed, concerned. "You want this Chambers, go after him. Let him know you're interested."

"Are you kidding? Me? Addison would laugh himself sick. I'm not his type, though I wish to God I were. Just once," she finished with a clip to her words, "just once I'd like to be the kind of woman a man like Addison would want. But there's not a hope of that."

"Why not? What kind of woman does this Chambers want?"

"Sleek, sophisticated, and sexy. Everything I'm not."

"And everything you'd like to be," he said with a shrewd glance at her.

She shrugged. He unfolded himself from the chair and ambled across to the beige phone sitting on a table at the far end of the couch. "What's your number?" he asked. She told him and he punched it in. A moment later he said hello and "I'm just checking in for Rhea. She got locked out, but she'll be on her way home in a minute. . . ."

Rhea imagined how Laurey must be enjoying that bit of news. Losing her apartment key was a habitual problem for Laurey, and Rhea had lectured her more than once about it. She didn't listen to the rest of the brief conversation; she simply looked up when Steve appeared before her.

"You don't seem to want to help yourself," he said, taking hold of her hands, "so I guess I'll have to help you."

"Huh?" she said, feeling ridiculously lost.

As he raised her from the couch, he grinned confidently. "You want to be Chambers's kind of woman, we'll make you into Chambers's kind of woman. We'll start first thing in the morning."

"Look, I don't know what you're talking about," she sputtered as he steered her into her jacket and boots.

"I'm talking about the way you don't like yourself. Though you look perfectly okay to me."

"I do?"

"Of course you do."

"You don't think I'm overweight?"

"Not by a long shot." His moustache suddenly danced. "I'm a man who likes to have something soft to hold on to."

Rhea blushed, wondering how they'd gotten onto this subject anyway. As if it mattered whether he thought her too heavy or too slim or just right. A fingertip nestled beneath her chin and forced her head up. She found herself looking into blue eyes as solemnly still as a clear, calm pond.

"I don't see anything wrong with you, but it's obvious you need to make some kind of change for your own satisfaction."

"What are you, a shrink or something?" she demanded in exasperation. "What's it to you if I'm happy or unhappy?"

"I don't like unhappy jogging partners," he replied mildly. He twirled her around and pushed her gently toward the door.

"Jogging partners?" Was the room spinning or just her head? What was this guy up to?

"I need a partner and you fit the bill. First thing tomorrow I'll pick you up and we'll start in."

She made a protest, but it was cut off by his cheery "See

you bright and early," followed by the closing of his door. She stared at the brass knocker in stupefaction. With a long sigh she concluded he couldn't possibly have meant a word of it. All that talk had been a speedy and effective method of getting rid of her. Which was, she told herself as she made her way down the stairs, all for the best in the long run.

CHAPTER FOUR

Her head was pounding. She burrowed into her pillow, but though now muffled, the banging increased in vigor. She experimentally opened an eye. A vague gray light slid from beneath the window shade. Morning was rousing as drowsily as she. A thoroughly impatient rapping resounded imperatively. She opened both eyes and sat up. It wasn't her head. It was the door.

Rhea scrambled from within the warm cocoon of the blankets, cursing Laurey beneath her breath. She'd like to staple the apartment key to that girl's wrist, but after all the teasing she'd endured last night about getting locked out herself, she wouldn't be able to say so.

The hem of her flannel nightgown grazed her bare feet as she padded soundlessly over the carpet. The harsh clangor of the knocker filled the air to the exclusion of all else. "All right, all right, hold your horses, I'm coming," muttered Rhea as she fumbled to unhook the chain. She wrenched open the door, ready to tell Laurey what she thought of such a rude awakening.

"You must sleep like the dead," said Steve Bradley as he dropped the clapper with one last ringing echo. "I've been trying to wake you for the last fifteen minutes."

She gaped, then gasped as he breezed past her. She flung the door shut and chased after him. "But what are you doing?" she demanded of his back. "You can't just barge in here—"

52

In the center of her living room he abruptly spun around to face her. Not expecting this, she skidded to a halt just inches from his chest. The soft gray sweat suit blurred before her eyes. She took a quick step back, and craning her neck, glared up at him. He smiled down at her.

"We're going jogging, remember?" His gaze inched over her. His moustache twitched and his eyes twinkled. "That is, if you can find something a little more appropriate to wear."

Glancing down, she took in the flaring width of her plaid nightgown and clutched a handful at the front. She returned her resentful gaze to focus myopically on his amused face. She wished she'd put on her glasses. "Well, how was I to know you'd be here before daybreak? What are you doing here anyway?"

"We had an agreement. I'm going to help you get in shape to snare this Addley Chambers fellow."

"Addison," she corrected him absently. She chewed her lower lip a minute, then said in a voice of careful exploration, "You mean you were *serious*?"

"Indubitably," he answered, and grinned the friendly grin that had so charmed her the day before. It did not charm her now. She eyed him with suspicion.

"Why?" she asked warily. "And don't give me this stuff about needing a jogging partner. I thought about it a lot last night and I couldn't come up with one sane reason for you to involve yourself in my problems. So I decided you hadn't meant it. But if you do mean it, I want to know why. What's in it for you?"

"Hmmm, so you're a cynic," he murmured, and glanced past her shoulder toward the kitchen. "We'll discuss it over breakfast. So why don't you go shower and change while I put something together for us to eat?"

Recognizing that tone as the same authoritative command she'd instinctively obeyed yesterday, Rhea sighed and trotted back to her bedroom. Though she told herself she was totally insane to let a man she scarcely knew walk in and take over without protest, she meekly gathered together a pile of clothes and headed for the bathroom. A quarter of an hour later she emerged, refreshed and, she fervently hoped, clearheaded. She followed the smell of sizzling bacon into the kitchen.

Steve stood before the stove, manipulating two frying pans with apparent ease. He'd discarded the outer jacket of his gray jogging suit, revealing a white woven thermal undershirt. As she rounded the corner, he looked up and grinned. "You'd better like your eggs over easy, 'cause that's how they're coming out."

She had to admit that with her glasses on, the effect of his grin was brilliant. In fact, it was so brilliant, it worried her. Why was he here, grinning at her like that? While she tried to puzzle it out, she poured coffee into cups and flipped toast onto plates. He added the bacon strips and eggs and together they moved into the dining room.

Once seated, Rhea eyed him resolutely and got right to the point. "Okay, you said you'd explain, so explain. Why bother yourself over me?"

He buttered his toast with the same deliberation that exemplified all his actions. "It's the old white knight syndrome. I can't stand to see a damsel in distress, and if ever I've seen a distressed damsel, you were she. After our accident, I thought if I could do anything to help you, I would. Besides, you're nice and have a great laugh and I really could use a jogging partner. I'm tired of pounding the pavement alone at six A.M."

"Six A.M.?" She set her coffee cup down with a disbelieving thump. "Six A.M.? Are you telling me that it's only six A.M.?"

"Well, it's closer to six thirty by now," he pointed out.

"You got me up at six A.M. on a Saturday?"

"Too much sleeping's not good for you. Eat."

She glanced dubiously at her plate. "Are you sure about

54

eating all this? I mean, should we be eating if we're going running? Won't we get cramps or something?"

"That's swimming. Eat, you'll need the energy." When she continued to hesitate, he picked up her fork and set it in her hand. "There's two schools of thought about eating before running. Some do, some don't. It's true most serious runners won't eat before a long run, but as we're not about to run very hard or very far, I suggest you have something to sustain you. You're not used to expending much energy, and you'll need the boost. Later, when we've built up your speed and distance, we'll eat after we run."

Somewhat reluctantly she began eating, then found herself digging in with a relish she normally didn't have for breakfast. Her morning meal generally consisted of coffee, more coffee, and the occasional doughnut. This morning, however, the full meal tasted warm and satisfying. She flashed a smile and said, "This is delicious. Are you this handy at everything?"

"Now that's a double-edged question if ever I heard one. If I say yes, I'm conceited, and if I say no, I'm a liar."

Rhea laughed and felt unusually light. Her buoyancy was weighted down a bit by the program of diet and exercise he outlined as they ate. It sounded ominously rigid to Rhea. Her idea of exercise, she told him plainly, was answering the telephone. He simply chuckled and told her he'd have her in shape in no time. "But," he added, casting an eye over her maroon turtleneck and blue jeans, "we'll have to get you some proper clothes first. Those'll have to do for today, but you need something your body can breathe in."

"What makes you think I want my body to breathe?" she asked in mock indignation.

"Aside from the fact that you should work out to tone up your muscles and keep yourself healthy, if you want to get sleek for this Addiman of yours, you will."

"Addison," she said, and picked up her empty plate.

"So even if I do lose weight, that still won't make me sophisticated or sexy. I mean, either you've got it or you ain't, and I ain't."

"I don't think that's true," he countered, and Rhea wondered whether he referred to the general statement or to her personal lack of sex appeal. Before she could ask, he said, "Anyway, we ought to take one step at a time. First we'll get you slim and trim, and then we'll worry about image. Now, do you have some tennis shoes?"

She nodded, stacked the rinsed dishes in the sink, and left to rummage through her closet for the sneakers she last remembered wearing at an office picnic two years ago. Eventually she reemerged, triumphantly decked out in grass-stained sneakers and thick argyle knee-highs. Seeing her, Steve shook his head.

"You'll need proper shoes too," he said with that dictatorial manner that just stopped short of being despotic. "I'll make out a list of what you should buy. Now we'll start by warming up. Always take time to stretch before running. If you don't, especially in the beginning, you could strain your tender muscles."

She eyed him warily. "Stretching and straining are not activities with which I like to associate."

"Do you want my help or not?" he asked, and she sighed.

"I don't know what I want," she said.

"I thought you wanted this Anderson."

"Addison. And I do."

He grabbed her hand and pulled her into the center of the living room. While she'd been searching for her sneakers he had shoved all the furniture against the wall, clearing a square section of it. Issuing commands in that not-to-be-disobeyed tone of his, Steve harried Rhea through a series of bending, stretching, twisting, and even mild jumping exercises. None of them were strenuous, and she began to think this wouldn't be so bad after all. It was even kind of fun. And despite his autocratic manner, Steve was fun to be with.

When they'd gone through a fifteen-minute routine, he threw on his sweat-suit jacket and pulled a black-and-red patterned stocking cap from his pocket. He jammed the cap over Rhea's brown hair. His fingers brushed her ears and a tiny tingle pulsed through her. She ignored it. Tingles, no matter how tiny, had nothing to do with their arrangement.

She donned her jacket and a pair of wool mittens and he put on a white cap and gloves. They walked wordlessly outside. Their breath danced visibly on the crisp morning air. Their steps rang in a synchronized rhythm on the dawn-lit pavement. Rhea cast a quick sidelong glance at him, wondering just what their arrangement really was. Why would he want to help her get herself together for Addison Chambers? His explanation hadn't satisfied her, though she couldn't pinpoint why it didn't. With an unconscious thrust of her chin, she returned her gaze to the view ahead. If he did want to help her, she'd let him, but that was as far as it would go. If he had any ulterior motives, he was in for a big disappointment.

It soon appeared that Steve's only motive was to coach her through their morning jog. He issued a series of instructions, stressing that she not try to overdo it this first time out. They ran along the side of an infrequently traveled back street, and at first, Rhea thought he'd been overly cautious. It was much easier than she'd supposed it would be. The pace was slow and easy. Her dimples appeared in a confident flash.

"This is okay," she said on little gray puffs of breath. "Kind of like running in slow motion. Maybe we should speed up."

He gave her a knowing look that oddly disconcerted her. "And maybe we shouldn't. Don't get too cocky; you'll regret it."

They ran on. "How long have you been jogging?" asked Rhea after a time.

"Nearly four years. I needed something to take my mind off my divorce, and running provided an easy solution."

"Oh," she said, feeling a surprising prick of shock. Although she'd realized he must be well into his thirties, it hadn't occurred to her that he might have had a wife. She wished she could dare probe into the subject, then immediately chided herself for it. What did it matter to her? It was really none of her business.

They plodded on together, accentuating the silence of the early hour. The hum of an engine grew in the distance ahead of them. They sidled closer to the curb and silently watched the car whizz past. Rhea's lungs began to heave.

"So what," she asked, each word coming out with a huff, "do you do when you're not running?"

He laughed. He obviously wasn't even slightly winded. "I walk," he said, and laughed again at her look of disgust. "You could say I'm in construction, or rather, reconstruction. My company buys old houses, renovates them, and resells the remods, hopefully for a tidy profit."

"Re"—huff—"mods?"

"The remodeled houses. We specialize in turn-of-the-century restorations."

She thought it sounded interesting and would have liked to say so, but now her lungs were aching. They felt, she thought, rather as if they'd been invaded by an army of pygmies bearing sharpened spears. And the harder she breathed, the worse they stung. Her glasses, too, were steaming over, a chronic winter problem that was a source of great irritation for her. She was just about to tell him to go on without her while she collapsed to the ground when he gently tugged her to a stop.

"Rest a few minutes, get your breath, and then we'll walk back."

What breath? she thought, expelling what she was certain would be her very last. She doubled over, propping her hands against her knees, as much to steady her quivering legs as to enable air to rush into her lungs. Gradually the sting in her lungs eased, the wobbling in her legs settled, and she was able to gasp, "How far?"

He lifted her glasses from her nose, wiped them on his sweat suit and replaced them. "About a mile, maybe a little less."

"Less than a mile?" Her voice squeaked in an astonished wail. She'd have sworn she'd gone twice that far. She glared at him. He had yet to draw a single harsh breath.

"Don't worry," he said as if reading her thoughts, "you'll build the stamina. We'll be doing five miles before you know it."

"Humph," she snorted, packing a wealth of disbelief into the syllable.

They crossed the road and began retracing their route. "So have you ever been married?" he inquired with casual ease.

"No."

His brows rose. "Never?"

She shook her head. "It just never seemed to come up with the right guy. What about your marriage?"

"It came up with the wrong gal," he said, then paused. He seemed to gather his thoughts before saying, "The trouble was, we got married right out of high school and it took us years to admit we'd made a big mistake."

He didn't sound upset, but Rhea couldn't think of anything appropriate to say. They continued the rest of the way in silence. At her apartment door, however, when she turned to thank him, he surprised her by striding past her. For the second time that day, she hurried into the kitchen after him.

"First thing we need to do," he was saying as she caught up with him, "is clear out all this junk."

59

He threw open a cupboard door and grabbed a half full bag of potato chips, which he tossed into the trash beneath the sink. It was followed by a bag of pretzels and a box of chocolate cookies. Rhea watched for several stunned seconds before protesting.

"Hey, wait a minute! You can't just throw that away. I have a roommate, you know."

He glanced over his shoulder at her. His eyes narrowed slightly. "Who usually eats this stuff?"

More than anything, she wanted to deny the truth. But Rhea felt trapped in the clear blue shaft of his gaze. She shrugged. "I do, but still—"

"Chips and cookies won't make you sleek," cut in Steve. He smiled abruptly. "Now, if it's me you're interested in snaring, go ahead and keep the goodies. I don't care if you're sleek or not."

"What are you implying?" she inquired with icy hauteur.

"I'm not implying anything. I'm stating loud and clear that if you want to go after this Addleman—"

"Addison," she bit in through clenched teeth.

"Chambers fellow," he continued easily, "you'll toss out the junk food. If you'd rather settle for a lesser mortal —like myself, for instance—you'll stay just the way you are."

She looked mulish for just a moment longer, then yanked off the stocking cap with an unnecessary force. "Oh, go ahead and toss it. I think you would anyway. You seem to think you own the place."

He returned his attention to the cupboard without comment. Rhea fluffed her sweat-matted hair and watched as he cheerfully disposed of her favorite snacks. When he'd emptied the cupboard, he moved to the refrigerator. When he pulled out the last piece of banana cream pie, she decided she couldn't stand it any longer. She retreated to the hall closet, where she hung up her jacket and removed her sneakers. She then wandered down the narrow passageway and peeked in Laurey's bedroom. As expected, the bed was rumpled, but it was obvious from the clothes heaped atop it that Laurey hadn't slept in it. Sighing, Rhea went back to the kitchen. She arrived in time to see the last forkful of pie engulfed by Steve's mouth.

"Oh! I thought you were throwing that away!"

"And waste a good piece of banana cream pie?" returned Steve, sounding shocked.

"You could have shared," said Rhea, sounding offended.

"Uh-uh. Your diet does not include banana cream pie." He licked the remnants of the pie from his moustache and grinned. "Some day, Rhea Nichols, you'll thank me for this."

"Can I get that in writing?"

"You, my dear protegée, can consider it carved in stone. By the time I'm through with you, ol' Addlepate will be putty in your hands."

She laughed, but admonished him with a wagging finger. "You know perfectly well his name is Addison. And I'm going to hold you to this promise, Bradley, so you'd better deliver."

He swept his stocking cap from his head and flourished a grandiose bow. "Of course. But I would remind madam that I cannot do so alone. Thus, if madam will provide me with a pen and paper, I shall instruct madam in the dietary arts."

She couldn't help but laugh again, and she continued to grin as she fetched the requested pen and paper. He wrote out a sample meal for both lunch and dinner, telling her as he did so to eat her dinner as early as possible. "A calorie at night is a whole lot more damaging that a calorie earlier in the day. I'll bring by some diet books when I pick you up in the morning. And be sure to go through the exercise routine again tonight, sometime between four and seven would be best."

"How do you know so much about this stuff?" she asked, looking from the menu to him. "I mean, you don't look as if you're the type who needs to diet much. Did you used to be heavy or something?"

"Or something," he answered. "My older sister runs a body shop. You know, a women's workout gym, and I've grown up listening to lectures on the proper care of one's body. By the way, I'll see if she'll take you on a discount."

"That's not necessary."

"Hey, why not?" He winked at her, looking devilish and angelic all at once. "If you can't use your friends, who can you use? I've got to run, but I'll see you first thing tomorrow."

With a jaunty salute he was gone. Rhea heard the door click, but still wondered if she hadn't just imagined the entire episode. She looked down at the piece of paper fluttering in her hand. No, she hadn't dreamed it up. In a clear, bold print she read that she was to have tuna served on lettuce with melba toast for lunch and baked fish with broccoli for dinner.

A dozen reasons why she should call him up and cancel the whole deal proclaimed themselves inside her head. It was idiotic, to begin with. You couldn't just set out to capture someone's attention. It wasn't like studying for an exam or preparing to compete in the Olympics. Attraction wasn't something you manufactured. It just happened. Steve was crazy to think Addison would look twice at her, no matter how thin she got. He only squired the most polished women in town. And she had as much polish as a rusty bolt. She must have lost all her marbles to have even considered going along with Steve's insane idea.

Besides, she didn't have to change herself to be happy. Rhea didn't like change. She liked fitting into an accustomed pattern, knowing exactly what to expect of herself and the world around her. If she wasn't perfectly satisfied with her life, she was by no means thoroughly disgusted with it. She'd just tell Steve Bradley that this very minute.

Rhea thrust the menu onto the dining table and marched into the kitchen, where she extracted the phone book from beneath a stack of loose coupons and recipes. When she had Steve's number, she reached for the white phone hanging on the wall. The door slammed and she paused, looking over her shoulder, wondering if Steve had returned.

Laurey skipped in through the dining room. Her hair tumbled in honeyed disarray about her shoulders, her eyes held starry gleams which couldn't be dimmed by the faint purpureal shadows beneath them. "Morning," she said in a voice ringing with cheer, though deepened by lack of sleep.

"Hi," said Rhea. "I'll ask the obvious, have a good night?"

"Would you believe champagne for breakfast at dawn?" murmured Laurey with a drawn-out sigh.

"This Cal must have class."

Silvery chiffon swished as Laurey twirled. "Ummm, wasn't Cal. Vincent. Vincent," she repeated breathily and floated toward her bedroom.

The chiffon wisped out of Rhea's view. She looked from where Laurey had stood, dewy-eyed and full-lipped after a night of passion, to the receiver still clutched in her hand. She put the phone down.

CHAPTER FIVE

Handel's *Messiah* soared from the stereo. A pair of fuzzy blue slippers, a cranberry knit pullover, and a colorful floral-patterned needlepoint kit reposed beneath the scrawny tree standing with a decided tilt in the corner. Neatly folded wrapping paper bedecked with carefully detached ribbons lay beside the gifts. Twinkling lights danced about the branches, reflecting a cheery glow that Rhea was determined to feel.

She finished removing the silver foil from her last package and creased it into a perfect square, which she placed with the other wrap. Adhering to a family tradition, she held the long, flat box to her ear, shook it twice and said, "A tie."

For one instant Rhea felt foolish. At home, her parents would have laughed and exhorted her to open the box. Here, alone, it seemed remarkably silly to be making guesses that no one could find amusing. But when Laurey left the day before, Rhea had promised herself she'd not spend Christmas feeling sorry for herself. She meant to keep that promise. So she shook the box again and repeated with resolution, "Definitely a tie."

A slender, finely linked gold chain nestled within white tissue. Rhea watched the tree lights catch the sparkle of it before lifting the chain and, with a genuine smile, putting it around her neck. Imagine flighty Laurey remembering a thing like that. It must have been eight months ago that she'd seen the necklace in one of Laurey's careless tangles of jewelry and remarked how lovely she thought it. Whispering a thank-you to her absent roommate, Rhea rose and wandered into her kitchen.

She poured a cup of coffee and glanced at the clock. Her parents would be calling anytime now to wish her a Merry Christmas. She looked down into the dark liquid. With a surge of defiance she added a heaping teaspoon of sugar and a generous sloshing of milk to her coffee. What Steve Bradley didn't know, she told herself, wouldn't hurt him. Besides, it was Christmas; she deserved a treat.

After two weeks of bitter black coffee, meagerly portioned meals, and more exercise than she cared to think about, Rhea had lost four pounds. She had also lost her earlier resolve to become the woman of Addison Chambers's dreams. Coming home from being pulled in ten different directions by ten different attorneys, all wanting information immediately if not sooner, the last thing she wanted was to huff and puff while listening to her stomach growl. Her attempts to tell Steve that the cause was hopeless, however, had met with an overwhelming lack of success. He grandly ignored her moaning pleas and put her through her paces, stretching, bending, running, until she was too worn out to moan. He had, she wailed to an unsympathetic Laurey, all the makings of a Nazi commandant, issuing terse orders and expecting unquestioning obedience.

She slowly sipped her coffee. The sweetness almost overpowered the taste, but she reminded herself this was how she liked her coffee. She settled against the counter, cup in hand, and let her thoughts linger over the past two weeks.

Although at first she'd met him warily, being highly suspicious of his motives, gradually Rhea had accepted that Steve was simply as neighborly as he seemed. Other than treating her like a drill sergeant, his behavior hadn't inched one degree over the imaginary lines she'd laid down. His most intimate manner remained strictly brotherly, which oddly pricked at her more than his authoritative commands. But despite his dictatorial demeanor, she couldn't deny that Steve was fun to be with. When he wasn't bullying her into shape, he was making her laugh with outrageous visions of herself as the new vamp of Denver's legal society.

"Can you slink?" he'd asked her two nights before when they'd last gone running. "You'll have to learn to slink. That's a major requirement of sex objects."

"How do you know what's required of sex objects?" she demanded on a staccato breath that matched the slap of her Nikes.

He flashed a broad grin. "It takes one to know one, pal."

And then he raced ahead of her, running without effort while she struggled for each whiff of air. His legs and arms worked rhythmically together like well-oiled machinery. His back and shoulders displayed silent strength. Even in the baggy gray sweat suit the firm tone of his body was evident. She didn't think he quite rated as a sex object, but she had to admit he wasn't bad, not bad at all. Not, of course, that it mattered to her one way or the other. He turned, slowing to a trot as he reached her side.

"So, show me how to slink," she immediately challenged him.

"Show you?" he repeated, eyeing her narrowly.

"You said you were a sex object, right? You must be able to slink with the best of 'em. How do you expect me to learn to be sexy if you don't coach me properly?"

They halted on the pavement, the brisk, dusky air cool and pleasant around them. The halo of a nearby streetlamp crowned Steve's hair with a lustrous gloss as he deliberately postured, hand on hip. "I wouldn't have it said that I didn't give you the finest training available, so prop those eyes of yours open, kid, and watch how a pro does it. First off, the slink starts with a sway of the hip and slowly slithers the rest of the body along."

"Do tell," murmured Rhea. She managed to keep from laughing when he sashayed, with tiny, mincing steps and undulating hips, down the street. But when he pivoted on his toes and struck a dramatic pose, head flung back and lips breathily parted, she could no longer restrain herself. She plopped to the curb and laughed until her sides ached.

"Are you quite through?" he asked when her laughter wheezed to a gasping echo. "I'd like to see you do better."

She promptly rose to the challenge and, disregarding the bulk of her sky blue jogging suit, slithered in a manner guaranteed to make Mae West envious. Her hips jutted to the left, the right, the left. She smirked, enjoying the satisfaction of a slink well-slunk, and added an extra jounce to her gait. A snowball splattered directly on her swinging behind. She lurched, then whirled. Steve smiled with saintly innocence and hurled a second snowball her way.

Remembering the vigorous exchange of cold missiles that had followed, Rhea smiled to herself. Yes, he was fun. In many ways he reminded her of her brother, Fletch. He was a good friend, comfortable and undemanding. Well, she amended, he could be pretty demanding. Very demanding. Her smile faded.

She set aside the remainder of her coffee and crossed to examine the week's menu taped to a cupboard door. Nothing was listed for the day, and disliking to prepare a traditional meal for one, she had planned to repeat one of the low-calorie meals from earlier in the week. Now, still feeling defiantly determined to enjoy her solitary Christmas, she ripped the menu off the door and crumpled it into an unrecognizable ball. In one motion she reached for the flour tin and a well-thumbed cookbook.

The tantalizing aroma of bread baking drifted throughout the small apartment, overpowering the warm fragrance wafting from a platter heaped with sugar cookies. Rhea, her hair thrust behind her ears, her nose freckled with white smudges, and the sleeves of her ivory sweater bunched to her elbows, absently munched a cookie while flipping the pages of her cookbook. She decided to make a batch of butter drops and shoved the last of the sugar cookie into her mouth.

The resounding rap of the door knocker startled her. She inadvertently swallowed, sucking in fragmented cookie crumbs and choked. The knocker repeated its demand to be answered. Gasping, hacking, and chewing frantically, Rhea raced to the door, and without pausing to check through the peephole, flung it open.

"Hi," said a voice hidden behind a bulging paper bag. She coughed. Steve peered at her from around the sack. She drew in a breath and imitated a seal barking out a demand for dinner. He stretched out a hand to pound her back. Her glasses slid down her nose. Incriminating crumbs bedaubed her lips. He pushed her gently aside, entered, set down the bag, and encircled her waist with one arm. She was beyond trying to struggle. She was, in fact, feeling grateful she wasn't going to die alone.

As he slapped her back he remarked amicably, "I think this comes under the heading of just deserts. It's a good thing I came to check up on you."

Gratitude left her. "I-if you hadn't c-c-come," she sputtered, "I w-wouldn't be ch-choking to death!"

"Perhaps I should attempt a bit of mouth-to-mouth to save you," he offered.

She stopped coughing long enough to firmly squash that plan of action. He chuckled and released her. As her spasms eased, he cupped her chin and dusted her lips with feathery fingertips. "Hmmm, from the evidence all over your mouth, I'd say I wasn't the cause of your near demise. Looks more like cookie crumbs."

"It's Christmas," she said in self-defense. She tried vainly to frown at him. But she couldn't hide her sudden happiness.

His eyes crinkled up as he studied her. After a moment he flicked a last golden crumb from the bottom curve of her lip. Then he lifted his finger and pressed her eyeglasses back into place. "So it is. You planning to do anything besides stuffing yourself on cookies?"

"I wasn't stuff—" she began hotly, then caught the teasing gleam in his gaze and switched to what she hoped passed for nonchalance. "No, no plans at all."

"Good. I've got a deal you can't refuse."

"What's that?"

He lifted the sack and thrust it into her arms. She glanced down, saw the turkey, celery, and other groceries and looked up at him questioningly.

"You cook," he said, "and I'll eat."

"That's the deal?"

"I knew you couldn't refuse," he said with a laugh as he spun her by the shoulders and sent her toward the kitchen. "God, it smells great in here. What's baking?"

"Just bread."

"What do you mean, just bread? If it tastes as good as it smells, I'll order a dozen loaves." He collected a cookie from the platter and demolished it in two bites. "Ummm. Definitely worth choking to death for. You must be pretty accomplished in the kitchen."

She set the sack on the counter and shook her head. "That's how much you know. Sugar cookies are probably the easiest thing in the world to do."

"Bread isn't."

"Maybe you should wait till you've tasted it before you lavish such praise on my culinary abilities," she said dryly. But her voice lilted with a cheer she hadn't felt before, despite all her attempts to manufacture it. Steve had entered like a north wind, crisp and brisk and invigorating. She wanted to sing and didn't care why.

He shucked his coat and cast it over the back of a dining-room chair. Her eye caught by the motion, Rhea glanced his way, then paused. The dark snuff brown of his cord jacket seemed to darken the brown of his hair, while the form-hugging fit of his biscuit turtleneck emphasized the firm musculature of his chest. For no reason she suddenly wished she were wearing something other than an old bulky knit sweater and faded blue jeans. As he moved to join her his thighs strained against the brown corduroy of his slacks. Disconcerted that she'd even noticed such a thing, Rhea quickly returned her attention to the sack.

Together they emptied the bag, spreading the contents over the countertop. Rhea forgot her momentary discomfort. She was thrilled. She would have a traditional dinner after all. Turkey with stuffing, peas, mashed potatoes, cranberry sauce, and even white wine. She held the bottle aloft and grinned.

"Is there anything you didn't think to bring?"

"Well, I don't know. I think I brought everything. On the other hand . . ." He ruffled his hair and ran his eyes over the groceries on the counter. He stroked his moustache, then slapped his pockets. "It seems there's something . . . ah, yes, here it is." He pulled a small box from his jacket. Smiling, he extended his palm toward her.

She gaped first at the package and then at him. "For me?" she said stupidly. "What is it?"

"Why don't you take it and see?"

"But I didn't get you anything."

He waved the box under her nose. "Take it."

She took it. Carefully undoing the tape, she slid the Santa-print paper off, then set the box aside to fold the wrap. She heard Steve click his tongue and looked at him. He rolled his eyes at her. "I like to save the paper," she said with a bare hint of apology. Then she picked up the box and opened it.

For a moment she just stared. "What is it?" she asked again.

"A talisman. For good luck."

She lifted the carved ivory amulet and examined it closely. An almost three-dimensional figure squatted, arms folded proudly over his protruding belly. His nose was broad and flat, his mouth pressed in an everlasting grimace. She half smiled at Steve. "He doesn't look very lucky."

"Ah, well, appearances can be deceiving. The ol' boy's supposed to be overflowing with luck."

Rhea slipped the thin leather thong over her head. The leather settled against the gold chain; the charm nestled between her breasts. "I presume he's from your African collection? Are you sure you want to relinquish the good luck?"

He reached out and rubbed a fingertip over the sculpted surface of the amulet. Beneath the ivory, Rhea's heart beat a little faster.

"I don't think I'm giving up the good luck," he said. "I'm sharing it with a friend."

Now, why should that leave her feeling breathless? It was just Steve, after all, just Steve being her friend. But Rhea was unable to find the breath to speak a single word until he withdrew his finger and twitched his moustache at her. Then at last she managed to stammer her thanks. "I'm sorry I didn't get—" she began, only to be cut off.

"If you'da known I was comin' you'da baked me a cake." He strolled over to the table and grabbed a cookie. "As it is, you made cookies and bread and you're fixing the meal while I lounge around and enjoy myself, so I'd say we're more than even."

She grinned. Presenting him with a paring knife, she said, "So who said lounging was part of the deal? Celery, onions, and potatoes await you."

They worked together with an easy efficiency, Rhea

71

chattering happily as she prepared the turkey for roasting and Steve calmly listening while chopping and paring. She moved with a confident grace, filled with a glow that felt magical. Though it still wasn't the same as being with her family, she decided being with Steve was the next best thing. How wonderful that he'd come to spend Christmas Day with her.

Rhea paused in the act of pulling the bread from the oven. She glanced at Steve's back. As she tipped the bread onto a cooling rack, she asked herself why he had come to her. Why wasn't he spending the day with his family? She knew his sister lived in the Denver area. It seemed strange that he would come see her instead.

"Why aren't you with your family?" she asked on a rush.

"Why aren't you with yours?"

"I asked you first."

He grinned and waved the paring knife. "You should be less belligerent to a man holding a weapon."

She hoisted the roasting pan. "And you should be more cooperative to a woman holding the turkey."

"Ummm, good point. Well, as a matter of fact, the rest of the clan has gone to Illinois—"

"Illinois?"

"My grandmother, a matriarch in the truest tradition, lives in Chicago, and every year she issues a royal command demanding our presence for the holidays—"

"Commanding, huh? Sounds just like her grandson."

"Do you or do you not want to hear this?" demanded Steve.

"Sure."

"Then shut up," he said, but with a friendly grin as he picked up a stalk of celery, which he crunched as he talked. "As it happened, this year I had too many commitments to get away—I'm up to my ears in prints for no less than three projects—so Lou and her brood packed up and

72

left me here alone. Knowing Grandmother would be calling to express her extreme displeasure at my lack of familial compliance, I cravenly vacated my apartment and dashed over here in search of sympathetic succor. Instead of which," he finished on a mournful note, "I'm subjected to having my turkey held hostage."

Rhea giggled, feeling absurdly merry. He was definitely the next best thing to family. She thrust the turkey pan into the oven, snapped shut the door, and said gaily, "How much sympathy could you expect from someone you've been torturing for two solid weeks?"

"The torture, little lady, has all been self-inflicted. If you'd just forget about Addleson—"

"Addison," she said automatically.

"Who probably isn't worth a penny per thought—"

"Addison Chambers is the most sought-after bachelor in—"

"And concentrate instead on yourself—"

"By which I suppose you mean on *yourself*."

She was teasing, fully expecting him to come back with one of his bitingly witty retorts. Instead, he paused long enough to make her breath catch, then said soberly, "That might not be such a bad idea. At any rate, you can't blame me for letting yourself get out of shape. Now, tell me, why didn't you go home to be with your family?"

"I couldn't take the time off from work to drive to Canon City and back, and what do you mean that might not be such a bad idea?" Word by word, her voice had steadily escalated, ending on a glass-shattering shriek.

"Anything to improve the direction of your thoughts," he replied with a flash of his teeth. "So you come from Canon City. Large family?"

"Some improvement," she humphed, uncertain whether she was peeved or relieved. His smile was so engaging, however, she decided she couldn't be even slightly angry. "No, not a large family. I've an older brother who's married with three kids, and believes firmly that any female unmarried at my age is a disgrace to womankind, not to mention the Nichols family."

"An MCP, is he?"

"Of the highest order. But he means well." She sighed, thinking of the call earlier when with pointed nonchalance, Fletch had mentioned an old army buddy of his being transferred to Denver. She shrugged it off. She didn't need a matchmaker. She had a coach. "What about your family? Anyone besides the fire-breathing grandmother and your sister?"

"Lou's my older sister. Jennette's younger by four years and Warren's the kid of the family. Unlike myself, all are respectably married, and anything your brother has to say on the subject of marriage pales, I am certain, beside what Grandmother has to say on the subject of divorce."

He shuddered dramatically, then grinned as Rhea laughed. Looking at him, her mind wandered into unexpected territory. What, she wondered, would that smile taste like? How much warmth burned in that tempting curve? How would those lips feel if pressed upon hers?

She swiftly jerked on the mental leash of her straying thoughts. Just because she hadn't had a date in months, she was conjuring up utterly ridiculous images. As if she'd want to kiss Steve! Steve was her *friend*.

"Well, what's next, kiddo?" her friend was asking.

A subtle hint of an indefinable something underscored the simple query. For one horrifying moment Rhea had the impression that he knew what she'd been thinking. Then she pulled herself together enough to answer with a semblance of composure. "We indulge in some of that lounging you were yearning for while the bird does its thing."

As she walked out of the kitchen, she was unbearably conscious of him behind her. The faint scent of his aftershave, the hushed scraping of his cords, the meeting of his

74

shadow with hers on the wall. She was acutely aware of his slightest movement. At once she felt both thrilled and disturbed. Rhea's usual reaction to any emotional crisis was to eat. This was no exception. Passing the dining table, she snatched up a cookie with an unconscious sweep of her hand.

A ringing rap was delivered to her knuckles. Her hand jumped back and the cookie fell to the floor.

"Ouch," she said with more indignation than pain.

"You've more than exceeded your cookie quota, even for Christmas," said Steve complacently.

The back of her hand still tingled. She looked down at it in surprise, as if she'd never seen the back of her hand before. His quick slap hadn't been *that* heavy. Why was her hand still quivering? Why was *she* still quivering?

Half puzzled, half resentful, she looked back up at him and nearly glanced over her shoulder to see who was behind her. Steve gazed at her with the heated intensity of a man eyeing a woman he wants. It was the sort of look that could have turned a stone brick into whipped butter. It was having a rather similar effect on Rhea's bones.

She blinked, then blinked again as Steve smiled in a friendly manner and popped a cookie into his mouth. Had she imagined that hot blue gaze?

"So what's on the tube?" he asked on a muffled mumble around his cookie.

Deciding it was time to have the prescription for her glasses checked, she told him she didn't have the faintest idea. He strode on into the living room. She followed him just halfway, watching him from a safe distance as he turned on the portable set and flicked channels. Once he tossed a casual smile her way. By the time he selected an old movie and flopped onto the sofa, she realized the bones-to-butter gaze had been a figment of her overripe imagination. She resolutely ignored the ripple of disappointment that immediately followed this conclusion.

Steve glanced over his shoulder. "Aren't you going to sit down?"

"You go ahead and watch. I'm going to take a quick shower and make myself a wee bit more presentable."

"Need a partner for that quickie?"

She sucked in her breath. He chuckled. She let out her breath and said flatly, "No."

"Thought not," he said without the least hint of regret.

She thought of throwing the nearest available object, which happened to be a glass jar filled with colorful agates, at his head. But, instead, she pivoted and marched down the hall to her bedroom. Why had she felt such animosity anyway? She decided it was her insecurity. She'd never been very accomplished in the art of flirtation. She didn't even know how to respond to a suggestive comment, especially a strictly friendly suggestive comment. Making such comments obviously came naturally to Steve. With him it was a reflex action to a woman's presence, like squinting when stepping into bright sunlight.

Somehow this reasoning wasn't as comforting as Rhea had expected it to be.

CHAPTER SIX

The candle flame wavered, then struggled upright. Its glowing tip cast a soft light on the lazy curve of Rhea's smile. She glanced over the remains of the meal and looked up to meet Steve's eyes beyond the flickering flame. Her smile broadened.

"Now that," she sighed happily, "was a Christmas dinner."

"My compliments to the chef," he said, and she sighed again.

She'd stepped from her shower determined to enjoy the rest of the day, whether he teased her or not, but she hadn't expected to enjoy it quite so much. The food had been delicious and the conversation had been stimulating. They'd gone from talk of past Christmases to discussion of Steve's latest project, a renovation of one of the oldest homes in the heart of Colorado Springs. Watching him sketch an invisible diagram with the edge of his knife, Rhea had felt lightened inside. She imagined herself getting lighter and lighter until he'd have to tie her to her chair to keep her from floating away on a cloud of happiness. The vision of herself swaying above her chair with a string tail made her giggle.

Steve stopped talking. Leaning back in his chair, he stroked his moustache and drawled, "So stained glass amuses you. Or was it the fantail arch?"

77

"I'm sorry. I wasn't laughing at either one really. I was just feeling . . . happy."

He solemnly raised his wineglass. She lifted hers in return, eyeing him quizzically. "To your happiness, Rhea Nichols. Now, and for all your tomorrows."

That magical, radiant animation expanded, filling Rhea to overflowing. As she'd sipped her wine, she felt she *would* be happy, now and for all her tomorrows. Nothing, no one, could tarnish the brilliance of her future. It was absurd, unfounded, but she'd felt it nonetheless. She felt it still. Looking over the dirty dishes, the rumpled napkins, the empty glasses, she ridiculously wanted to giggle. Maybe it had been the Chablis. . . .

"Shall we clean up, or let it sit while we digest?"

She let out a last, lingering, gusty sigh. "We'd better clean it up. The way I feel right now, if I leave these dishes, they'll be here till New Year's."

He slid back his chair and stood. Bending forward, he cupped his hand around the flame of the slender red candle and blew. With a whiff of smoke the flame was extinguished. Rhea stifled an urge to protest. It had been such a lovely meal, she hated to see it end. Steve paused by her shoulder and she reluctantly rose. The turquoise silk of her sleeve rustled as it brushed against his extended arm. A thoroughly unwarranted spark crackled through her. She hurriedly gathered up her plate and his, telling herself not to be any more foolish than she could help. Visualizing herself as a human kite was one thing; imagining herself as electrified by the merest contact with Steve was something else altogether.

She could not quite, however, suppress a sense of satisfaction that she'd changed into the clingy, billowy silk blouse and pleated camel slacks. Not that she wanted to look appealing for Steve, but . . .

Reaching the kitchen, she cast an oblique glance in his general direction. He'd discarded his jacket before following her, and the tight fit of his turtleneck had an oddly constrictive affect on her ability to breathe. She began rinsing dishes with an absorption that would have astounded even Laurey, who thought her insanely absorbed in cleaning as it was.

He worked beside her, competently slicing and wrapping the leftover turkey. Each motion, each shifting of bone and muscle, of arm and shoulder, swept over Rhea's periphery to the exclusion of all else. A vegetable bowl slipped from her fingers to clack against the rim of the sink. Retrieving it, she examined it for cracks or chips, then thrust it into the dishwasher. *It's time to get a grip on yourself, Rhea Marie,* she mentally scolded herself. But she was intensely aware of Steve's quick glance at her.

"Won't you need to go feed your cat?" she asked abruptly.

"Socrates could stand to skip a meal or two," he replied. "But being the merciful, caring sort that I am—"

"Ho!"

"I left him a full bowl of Cat Crunchy to keep him occupied when he's not sleeping."

"Well, don't you think he'll get lonely?"

"What is this, a not-too-subtle hint that it's time for me to go?"

His query held a hint of laughter, but when Rhea spun to face him, she caught a glimpse of a shadow crossing his features. Before she had a chance to wonder at it, it was gone, and he was once again teasing her with his crooked smile.

"Of course not," she said, only in that instant realizing how much she wanted him to stay. "I was just making a poor attempt at conversation. I don't want you to go. That is, unless you want to go. But you don't have to go, if you don't want to. But if you want to—"

He gently pressed his fingers against her lips. They tasted of turkey. Her sputtering discourse broke off beneath his light muzzle. On the other hand, her pulse throbbed into overdrive.

"Okay, pal, no need to get worked up," he said. "I'll stick around for a while longer."

Though that was precisely what she'd wanted to hear, the thought that he could think she was practically begging him to stay pricked at her pride. She pulled back from his touch. Her spine stiffened. "You do not," she said with all the haughty indifference she could muster, "need to stay on my account."

"Who said anything about your account? If I go back to my apartment this early, Grandmother will be raking me over the coals for the rest of the night. I've got to stay away long enough for her to be grateful by the time she gets ahold of me. It's my only hope to escape a blistering lecture."

He held out his hands palms up and looked at her with the eyes of a sad puppy. She only hesitated a second before lightly slapping his palms.

"Oh, all right. Stick around here. But you have to tell me how you do it."

"Do what?"

"Make me feel foolish without a single bead of sweat."

He laughed, the nice laugh that Rhea thought should be bottled and marketed to replace medical relaxers. It relaxed her so much now that she didn't feel the least little nerve jump when he settled his arm about her shoulder for a short, comradely hug. She tipped her head to the side and smiled at him, enjoying the way crinkles appeared beside his laughing eyes and the merry way his moustache tilted above the broad display of teeth.

"I don't think you should blame me for that, sweetheart," he said on the end of his chuckle. "You seem to do that well enough on your own."

Her nerves returned to action, springing off the trampoline of that too tender "sweetheart." She shrugged out of his embrace, which was annoyingly easy to do, and sidled toward the living room, muttering, "Let's see what's on the tube."

"Funny, you don't strike me as the TV type," he remarked, ambling in behind her.

"Well, I'm not usually," she confessed. "But you nixed any dessert and I'm too full to do anything energetic."

This last was said firmly, with an eyeful of implacability directed at him. He merely grinned. Warning bells pealed in her head. He held out a hand. She glanced at it with the cordiality of greeting one of the living dead. She backed up a step.

"Now, listen here, Steve Bradley, this is Christmas and I'm not—repeat *not*—stretching, bending, or running. Especially not on this full stomach. Got that?"

"All we're going to do at the moment is sit and digest."

"At the moment? What do you mean, at the moment?"

His hand snaked out to grasp her wrist. Caught by surprise, she offered no resistance as he tugged her to the sofa. There, however, she made her stand. She dug her heels into the carpet. She opened her mouth to protest.

"Sit," he said, sounding rather like the headmaster at an obedience school.

She sat.

"That's better." Satisfaction dripped from those two words. He turned and crossed to the stereo stand. Rhea childishly stuck her tongue out at his back and wondered at the blithe gratification she felt in the silly act. It was the lighter-than-air feeling all over again. He glanced over his shoulder at her and she hastily licked her lips. He smiled a knowing smile and returned his attention to the stereo.

"Hmmm. I take it this record collection isn't yours."

"No, most of those are Laurey's. How did you know that?"

"After seeing you constantly for two weeks, it wouldn't take Sherlock Holmes to figure out your tastes do not run

81

to new wave punk rock. Even Watson could see you're too repressed for a song like 'Baby, My Body Burns for You.' Where do you hide your LPs?"

"On the bottom shelf, left corner, and I am *not* repressed."

His only reply to that was another quick glance with a knowing smile. She shifted restlessly on the sofa. "Well, I'm not," she said as he pulled out a John Denver album. He settled the record onto the machine and strolled back to her, smile intact. He nestled beside her. She glared at him. "I'm not. I just have more elevated tastes, that's all."

"Sure," he said, and she knew she might as well have saved her breath. He crossed an ankle and rested it on his knee. The supple motion distracted Rhea's attention. His thighs were solidly muscular. He really was in magnificent shape. How would those muscles feel beneath her fingertips?

"So this Dave fellow you used to date, tell me about him."

She jerked her gaze from the mesmerizing vision of his cord-clad thigh. A slight warmth began creeping up her neck. Had he realized what she'd been thinking? "Dave?" she squeaked. "What do you want to know about Dave?"

"You said something about his being the sort who expected you to do what he wanted. I wondered what you meant exactly."

"Oh. Well. Dave wanted to change me, you know, to be his kind of woman rather than accepting me for who I am."

"And you went along with that."

"It wasn't ever anything major, not at first, so it took me a while to see what was happening." Her brow wrinkled as she remembered how it had been in the beginning. "One of the first things he did, and it was only our second date, was to ask me to wear more jewelry. He liked dangly earrings, and I was happy to wear them, thinking I was

82

pleasing him. Then he wanted nail polish—bright red polish. And then it was doing my hair differently and on and on. He just expected me to fall into line with whatever he wanted. I mean, he quit asking me what I'd like to do when we went out and began telling me what we were going to do. So he was telling me what to do, what to wear, what to think. I was always dancing to his tune."

Steve patted her knee. "But you decided to stop dancing."

"Ummm," she murmured, intent on the firm warmth of that hand now resting on her knee. Large, square, capable, callused, it was a worker's hand. It was also gentle, comforting, and loving.

"Tell me about it."

She dragged her eyes upward. He was regarding her keenly. She reminded herself he was simply concerned about a friend. "What is this? You ask more questions than any attorney. You know what I think it is? I think you're a frustrated shrink. I'm surprised you haven't made me write down my dreams for you to analyze."

"You have interesting dreams, do you?" He quirked his mouth in a suggestive smirk. He leaned a breath closer. "Any dreams I should know about, Rhea?"

A mischievous light brightened the gold flecks of her eyes. "Are you asking if I've dreamed about you?" she inquired in her best Marilyn Monroe imitation.

"Have you?"

"Well, I have had one or two," she drawled, then paused. She sighed breathily. "Terrible nightmares they were too."

"You little—" he growled as he lunged forward. She shrieked and slid over in an attempt to evade him, but couldn't escape. He grasped her shoulders and shoved her down into the cushions. He stretched his length atop her.

John Denver was singing a love ballad, but Rhea didn't hear it. The soothing echo of the thump of her heart drumming against the steady beat of Steve's muffled her ears to all else. The vague notion that she should be struggling crossed her mind. But lying beneath the solid weight of his chest wasn't at all unpleasant. In fact, she thought she could all too easily become accustomed to the cozy warmth of it. She decided she was enjoying it far more than she should be. She jostled against his shoulders. "Steve, let me up. You're crushing me."

"That's the penalty you have to pay for being such a poor hostess and insulting your guest." The heat of his breath caressed her cheek.

"Humph! Some guest," she huffed. "Uninvited and unwel—"

"Don't you dare say it," he cautioned softly.

She stared straight up into his deep blue eyes and wished more strongly than ever that she'd been gifted with wide, lovely eyes like Laurey's instead of a myopic pair forever hidden behind thick lenses. Before she had time to explore the meaning of such a wish, Steve pulled away from her. It was very like having a quilt abruptly yanked off on a chilly morning. She actually shivered with the sense of loss.

He stood looking down at her with a fixed intensity, almost as if he were enraptured. Rhea knew that was absolute nonsense. Yet her heart began imitating a Ping-Pong ball in a national tournament. If this were a cardiac test, she had one heck of a strong ticker. He continued to stare at her. She opened her mouth to inquire if something was wrong, but said nothing as Steve bent, gripped her hands, and easily lifted her to her feet. Smiling crookedly at her, he pressed her wandering glasses back up her nose.

"Go get changed," he said. "We're going to work out."

"Un-uh. No way. I said I'm not exercising today, and I meant it." She'd never been more definite. The sooner he realized she meant what she said, the better for him.

With a shake of his head that seemed to say Haven't you

learned by now?, he twirled her around and patted her rear. "Sure we are. I'll give you ten minutes."

Marching into her bedroom, the imprint of his hand still warm upon her fanny, Rhea rationalized her obedience to his command. He wouldn't leave, she knew, until he'd tortured her a little. He'd hang around all night, waiting for the opportunity to make her stretch and bend. Seeing her sweat and suffer was how the man got his kicks.

She stuffed herself into the plain black leotard Steve had given her. She hated it. The stretchy material clung to her body, emphasizing every lump she possessed. But he never seemed to notice, a fact for which she should have been grateful, but found herself resenting instead.

After banding her hair into a haphazard ponytail, she stomped back to the living room, a rare accomplishment in bare feet on thick carpeting. He waited for her in the center of the room. At the back of her mind she noted that he'd pushed the furniture out of the way. The front of her mind was taken up with the sight of Steve in white gym shorts and yellow T-shirt. While trying not to notice how terrific his legs looked bare, she couldn't help staring at the muscles bulging beneath the thin T-shirt.

"Ready?" he asked, charm oozing from his ready grin.

"You planned this," she said in tones thick with accusation.

He shrugged. "I knew you'd be eating more heavily today, so you'd need a special workout."

"You're a treacherous, underhanded rat."

Her disgruntled snarl didn't deter him in the least. He simply reached for her hand and hauled her next to him. "If it makes you feel any better, we'll work in tandem today."

She had to admit her interest was piqued. Previously, all her exercising had been solo, with Steve directing and encouraging. Now, however, it appeared he meant to work with her, exercising together. Her frown faded. This could be very interesting.

After a short warm-up of running in place, he turned her toward him, standing so closely, his toes nearly touched hers. "We'll start by working on the head and neck, like so."

She eyed him warily as he set her hands on each side of his head. He then clasped the sides of hers. Trapped by his palms, waves crashed in her ears. "This is an exercise?" she asked.

"Yes, my little skeptic, it is. Press your head against my hands while pulling my head toward you. We'll hold it five counts, then relax. Got it?"

Concentrating on pressing and pulling helped distract her from his near-suffocating closeness. Though in actuality they were an arm's length apart, to Rhea it seemed as if Steve were once again atop her. Her blood seemed to pulsate with the strength of his fingers as they entwined in her hair. Her skin seemed to heat with the warmth of his breath as he counted. Cupped beneath her palms, his hair was soft and springy and she had to work not to forget the pulling in favor of teasing her fingers amid the dark softness.

What on earth is the matter with me? Rhea scolded herself sharply, fighting to ignore the way in which her pulse was galloping, her nerve endings were catapulting. Whatever this was supposed to be doing for her head and neck, it was most certainly a vigorous drill for her blood pressure. Had she been so long without a man that she reacted to anyone who came near? It disturbed her to feel such an attraction for a man who was nothing more than her friend. She nervously looked beyond Steve's shoulder, hoping he couldn't detect her quite ridiculous reactions.

They counted, relaxed, counted, relaxed. Or, rather, Steve relaxed while Rhea pretended to relax. When his fingers loosened from her hair and he shifted, an inner sigh of relief surged up from her lungs. It got caught in her throat as he slid closer, pressing his shapely body lightly against hers. The length and width and breadth of him overwhelmed her. She couldn't move as his legs brushed a hairsbreadth on either side of hers, his arms slipped around her shoulders, and his hands swept down her back.

A husky, teasing laugh drew her startled gaze to his face. The sigh at last escaped from her dry throat, but it no longer held a speck of relief.

Desire, hot and raw, imprinted his features. From the blinding blue of his eyes to the set of his strongly sculpted jaw, she clearly read his intention. And still she asked, "W-what are you doing?"

"Another exercise," he murmured. "For the lips."

She did not, as she knew deep down she should, make even a show of resistance. She rather feared, in fact, that she tilted to meet him.

He lowered his mouth to hers, slowly, surely. A quivery surprise rippled through her. His lips were so cool, his kiss so feathery light. He nibbled gently. Her quivers became tremors of pleasure. He flicked his tongue once; she parted her lips willingly. But he merely tantalized her with another airy kiss. A mewing protest trickled from her.

"Shhhh," he breathed, and the warm hum of it throbbed through her veins. "There's no need to rush, sweetheart. We've got . . . all the time . . . in the world."

He kissed her again, another kiss curiously without pressure, yet capable of arousing a fierce response unlike any Rhea had ever known. Yearning dizzied her. She yearned to bathe in the moist delight of his lips, the gentle rapture of his hands, the hard pleasure of his body. At some vague level she wondered at the intensity of need pulsing through her, but reasons *why* she felt were quickly overshadowed by *what* she felt.

She surrendered to her desire to tease her fingers through his hair. Like his kisses, the strands were silken soft. It amazed her that someone so strong, so firmly muscled, could be so sensitive, so light. Would his hands stroke her so gently? Would his body enfold hers so tenderly? Hunger to know filled her. She swayed toward him in a silent plea.

Murmuring her name, he tightened his arms about her. Her glasses dug into his shoulder and slid askew. The wisp of his low chuckle stirred her hair. The vibration of it thrummed where her breasts pressed into the hardness of his chest. He tipped her slightly away. She blinked and raised a hand to push her glasses back into place. He stayed her hand, lifted the glasses off her nose, and dangled them a moment before tossing them carelessly onto the sofa. As they landed without a sound, she squeaked an objection.

"You won't need those for a while," he said. "They'll only get in the way."

For a simple statement his words had an effect that was decidedly complex. Rhea was torn between dashing to don her glasses, as if girding her armor for protection, and casting her body eagerly into the bonfire of his embrace. She squinted up at him, longing to see the possessive passion she'd thought she heard. But passion wasn't distinguishable in his blurred features. She squinted harder and he laughed.

"Sweetheart, sweetheart," he whispered on a note so loving, Rhea knew her ears were no more reliable than her eyes. "You shouldn't squint. Squinting will get you nothing but wrinkles."

"But I can't see you."

"You don't need to see me. I'll show you all you need to know."

"But I want to—"

"You, my sweet, don't know what you want," he cut in.

She arched her head back and eyed him narrowly, if still fuzzily. Irritation pricked her. He'd sounded so unalterably certain. "Oh?" she said with all the frost she could muster while her blood was burning with desire. "And I suppose *you* know what it is I want, Mr. Know-It-All?"

A blistering inferno would have had a more gelid effect. He flashed his teeth in a confident grin. "Absolutely. What you want, right now, is this."

He muffled any further argument with a kiss, a kiss unlike any preceding it. His lips were no longer cool and persuasive. They were hot and demanding. Tender coaxing had been replaced by impatient claiming. He stroked with hands that were restlessly insistent. From her shoulders to the small of her back, down over the curve of her buttocks and back up, his hands declared his intention to possess her.

He was, of course, right. This was precisely what Rhea had wanted. She couldn't remember ever wanting anything quite so much as she wanted to be held, caressed, loved by him. She didn't stop to think it out; she simply gave herself up to the delicious joy of the feeling.

And it was delicious, indescribably so. She hadn't experienced such trembling eagerness since her first kiss. These kisses consumed her, fused her body and mind and soul into one explosive need. She felt as if she were dissolving in the white-hot flame of passion. . . .

Plush carpeting rubbed sensuously against her bare legs. She opened her eyes and discovered they'd somehow slid to the floor. She lay tangled within his arms. His body stretched over hers; his head burrowed into her neck. The gloss of his sable hair changed with each colorful flash of the tree lights. On a bright blink of red, she closed her eyes, shutting out the world beyond the thick cushion of the carpet, the supple blanket of his body, the exquisite stimulation of his lips, his hands.

He nuzzled her cheekbone, tracing a delicate spiral to the corner of her mouth. The downy brush of his moustache, the faint scent of soap and tobacco, the quickening rasp of his breath as he caressed her, all roused her to a thrilling excitement. She kissed him with an abandonment that would have shocked her, had she been capable of thinking about it.

She was beyond thought. She was beyond everything but feeling, tasting, enjoying.

His hands slid over her leotard, pausing to encompass each breast. Her nipples thrust tautly upward, protesting the material covering them. He bent his head and kissed each in turn before trailing downward. Rhea thought of ripping the cloth from her body. His fingers danced over her belly, then moved slowly back toward her breasts.

"What do you want, sweetheart?" he asked, blowing light kisses into the hollow of her throat.

"I . . . want . . . you," she breathed.

Raising his head, he gazed down at her. She tried to focus on his smile. Even blurred, she clearly saw her desire mirrored in his face. There was something else there, too, something she couldn't quite define with her myopic gaze. Satisfaction? Triumph? What?

"You want me," he said.

She nodded and pressed hot little kisses against his chin. What was he waiting for? Fireworks? She wriggled suggestively beneath him. His fine lips slowly curved upward. The quirk of his moustache held that indefinable something.

"Not Addiboy?" he asked in velvet tones.

Later, much later, Rhea would ponder what would have happened if he had not said that; she'd ponder it with a curious mixture of relief and regret. But at the moment she didn't think at all. She heard the name and simply reacted. Shame, ice-cold sickening shame doused the heat in her veins. How could she offer herself to one man while loving another? How could she respond with such ardor to Steve when it was Addison her heart yearned for?

Her body went rigid with self-disgust. She thought she

would be sick all over the carpet. She thrust wildly at his shoulders. "Let me up, get off me," she urged in a shrill voice she didn't recognize as her own.

"Rhea, what—"

"Off!" she shrieked, and shoved with strength enough to topple him to the side.

She leaped up and rammed her fist to her mouth. How could she? She spun away from her guilt and made her way to her glasses. Behind her she heard his breathing slow, evening to a normal rate. It annoyed her. Her own lungs still heaved, though no longer from passion. She set her glasses on her nose and whirled to glare at him.

He sat, hands resting on his knees, looking perfectly at ease. His hair was mussed, his T-shirt was rumpled, but otherwise he looked as placidly composed as he always looked. Her annoyance gave way to sheer anger.

"Thank you for bringing the turkey," she said through stiff lips. Her tone was a decided dismissal.

He didn't move. He just watched her with a steady regard that disconcerted her even more. So many emotions roiled through her—guilt, reproach, anger, frustration—that Rhea had no idea what to do. Finally, as she was about to demand he leave, he came lithely to his feet.

"You don't know what you want, do you?" he asked.

"I know I want you to leave now."

He smiled. Obviously he was a man with a hide too thick to be pierced by rude insults. "Okay, pal," he said, moving to gather his clothes. "But think about it. You've got to work this out for yourself."

"There's nothing to work out."

"Isn't there?" was all he said before striding out.

CHAPTER SEVEN

The Christmas lights still winked merrily. For want of something more purposeful to do, Rhea strode to the tree, knelt, and angrily yanked the plug from the socket.

She sat back on her heels then and stared at the opaque ornaments dangling from the shadowed branches. How long she sat there in the darkened corner, she didn't know. It was long enough to work through her guilt. After all, she couldn't fault herself for being attracted to Steve. He was an attractive man. He was charming, intelligent, and though not a Greek god, engagingly handsome. She'd have to be made out of stone not to react to him. She'd simply had a normal physical response to an appealing man who'd kissed her.

And how he could kiss!

Steve was obviously very experienced in the art of seduction. Very experienced indeed.

For no logical reason this notion depressed her. Vague images of a forest of females being felled by Steve clouded her mind. She was certain he could have his pick. Why waste his time with her? Rhea Nichols wasn't anybody's idea of a fantasy woman.

Another cloud of gloom mantled her. She wasn't anybody's idea of a woman, period. Even Dave had dated her more for convenience, because she was there, rather than out of any true desire to be with her. It had been so long since any man had even seemed to notice she was alive, she'd blossomed to Steve's attention like a parched flower opening to the first raindrop.

Which brought her back to the point. *Why* had he paid that attention to her?

"Okay, what's he up to?" she said aloud, shaking a finger at the tilting tree. "Why did he stage that little love scene today?"

The tree, silent and still, had no answers for her.

She wrapped her arms around her knees and squeezed tightly. Closing her eyes, she recalled the tender touch of his lips, the gentle caress of his hands. Desire stirred anew. She opened her eyes. She kept them wide open as she clinically examined all that had happened. There was no doubt that Steve had initiated the lovemaking and little doubt that he'd planned to do so before he arrived. But he had seemed as intensely affected as she. He had certainly been aroused. . . . The deepening rasp of his voice, the harsh rapidity of his breath, the hardening tension of his body, all told her he had been.

Could he have manufactured such physical interest? Even as the question came to mind, Rhea dismissed it without a single doubt. Steve wasn't the sort to play such potentially hurtful games. He was too honest, too caring to toy with another's emotions. She could conclude only that he'd actually been attracted to her.

Rocking aimlessly on her heels, she let that roll around in her head, testing it. The more she considered it, the more certain she became that as unbelievable as it was, Steve had indeed wanted her.

A warm exhilaration flowed through her. She firmly ignored it. She set her mind to confronting this new problem. It was a definite problem. As warmly as she responded to him today—a response she firmly set down to not having been held and kissed and touched in a long time— Steve meant nothing to her. At least, nothing that way. As a friend, as a surrogate brother, he meant a great deal to her.

But Addison Chambers was the man of her dreams, the man she longed for. Even though he was an impossible dream, even though she was tilting at windmills to think she could ever have a man like him, the fact remained it was Addison, not Steve, who made her heart pound.

Rhea unfurled and stood. Shaking the cramps from her legs, she set that glowing warmth down to being flattered. It was highly gratifying to think a man like Steve could be interested in her as a woman. But she tamped down the elation this roused. It would be cruel to lead him on simply to pander to her vanity. She liked him far too much to hurt him in any way.

She headed for bed resolved to let Steve down gently, but firmly.

"Anybody home?" called a voice from around a wall of books. The query was immediately followed by the appearance of a mass of auburn curls and curvy hips.

"Over here, Janice," said Rhea, looking up with a smile. She leaned over an open drawer at the end of a short row of files, half obscured by a floor-to-ceiling shelf thrust into the room at a haphazard angle. She watched in amusement as Janice threaded her way through the maze of steel cabinets and wood shelves.

"One of these days, you're going to disappear back here and no one will ever find you." Janice laughed. "The case of the missing legal librarian. I've worked here four years and still feel as if I should leave a trail of bread crumbs behind me to find my way out."

Rhea smiled in understanding. Her domain was commonly referred to as "the catacombs" by everyone in the firm. Tiers of shelves crammed with books jutted this way and that throughout the small library with small chains of file cabinets squeezed in between, leaving short, twisting aisles to get from one point to another. Books and papers continually spilled from two tables at the front of this cramped labyrinth, beside which stood Rhea's square wood desk, the one haven of meticulously neat organization in the room.

Janice waved a scrap of paper. "Sir Stockard needs this reference as of ten minutes ago."

Taking the proffered paper, Rhea clicked her teeth. "Does he ever ask for anything he doesn't need ten minutes ago?"

"Do any of them?"

"If anyone ever did, I think I'd faint dead away, so I guess it's just as well he saved me the shock."

She slapped the drawer shut with a ping that underscored her sarcasm. She stepped around first one shelf, then another, with Janice following directly on her heels. After several turns through the maze, Rhea halted by a wall bursting with fat, black legal tomes, tugged a sliding ladder into place, and mounted it. As she selected a hefty, leather-bound book, she wobbled slightly with the added weight.

Below her, Janice laid a steadying hand on the ladder and asked, "So how was your Christmas?"

The book tumbled from her hands and hit the floor with a heavy thud. Janice jumped out of the way. The ladder skated to the side. Rhea clung tightly to it for a moment before looking down. To her intense dismay, she could feel the heat of a vivid blush mounting her cheeks. Worse, she realized from the widening of Janice's eyes that it was clearly noticeable.

"That good, huh?" said her friend pertly.

She strove for nonchalance. "Nothing special," she tossed off as she backed down the ladder.

"Sure," said Janice, and handed Rhea the book with a knowing look.

Rhea ignored the look, flipped open the book, and

marked the necessary passage for Peter Stockard in silence. Janice shrewdly changed the subject, rattling on about her own Christmas until she went on her way. Left alone, Rhea leaned against the shelf and sighed.

Once again the events of the day before rose up to taunt her. Her eyes closed. She traced the curve of her lip with a fingertip, remembering the kisses that had pressed there. She could almost feel those soft, cajoling kisses. She thought of how they'd turned fiery, insistent, rousing her to an aching need, a need she could almost feel.

She jerked her finger away and told herself sternly to quit being such a fool.

Yet she couldn't seem to stop such memories from invading her mind. All morning she'd been plagued by them. The time they'd shared had begun so comfortably, two friends enjoying each other's companionship. But somehow their feelings had escalated to a level that had nothing to do with friendship. It had seemed so special, so very special.

The more she recalled the conversation, the laughter, the passion she'd shared with Steve, the more her resolution to return to a platonic friendship with him wavered. Would it be so wrong? If she didn't love him, she at least liked him very much. They could have good times together. It was more than she'd ever have with Addison. She was kidding herself to think she'd ever have anything with Addison. He was nothing more than a dream. Why waste her life chasing after a dream?

Why indeed? she thought as she went back to the files. She reached the cabinet and a decision at the same time. It was stupid, childish, to let an infatuation, a mere fantasy, obstruct her chances for a real relationship. She plucked a manila folder from the drawer with determination. When she met Steve tonight, she'd let him know she was through with dreams.

A grin spread over her lips as she marched back to her

desk. The warm satisfaction of correctly settling a matter filled her. The depression that had hovered over her the last few months evaporated. Nothing could stop her now! She came around the shelf that divided the front from the inner sanctum of the library and lurched to a halt.

The man of her dreams lounged on her desk, idly swinging one foot as he thumbed through her Rolodex. He looked up, his foot halted, and he greeted her with a lazy smile.

The file slipped out of her hands to splash papers over the floor. Her grin hung foolishly on her face. She knew she was gaping, but could do nothing to prevent it.

Addison's pale, perfect brows drew together, then evened. He straightened from his perch on the edge of her desk and bent to rescue the file. Rhea, horrified, embarrassed, dove down to scoop it up first. Their heads met with a resounding thump. Each jerked back. She stared helplessly into his gorgeous eyes and prayed the shelf behind her would collapse, crushing her into oblivion.

"Are you hurt?" he asked.

Her heartbeat did a dance to the melody of his voice. Her pulse hummed just to be near him. She shook her head dumbly.

He smiled again. Her knees wobbled. He rose. She drank in the length and shape of him, thinking how beautiful he was. The perfectly pressed gray suit enhanced his classic good looks and enkindled all her secret hankerings to blazing need.

"I'm sorry. I didn't mean to startle you," he said, looking down at her.

"Oh, no, you didn't. I mean, you needn't—it wasn't you—I should've—"

The touch of his hand to her sleeve stopped the inarticulate gush. She decided her teal velour had been coated with asbestos. It was the only explanation for why those long, slim fingers didn't scorch right through the cloth.

She managed to scramble to her feet and stand out of his way while he gathered together the scattered papers and stuffed them into the folder. She even managed to squeak, "Thank you," when he handed it to her.

"It's the least I can do, considering I apparently frightened you half to death. You're still whiter than a sheet."

"It wasn't your fault. I—I've been having a clumsy day. I didn't hurt you, did I?" she asked, wishing she could pinch color back into her cheeks without his noticing it.

"No, not at all." He smiled again and ruffled his hair above the spot she'd bumped.

Rhea watched with hungry eyes. His lovely hand came down. Each silvery blond strand fell obediently into place.

"And you're certain I didn't hurt you?"

She shifted her gaze to his face. Masculine satisfaction glimmered in the slight lifting of his lips. She realized he'd seen the yearning stamped on her face and thought longingly of the tumbling bookshelf. How could she make such an utter fool of herself?

She looked away. "I'm fine, really."

"You're sure? That was a pretty nasty crack. I think you might have a bruise here."

The cool touch of his finger to her forehead ignited fulminating flames in her blood. He drew his finger away and still her body smoldered. She scarcely felt the heat. She'd have jumped willingly into a pyre to see such concern for her in his eyes. For the first time, he was looking at her and really seeing her, not just seeing the firm's librarian. She felt as if her excitement would consume her. Licking her lips, she shyly inquired, "Can I help you, Mr. Chambers?"

"Actually, I was searching for Janice Ekland. Stockard told me she'd come here. Is she back in the catacombs somewhere?"

Now she knew what a balloon must feel like when someone carelessly jabs it with a pin. Her excitement deflated in one big burst. "No," she answered flatly. "She was here, but she left about fifteen minutes ago."

"Do you know where she went?"

"If she's not at her desk, try the lounge. She might be taking her coffee break."

"Righto," he said, and turned to leave. He paused, glancing over his shoulder. "And thanks . . . er . . . Rita, isn't it?"

"Rhea."

"Ah, yes, that's it. Well, thank you, Rhea." He presented her with a final smile, one of his casual, smile-to-the-masses smiles. He strolled out, taking most of the light with him.

Dim and dejected, Rhea slumped at her desk. She leaned her elbows on the forgotten file folder and pondered miserably over the absurdity of her behavior. She reexamined each infinitesimal moment with Addison; she recalled the angle of his stance, the tilt of his head, the curve of his smile, the gleam in his eyes when he'd actually looked at her. With her pulse pumping furiously, she focused again and again on the instant he'd looked at her as if she were a woman.

And she knew that as ridiculous as it was, as long as there was the tiniest hope he'd ever look at her that way again, she couldn't stifle her feelings for him. She couldn't substitute Steve for Addison.

She renewed her decision to explain all this to Steve. Of course, she'd do so as gently as possible. She didn't want to hurt him. As she removed her elbows from the file and set to work, she mentally formulated a speech.

By the end of the workday, Rhea's outlook had brightened considerably. After all, Addison *had* noticed her, if only in passing. That was a start. She was convinced the four pounds had made the difference and resolved to throw herself body and soul into the "beautifying Rhea" project. When she was through, she'd make Addison see her again—and this time, do a double take!

Once home, she flew about the apartment, leaping into her leotard with only a passing thought of Steve's hands on it, on her. Grabbing her jogging shoes in one hand and her sweat suit in the other, she raced into the living room and began shoving furniture out of the way. There wouldn't be an exercise she wouldn't do tonight!

Laurey shuffled out of her bedroom, looking lovely despite her sleep-tousled dishevelment. She yawned widely. "What's going on?"

"I'm getting ready for my exercises with Steve. I'm sorry I woke you, I didn't realize you were here. When did you get back?"

"A couple hours ago. Anyway, you didn't wake me. I was just resting a little before getting ready for a date tonight."

"Good Christmas?" asked Rhea, hopping energetically as she cleared clutter.

"Umm, the usual family gathering," Laurey answered absently. She watched Rhea bounce about and said on a peevish note, "What's happened to you? You look positively rabid to exercise."

Rhea shrugged and turned aside to push an armchair against the wall. She felt slightly foolish, for that was a perfect description of how she was feeling, but she couldn't explain the whys of it to Laurey. It was bad enough knowing she was acting like a lovesick teenager. She couldn't imagine how awful it would be to have Laurey knowing it too. So she said instead, "Oh, it sort of grows on you, all this jumping around. I didn't get to it yesterday and sort of missed it."

"God, I hope it's not contagious," mumbled Laurey as she floated back to her bedroom.

The sound of confident rapping sent Rhea flying to the door. She didn't know which she was more eager to get

100

over with, her exercises or her speech. She reached for the knob, but hesitated. Poor Steve! How could she explain without hurting him? Another loud knock resounded in her ear. She inhaled deeply and, hoping she looked more composed than she felt, flung open the door.

"Took you long enough," said Steve cheerfully. "I was beginning to think you were chickening out on the exercises."

"Of course I wasn't—" she started, but stopped as she realized she was already speaking to his back.

He'd strolled past her and into the living room. Grinning broadly, he emitted a low whistle. "Guess I was wrong. What is this? A New Year's resolution?"

She couldn't help returning the grin. "I've finally figured out there's no sense trying to fight you."

A shadow passed so fleetingly over his face, she couldn't be sure she hadn't imagined it. All he said was, "It's about time." He threw off his jacket and shoved up the sleeves of his thermal shirt. "All right now, warm-ups."

She held back, digging her toes into the carpet. In all her imaginings of this, she hadn't expected him to be the same old Steve. She'd thought he'd be hesitant, maybe slightly embarrassed, or at the other extreme, eager and loverlike. She had not anticipated that he'd be back to dictatorial and brotherly. Although a large part of her prepared speech had been devoted to how they should act as if nothing had happened and return to their platonic friendship, to find him acting as if nothing had happened took the wind out of her sails. She eyed him with resentment. Didn't he think anything had happened yesterday? Hadn't those kisses affected him? The notion that they hadn't at all somehow disappointed her.

He clapped his hands, ending her reverie. "Hey, pal, let's get going, chop-chop. You know the circuit. Ten each."

"I'm going, I'm going," she muttered as she began

stretching to his count. The casual way he'd tossed off "pal" rang in her ears. She cast several furtive glances his way. From the top of his hair—which was, she inanely remembered, exceptionally soft—to the tips of his canvas jogging shoes, he exuded congeniality. This relieved her. It also piqued her. Hadn't yesterday meant *anything*?

"Quit scowling and wake up," he said. "You're supposed to be doing jumping jacks."

She allowed herself the satisfaction of sticking her tongue at him before jumping. He chuckled and, despite herself, Rhea began to relax. So maybe her ego was a little bruised; it was far more important to retain her friendship with Steve than to flatter her ego with his unwanted attention.

When they were zipped into their sweat suits and heading for the back street they used for jogging, she gave him her friendliest smile and inquired, "So did you ever talk to your grandmother last night? Did you manage to sweet-talk her?"

"As a matter of fact, no. All my subterfuge was in vain. She blistered my ears for a half hour and ended by demanding I put in an appearance at Easter or else."

"Or else what?"

"Or else I'm drummed out of the family in disgrace, never to darken the honorable name of Bradley again, my descendants stripped of their inheritance."

He was grinning. She quirked her lips and started trotting beside him. "My descendants," he'd said. She wondered if he had any children. He'd been married a long time. She wondered why she'd never wondered before. Why he'd never said anything. Why she wanted so badly to know now. But, of course, she couldn't pry into his private life.

"You have children?" she promptly blurted.

"No," he replied with unusual terseness.

They jogged in silence after that. Rhea wished she'd bit

102

her tactless tongue off at the age of two. When they stopped at their usual corner, a mile from the apartment complex, she jammed her mittened hands under her armpits and refused to look at him. Their breath vapors clouded the cold air. Halos from streetlamps melted in radiant pools between night's descending shadows. Bright beams of headlights streaked by, accompanied by the loud drone of engines.

The rough wool of his glove gently chucked her chin, startling her into looking at him. A dim aureole of light spilled over him, softening the lines of his face. She thought of the first time she'd seen him and how kind she'd thought his face. He looked even kinder now.

"I'm sorry, Rhea," he said quietly. "I didn't mean to be so brusque with you."

"I deserved it. I had no right probing into your affairs."

"Nonsense. You're my friend, and friends shouldn't be afraid to ask questions of each other. Come on, let's head back and I'll try to explain as we go."

"You don't need to explain anything to me."

"I may not need to, but I want to," he said, and started running. He was four paces ahead of her when she spurted after him. As she caught up to him, he cast a tender smile her way. "It's always been somewhat of a touchy subject with me, but I'd like for you to understand. You see, when Tammie and I married we agreed we didn't want children. We were young and didn't want to be tied down. But after a few years I began to want a family. Tammie didn't. As each year passed, our differing attitudes widened the rift between us. It wasn't the only reason we split up, but it was a major factor."

"Oh," said Rhea, feeling it was inadequate. But what else could she say?

"I still want a family, but it doesn't seem to be in the cards for me."

"Oh," she repeated.

103

He halted in front of her and grasped her by the shoulders. "Listen here, Rhea Nichols, friends have to be honest and open with each other. I'm glad you asked. It shows you're interested and care about me. I told you how I felt because I care about you. All right?"

Now was the time for her to launch into her speech. Now she should tell him how Addison was the only man she could care about. She should tell him that her only interest in him was strictly sisterly. Instead, she whispered, "Right," and waited for the kiss she was certain would come.

He ruffled the top of her crimson stocking cap and said, "Great." Then he turned and resumed running.

Rhea began to believe she'd summoned up all that passion out of her own vivid imagination. She must have. Steve didn't appear to realize that white-hot desire had flamed between them yesterday, that awkwardness should lay stiffly between them today. He didn't evidence any interest in her beyond his usual friendly, almost brotherly, concern. Though it was precisely what she wanted, she didn't know whether to grin or grind her teeth.

They parted in the parking lot, agreeing to get together at the same time the next day. "Night, buddy," were Steve's last words to her. Hot and tired out, Rhea trudged up the stairs to her apartment, lecturing herself every step of the way.

She hadn't wanted him to kiss her again, had she? How could she even think of it when she had Addison's smile to think about? She should be singing for joy that the attraction had all been in her head. She had no reason whatsoever to feel glum. She had Steve's friendship and Addison's smile.

And somewhere, tucked far away at the back of her mind, she had the memory of that magic on Christmas Day.

CHAPTER EIGHT

"I'm almost afraid to look down."

"Then I'll look for you."

"Oh, no, you won't!" Rhea negated with an intimidating glare at Steve.

He wasn't intimidated. "You'll be telling me anyway," he pointed out reasonably.

She wasn't to be reasoned with. "That doesn't mean you need to look. I'll look."

"So look already. You've probably gained a pound just hanging around on the scale."

Settling the argument by making a face at him, Rhea turned her gaze to the number showing between her toes. She blinked and looked again. She hopped off the scale and hugged Steve in one excited motion.

"I take it this means you didn't gain a pound," he said on a note dry as dust.

"Ten pounds! I've lost ten pounds!" she yelled, and jumped back onto the cream fur covering the square scale. The round dial spun crazily, then steadied. She stabbed her finger downward. "Look, just look!"

"But I thought," drawled Steve, hanging back, "that you didn't want me to look."

She threw him an aggrieved frown. He laughed and came forward. Slinging an arm around her shoulder, he squeezed her once lightly, then obediently checked the dial. He whistled.

"Good going, pal. Didn't I tell you last week you shouldn't get upset? You've got to expect you'll reach a few plateaus when you don't lose."

"You know the only thing worse than being continually, disgustingly, right is being an I-told-you-so." She came out of his loose clasp and stepped off the scale. "But you were right and I'm sorry I was such a bear last week."

Having declared at the outset that she could not bear to weigh herself on a daily basis, they'd established the routine of weekly weigh-ins before their Sunday-morning run. At first she'd lost one or two pounds every week, making the ritual a happy occasion that they followed up with a long run and a gigantic breakfast. Last week, however, the ritual hadn't been so happy. Rhea hadn't lost a single ounce. She'd spent the entire day sunk in gloom. She'd threatened to either give up the whole stupid project or to fling herself into one of those quick-loss crash diets. Steve had firmly nixed both, extracting her promise to continue for at least one more week. Now he offered her a cat-who-swallowed-the-canary smile and suggested they enjoy their run.

Usually when they ran, they bantered easily, with the familiarity of close friends, talking about everything from the day's headlines to family squabbles. After weeks of constant companionship, there were few constraints between them. Periodically the memory of Christmas would intrude and a shyness would come over Rhea, but it always faded quickly in the force of his easygoing charm. It was, in any case, patently clear she'd imagined those holiday sparks. The mood of the moment had brought them together, but that's all it had been—a moment in passing. She was grateful it hadn't ruined their friendship. She'd never had a friend who meant as much to her as Steve did.

When they stepped outside they were greeted by a steadily falling snow. Steve produced a key. "Come on," he said, and nudged her toward a black Bronco.

"What's this?"

"This is mine." He flashed her a grin full of devilment. "I'm somewhat cautious about using the MG these days."

"I meant *this*." She ignored the taunt and pointed an accusing finger at the key.

"It's for my sister's gym. Since it's snowing, I thought we'd go there for a workout. Get in."

Rhea halted, looking stubborn. "I've told you before, I am not about to jiggle my flab in front of a crowd."

"What flab? You're ten pounds slimmer these days. Get in."

"I'm not exhibiting my body to a group of strangers."

Exasperation flicked over his face. "Haven't you gotten over that nonsense yet? You look terrific. I'd think with the inches you've trimmed off, you'd want people to ogle your figure."

"There's only one person I want ogling my figure and he hasn't noticed how terrific I supposedly look." She had the sinking feeling that sounded petulant and whiny. She tried again. "It's just that I get embarrassed. I can't help it. I always have. I hated high school gym classes."

"You don't have anything to be embarrassed about. You never did have, but you won't believe me about that either. After all, it's not *my* opinion that counts with you, is it?"

Gone was the teasing smile, the twinkling gaze. She could feel his hostility as palpably as if he'd slapped her with it. She kicked her toe at the white powder paving the lot and waited. After a few seconds that seemed to stretch into decades, he said coldly, "We'll have complete privacy. The Body Shop is closed on Sundays. Now, get in before I toss you in."

She got in. He slammed the door and strode around to get in on his side. They drove off in a thunderous silence.

The cheery mood had apparently been shattered beyond repair. Rhea didn't fully understand why. She gripped her hands together and focused on her whitening knuckles. Steve had never been angry at her before, not like this. It both disturbed and irritated her. He was being unreasonable. He knew how she felt about exercising in front of others; why had he made such a big deal of it?

They were heading west, toward the mountains. She watched monolithic office buildings give way to patches of shopping centers surrounded by spokes of frame houses. This was an area of Denver she didn't know. She ventured a question. "Where are we going?"

"Littleton."

The pointed brevity of his reply decided Rhea in favor of the depressive silence. The purplish hues of the distant peaks evolved into dull browns as they drew closer to the jagged ridge that designated the beginning of the Rocky Mountains. A sandstone-colored quadrangle stood out in the midst of an expanding tract neighborhood. Steve turned into the parking lot and parked at the far end. Rhea followed him to a plain, unmarked door. He unlocked it and ushered her inside.

Despite the gloomy shadows shrouding the entry, she could clearly see a half wall of daffodil yellow splashed with spring green lettering which proclaimed this to be The Body Shop. Steve switched on the lights. A fluorescent glare washed over them. Rhea walked around the divider, took one look, and pivoted to retreat.

"Where do you think you're going?"

"Out of here. Have you seen what's back there?"

Steve laughed. Looking up at him, Rhea immediately decided that if she had to torture herself by getting into, onto, or around any of the hideous contraptions she'd glimpsed, she would do it. To have him smiling at her like that would be worth the sacrifice. She summoned up a weak smile and said gamely, "Well, maybe I could try one of them."

He grasped her shoulders and spun her around. "My little martyr," he said, sounding highly amused.

Feeling a kinship to all those thrown to the lions, she stiffened her spine and stepped back into the gym. Obviously the room had been furnished by the designer of the interrogation room for the Spanish Inquisition. Elastic straps dangled lifelessly from steel bars. Massive discs lay in heavy lumps beside a stack of poles. Stationary bicycles and mechanical rowers waited ominously. A padded cushion with weighted bars at the sides and stirrups at the foot looked about as inviting as a dentist's chair. In fact, Rhea rather thought she'd prefer the latter.

Her dismay must have stamped itself upon her face, for Steve took her hand and said soothingly, "Don't worry. I didn't bring you here to inflict any of this on you. Look up."

She obediently tipped her head back and gazed upward. An oval track ran above, circling the room. Her fear receded. She wouldn't have to become intimately acquainted with any of the horror machines. "Oh, thank God," she said on a gush of relief. "We're going running."

"Six times around equals a mile," said Steve. "Think you can go for five today?"

"Sure," she agreed happily. She'd have agreed to ten just to keep him smiling at her. Those minutes when he'd angrily shut her out were ones she never wanted to repeat.

He released her hand. "Let's make it interesting. If you make the five miles, I'll take you out to lunch tomorrow. If you don't make five, you take me."

"You're on. There's a place near the office that has a fantastic salad bar."

They warmed up, then mounted the stairs to the track. At first Rhea thought it would be a snap. Their pace was smoother, seemingly faster on the track than on the uneven pavement. She joked as they ran, telling him she'd eat extra portions since he'd be paying. But gradually she couldn't spare the breath for jokes. She hardly had enough for moving. Her lungs heaved. Her eyes blurred. The slap of their shoes echoed within the empty building.

Just under four miles, Rhea collapsed in a defeated heap. She dropped her head between her tired legs and struggled for breath. Every inch of her body ached. She would have welcomed the cushioned chair downstairs—bars, stirrups, and all.

Steve crouched beside her and asked in concern, "Are you okay?"

Gasping, she shook her head. He tenderly toyed with her hair, saying nothing. After a time, she rasped, "I'm going . . . to die."

He chuckled. She scowled. He stroked his moustache and remarked, "For a while there, I thought you just might pull it off. Don't feel bad though. It was a good three months after I started running before I reached five miles."

"You mean, you knew I couldn't do it?" she spit out.

"Well, I didn't know you couldn't, but the odds were against it."

Words failed her. She couldn't find any words scathing enough to tell him what she thought of him. He reached out to brush her hair away from her sweaty brow. His fingertips seemed to linger an extra moment. She glanced up at him. As she had so often before, she thought how kind, how comfortable he looked. He smiled at her and a warm happiness rejuvenated her weary muscles. She returned his smile. "You don't deserve it, but if you want to collect your lunch, pick me up at noon tomorrow."

"Noon tomorrow," he agreed, and lifted her to her feet. "I wouldn't miss it for the world."

An unconscious stirring rippled throughout the restaurant. The hanging ferns and potted rubber trees seemed to sway with the breeze of anticipation. Voices were hushed, clinking silverware was muted, and linen napkins were poised like banners waving. Rhea sensed it and glanced up from the oversize menu she'd been studying. Seated opposite, two women in classically tailored suits straightened slightly in their chairs. Their widened eyes were fixed on the entrance. Her curiosity roused, Rhea swiveled slightly to look over her shoulder.

The classically perfect profile was cast into stark relief by the bright sunlight streaming through the window behind him. The sun streaks haloed the fair head, bestowing a silvery corona to the iridescent blond hair. Rhea stared and felt her heart somersault.

"Have you decided on anything?" Steve asked, and she realized with a guilty start that it was the second time he'd asked.

"Uh, no, not yet," she mumbled. She riveted her eyes on the cream vellum menu, but failed to read a word printed there. Her pulse was clacking like a locomotive, repeating Addison, Addison, Addison until her blood thrummed with the message.

The flash of his blue suit caught her attention. She peered around her menu. As Addison strolled by, he smiled at his companion, a woman Rhea barely noticed. Watching the beauty of that smile, she wouldn't have noticed the ceiling caving in.

Steve tapped her hand. She jumped, then gaped at him dully. "You must be starving," he said dryly. "You're practically drooling on your menu."

Raising her menu like a shield to hide her flush of excitement, she leaned toward Steve. He obligingly lifted his own menu and leaned a conspiratorial ear toward her.

"That's him," she whispered with dramatic, if ungrammatical, fervor.

"What? Who? Who's him?" he whispered back out of

111

the side of his mouth while surreptitiously searching the room.

"Addison. It's Addison," she breathed.

"Where? Who? That man in brown beneath the hanging fern?"

"What? No, of course not! Addison doesn't have a pot belly! *That* man over there. The gorgeous blond taking the seat by the bay window."

"You think bald is gorgeous?"

He lowered his menu to eye her with incredulity. She glared, flapped her menu at him, and bit out a low rasp, "Not *bald*. Blond. The blond man at the next table over from the bald man."

Looking a great deal like Inspector Clouseau, Steve again hoisted his menu into place before his face, then edged his nose around the corner to stare theatrically across the restaurant. His gaze slithered from Addison's table to Rhea's expectant face and back again. Finally he returned his eyes to intently study the listing of meals before him, oblivious to the palpable impatience rising like steam from the woman near him.

"Well?" hissed Rhea finally.

"Well, what?"

"Well, what do you think?"

"I think I'll have the French onion soup with broccoli quiche."

"Steve Bradley, I'm warning you—"

"There's no need to snarl, pal." He set down his menu and gently tugged hers from her hand. He looked her up and down, then shook his head. "It's just that I can't believe it," he said with a touch of sadness.

"Can't believe what?"

"That that's Adley. Are you sure Adley's the blond over there?"

He stabbed a finger in the general direction of the bay window. She frantically clutched his finger and shoved it

112

down, glancing about wildly, praying no one had noticed. The horrible feeling that she was making a spectacle of herself in full view of the man she loved made her voice shrill. "*Ad-di-son!* Of course it's Addison. Why can't you believe it?"

"Because I can't believe," he said in tones throbbing with disbelief, "that *that's* the man of your dreams."

The pitying look that accompanied this momentarily stunned her into silence. Before she could regain her wits enough to demand a full explanation of his quite incomprehensible—and to her view, demented—attitude, a cheery young waitress sailed up, asking what they wanted. Though she no longer cared if she ate or not, Rhea ordered a salad and cup of soup, then glowered at Steve as he placed his own order. She rather hoped he choked on his onion soup. How dare he, she thought angrily, and only passingly wondered how dare he what? It upset her that he should dismiss Addison so casually. How could anybody dismiss Addison?

The waitress gave them an I'll-get-back-to-you smile and disappeared. Rhea immediately shifted in her chair, intent on presenting Steve with the full force of her frown. He, however, didn't notice her efforts. His gaze was fixed on the table by the bay window. She cleared her throat. He continued to stare, heedless of her attempts to gain his attention. She kicked his shin beneath the table. He faced her in surprise.

"Do you always get this violent when hungry?" he inquired with an air of injury.

She ignored the misplaced humor and unclamped her teeth. "Okay, out with it," she commanded. "Tell me what you can't believe about Addison."

His injured look deepened. Even the ends of his moustache appeared to droop sadly. "I thought I had. I told you, I can't believe he's the man of your dreams. You just

113

didn't strike me as that type of woman. Not that type at all."

"If you don't explain what you're talking about, I'm going to show you just how violent I can get when pressed."

His moustache ceased to droop. His broad grin was not appreciated by its recipient.

"Steve," she muttered on a warning note, and he chuckled.

"All right, all right. Before you leap over the table to do me in, I'll try to explain. I didn't think you were the sort to be bowled over by a walking mannequin. He's handsome, I'll grant you that, but he looks about as deep as his three-piece suit."

"How can you make a judgment like that? Besides, you're completely wrong. I'll have you know, he's one of the sharpest attorneys in town," she said on a snap.

"Oh, I don't doubt that he's sharp in the courtroom," he agreed easily. "He probably manipulates juries with ease."

His agreement annoyed her. There was the slightest hint of disparagement in his words. She thought his censure totally unfounded and yet . . . She looked over to where Addison sat, framed by the bay window. Handsome failed to describe him accurately. He was, quite simply, stunning. She turned back to Steve. She bit back the impulse to chant Sticks and Stones, and said, instead, "Addison Chambers is not just a pretty face—and don't look at me like that!"

"Like how?"

"As if you pity me. I can't understand your attitude. He's got everything a woman could want. Looks, position, brains."

"Don't forget ego," he murmured.

Rhea stiffened, but before she could leap to Addison's defense, the waitress arrived with their meal. Silence throbbed between them as they were served, and the polite clink of silverware prevailed. Steve remarked that the soup was tasty. She didn't bother to reply. She fixed her gaze on the bay window and told herself that if Addison had an ego, he deserved to have one. She couldn't think of anyone who had more right to be proud of himself.

She voiced the thought, then wished she hadn't. Steve immediately concurred and added, "But I wasn't talking pride. I was talking conceit. I think it's ridiculous for you to want a man who probably spends his free time looking in the mirror."

"As I recall," she said in her most frigid tones, "our agreement was that you'd help me get in shape. I've put up with being bullied, with starving and sweating at your command. I don't think I have to put up with suffering your arrogant opinions. I don't recall that being a part of our agreement."

"You asked me to explain," he said reasonably.

Rhea didn't feel like being reasonable. She dipped into her soup with an angry little splash and proceeded to ignore him. He had no right to say such things. He didn't even know Addison. He didn't know what he was talking about. Addison was the most sought-after bachelor in town. Addison was everything a woman could want. Steve's opinion didn't mean anything.

So why did she suddenly feel, well, ridiculous for wanting Addison?

Once again she found herself staring at the table by the bay window. Addison raised a wineglass to his companion and a small pang pierced Rhea. To be that lucky woman! A vision of herself sitting across of Addison, receiving his smile, his toast, his attention, filled her mind. It was a delicious fantasy and she relished each moment of it. Her soup began to cool; her salad went untouched.

"It's enough to put me off my meal," said Steve.

She looked vaguely at him. "What is?"

"The sight of you mooning over a man who's thoroughly immersed in the effect he's having."

She opened her mouth to refute this, but thought better of it. The horrifying certainty that she had been mooning over Addison was overshadowed by the appalling thought that he'd been aware of it. She indignantly resented Steve for pointing out her humiliation. Stabbing viciously at her salad, she muttered, "And to think I'm paying to have all this fun."

Steve set his hand over hers, stilling it. She moodily eyed that hand, then raised her petulant gaze to his face. He smiled crookedly, tilting his moustache comically and displaying more than his fair share of charm. Her animosity began slipping away from her, then was chased away altogether when he said, "If I offered to pick up the tab, would it erase that frown of yours?"

"Are you offering?" she queried in reply.

"Absolutely. If I see a smile, I may even go so far as to apologize for ruining our lunch."

That did bring a smile to her lips. "Oh, you didn't ruin it. Just dented it a little."

"Ah, well, that makes us even then."

Her brow furrowed in puzzlement. "Even?"

"You started our friendship off with a few dents."

"You're never going to let me live that down, are you?"

"Nope," he answered cheerfully. "And I am sorry, pal. You're right. I agreed to help you out, not to spout off."

They shared a grin and were friends again. As they resumed eating, he told her he thought it was about time for "phase two of our program."

"That sounds ominous. If it means more sweat, forget it. I've given all the sweat I mean to give for this project."

"No more sweat, huh? Not even for ol' Atterson?"

"Not even for Tom Selleck," she replied breezily, refusing to be baited again.

He chuckled. "Well, lucky for Atterson, phase two

116

doesn't mean more sweat." He paid no attention to her fervently breathed "Thank God," but continued to explain. "Now that you're well into the trimming and slimming, we need to start working on style—finding the right kinds of clothes and makeup for you. A friend of mine's a beauty consultant and I thought we could get her advice on what's best for you."

She greeted this suggestion with enthusiasm and they spent the remainder of their meal discussing when they'd get together with Steve's friend and what to expect when they did. The table by the bay window and its occupants were forgotten in the new excitement as Rhea tried to envision herself in different hairstyles and different kinds of clothing. It was only at the end of the meal, when the waitress had passed by with several refills of coffee and finally the check, that Rhea realized she'd failed to think of Addison once in all that time. It was incomprehensible that she'd been in the same room with him and not tingled with awareness throughout. She hastily sought out the object of all her endeavors.

He still sat framed within the embrasure of the window, looking elegantly polished as he conversed with his luncheon companion. As he spoke he scanned the restaurant, letting his gaze pause whenever he lit on one of the several admiring glances he received. Amid the fluctuating clatter, his eyes met hers, briefly lingered, then moved on.

Oddly, her heart didn't skip its usual beat, her pulse didn't flutter. The echo of Steve's words, *A man thoroughly immersed in the effect he's having,* slipped through her mind. She tried not to hear it.

Pushing her glasses up her nose, she rose to follow Steve out of the restaurant. At the entrance, however, she glanced back. It may have been the clouds scudding through the sky, and thus momentarily dimming the interior, but for once, Addison's image didn't glow.

CHAPTER NINE

Each little snip reverberated in Rhea's ears, resounding over the surrounding chatter, the low hum of dryers, and the radio buzzing in the background. She knotted her hands together and tried not to look panic-stricken. In this, she failed miserably.

"Buck up. It's only hair," said Steve. "If you don't like it cut, it'll always grow back."

She pouted at him. He leaned negligently against a hip-level shelf jammed with shampoos, lotions, creams, and other miscellaneous bottles and jars. His arms were crossed over his chest and one leg scissored the other. But it wasn't his casual stance that rubbed Rhea the wrong way. It was the air of amusement that fairly dripped from him. Of course he wasn't perturbed. It wasn't *his* hair that was being hacked off.

Before she could utter any of the blistering set-downs her mind was struggling to produce, Ilona Drake spoke up. "Don't listen to him. You're going to love it. Terence is the best stylist in town, aren't you, Terry love? Don't you pay any attention to Steve, Rhea. He's nothing but a terrible tease."

Her glossed lips curved upward as she cast him a coy look that purred, *I ought to know.* He grinned a slow grin, the sort of warmly intimate smile of a longtime friend. Or lover.

Rhea watched the exchange and came to a decision. She

decided she hated Ilona Drake. It was unreasonable, she knew, for over the past few weeks Ilona had offered invaluable advice and services, helping Rhea select a new wardrobe, coaching her on makeup and fashion. She'd taken Rhea under her wing zealously, taking complete command, determined to make a swan out of the duckling. Under any other circumstances, Rhea might have sincerely liked her. Ilona was gregarious, astute, confident, the kind of assertive achiever Rhea admired. But absurdly, the familiar play between Ilona and Steve irritated her.

They went "way back," he'd told her. Just how far back she didn't know and insisted to herself she didn't care to know. But it was obvious they'd been close, very close. Their banter, their smiles, their looks, all whistled with suggestion.

She shrugged her irrational annoyance off and said she was certain she'd like the new cut. She was lying. She wasn't certain in the least. Change had never come easily to her, and though she'd thrown herself with enthusiasm into the project, her exuberance was tempered by lingering apprehension. As much as she'd wanted to be someone new, Rhea wasn't really sure she wanted to be anyone different.

But as winter sluggishly melted into spring, the metamorphosis continued. She'd lost more weight, picked up on accentuating her features with makeup, and altered her style of dressing. Throughout it all she wavered between excited exultation and quivering disbelief. Each time she put on one of the new, bolder, more colorful outfits Ilona had chosen, doubt pricked her. Was that *really* Rhea Nichols wearing the splashy yellow-on-red crepe blouse? The billowy black silk slacks with patent heels? The dangling gold teardrop earrings? Whenever she looked in the mirror, she wondered who was looking back at her.

Her hair had been the last vestige of the "old Rhea." Straight, longish, without particular style, she'd twisted it into the same old mousy brown knot until Ilona had decreed it must go. Surprisingly, Steve had disagreed, saying he thought Rhea's hair looked fine. Rhea was about to second this opinion when Ilona yawned widely.

"Oh, yes, darling, I quite agree," she said, stifling her yawn with scarlet-tipped fingers. "It's perfectly fine for an old-maid librarian."

Rhea's reluctance instantly gave way, and she'd found herself sitting in the plushly upholstered beautician's chair, fuzzily watching strand after strand fall to the floor. In a way, she was grateful she was too nearsighted to clearly see herself being shorn. Or to see the play of expressions being exchanged by Ilona and Steve as they hovered on the sidelines.

They tossed light jokes back and forth, the kind of inside jokes that kept others from sharing. An odd depression lowered itself on Rhea. She focused blankly on Terence as he cut, then dried and styled. She began to wonder what she looked like. Just when curiosity threatened to eat at her, Terence set aside his brush and put her glasses in her hand. She put them on her nose.

The cut was short and tapered, brushed back with a light sweep of hair across the brow and a lift at the crown. The hint of blond seemed brighter, the color overall less drab. And though the cut emphasized her cheeks, they seemed less round and more dramatic. She squinted narrowly, trying to assimilate the sexily chic style as hers.

Terence ran his fingers through her hair, drawing her attention to him. Though he didn't smile—he didn't seem to her to be the sort of man who possessed a smile—his eyes crinkled slightly, indicating he was pleased.

"Shake your head," he directed.

Rhea shook her head. Her hair instantly, obediently, fell back into place.

"Ah," said Terence, with what for him was rousing satisfaction and in anyone else was a quirk of the mouth.

"A good cut should always fall right into place. A good cut gives you all the volume and style you need."

"Thank you," she said, feeling it was inadequate, but not knowing what else to say. Her eyes sought Steve's. He rose nobly to the occasion.

"Outstanding, Terence. She looks fabulous. You're a master."

"Yes, of course," agreed Terence. He fluffed the top, then frowned into the mirror. "A pity about the glasses though. Ummm, yes, a real pity. You see the way I've cut, here and here, accents your cheeks, your eyes. You've lovely eyes, but the glasses spoil the effect."

"Terry, darling!" shrieked Ilona, widening her already-wide eyes in mock indignation. "What do you think I am? *Of course* she's getting contacts. The very instant we leave your salon, we're taking her to my optometrist."

"Contacts?" squeaked Rhea as Terence permitted himself to emit a sigh of pleasure. She ignored him to gape questioningly at Steve. He shrugged.

Ilona swept a hand over her own sleekly cut dusky hair and murmured, "I'll be needing a trim soon, Terry. Next week?" The hair stylist agreed, and as the two of them worked out the schedule, Rhea pounced out of the chair.

"What's going on?" she hissed at Steve. "What does she mean, contacts? I can't afford contacts. After this haircut I can't afford lunch!"

"Hey, hey, settle down," he calmed. "I don't know what she's talking about, but I wouldn't worry about it. My guess is she picked up on what Terence had to say and strove to outdo him. Ilona likes to be the originator of ideas. It's just talk."

She wasn't totally mollified. To be told her new, unbelievably expensive hairstyle was ruined by her glasses filled her with new doubts. Why had she let them cut her hair? She peered into the mirror. She flicked her fingers at the crown, the sides. She tipped her head to one side, then the other. It may not look like the Rhea she knew, but she had to admit it looked good.

"Maybe it's not such a bad idea. Maybe I should get contact lenses." She pushed her glasses up her nose and frowned. "What do you think?"

"I think you look terrific just as you are."

A slight intimation of warmth was revealed in his voice. Her gaze flew to meet the reflection of his. The lids drooped, screening his eyes from the probing of hers. She hesitated, then asked, "You think I look okay with the glasses?"

"You always look good to me, pal," he said softly, so softly she had to strain to hear it over the babble of voices, the drone of dryers.

Inch by inch her depression gave way to happiness. Held within the spell of his half-lidded gaze, she stood stock-still and let the joy fill her. She didn't question where it came from or why; she simply welcomed it, reveled in it.

"Well, troops," said Ilona, coming up to take each one by an arm, "let's push onward in our quest to produce the perfect Miss Nichols."

Rhea somehow managed to shake free of the spell immobilizing her. "Did you mean it about the optometrist?" she asked as she was led to Ilona's silver-gray Mercedes.

"Of course I meant it. I'd thought I'd told you. Didn't I tell you about the appointment?"

"I must have forgotten," she murmured. She got into the car without looking back at Steve. She didn't have to look at him to be aware of him. She could feel his presence behind her.

At the optometrist's Steve voiced his opinion that Rhea didn't need contacts. Ilona immediately contradicted him. "Of course she needs them. Her eyes are gorgeous, perfectly shaped, but who can tell? They're hidden behind those godawful owlish lenses. If she really means to have this mystery man, she's got to get rid of the glasses."

"She doesn't even want contacts," said Steve.

"Yes, I do," objected Rhea. The reference to Addison had decided her. If she had to scrimp for the next year, she was going to get the contacts. It would be perfectly stupid to have worked so hard to make herself into Addison's kind of woman and let it go to waste over a pair of contact lenses. "Ilona's right. I need the contacts to get Ad—to make this whole thing work."

Steve withdrew from the fray, agreeing to her decision with an indifferent shrug. For some reason a bit of Rhea's happiness dimmed beneath the cloud of his silent disapproval. In the process of the examination, however, she forgot everything but her anticipation of the day when Addison Chambers saw the new Rhea Nichols.

She responded to the soft buzz by pressing the blinking light on the console. "Chambers, Chambers," she said, then connected the call before greeting the client who'd approached the well-polished walnut desk. After directing the gentleman to one of the floral wing chairs, she notified Catherine Young that her client had arrived and resumed sorting the message slips she'd written out earlier.

A sense of satisfaction glowed within her. It had been a long while since Rhea had manned the front desk and at first she'd panicked at the thought of the switchboard. But she'd found it was rather like riding a bike; once you learned, you didn't forget how to operate a PBX. When she started working for the firm, she'd also acted as relief receptionist, but as her library chores increased, the relief duties had been given over to the firm's docket clerk. Today, though, both Pat and the clerk had succumbed to the spring flu making the rounds, and she'd been asked to take over as receptionist for the day.

She heard a rustling and glanced up to see the waiting

client eye her with blatant male appreciation. Being the recipient of such looks was still new enough to both thrill and amaze her. She smiled shyly at the man and sent a silent prayer of thanks to Ilona.

For the first time in her life Rhea felt pretty, feminine, and desirable. A year ago, three months ago, she wouldn't have dreamed of wearing a whispery lilac dress with a pleated bodice and fluttery sleeves to work. Three months ago such a dress would have clung to flabby lumps she hadn't wanted anyone to see. Today it clung to shapely curves. All the skipped desserts, all the endured exercises had been worth it.

But it was the new style, the fashionable clothes, and the short, sexy hairdo that made the difference. And, of course, the contacts. More men had seemed to notice her this past week than in all the years preceding it.

Catherine came out to get her client. She paused by the desk. "How do you do it?"

"Do what?" returned Rhea, puzzled by the query.

"Manage to look better and better every day. With eyes like yours, it's easy to see why the library's suddenly become so popular with the male attorneys of this firm. Clients, too, it seems," she added with a wink before sliding smoothly to her client's side.

The double doors swished open. Shining with pleasure from Catherine's compliment, Rhea looked up with a smile of welcome. Her smile melted. She quivered from head to toe. Addison ambled in. He nodded absently in her direction. She strove not to be disappointed. Two steps past the desk, he abruptly halted and did a double take. He pivoted and examined her intently. Rhea's heart pounded so loudly, she didn't hear the buzz of the console.

A slow, breathtaking smile played over his mouth. "Aren't you going to answer that?" he asked.

For a second she continued to stare at him, then snapped to herself at another summoning buzz from the console. She took the call with shaky fingers and a voice that barely refrained from trembling. Out of the corner of her eye she saw Addison stroll to the desk, lounge on the polished edge, and riffle through a stack of pink message slips. How she placed that call, she'd never know. In fact, she wasn't certain she had placed it. She simply pushed some buttons and disconnected herself before turning her gaze to Addison. She wondered how her heart could keep working under the bursting brilliance of his patent admiration.

"Did you enjoy your trip, sir?" she inquired. Her nervousness deepened her voice to a smoldering rasp. His thick lashes came down over his violet eyes, then slowly rose again.

"Not nearly as much as I enjoy being back. I had no idea my father intended to redecorate the office or I'd have come back even sooner."

"Redecorate?" she breathed.

"You are quite definitely the prettiest ornament to grace this desk in years," he murmured, and her heart gave up the attempt to keep working.

"Oh—I—thank you."

He smiled. It was the smile designed to make mush of a woman's innards. It accomplished its purpose in record time.

"Let me thank you," he said.

"F-for what?"

"For being here to brighten up my day."

Rhea had fantasized about this so often, she'd rather expected to be disillusioned. She wasn't. Fantasy, she decided, couldn't hold a candle to the reality of his smile, his charm.

He reached out and lightly set his fingertip beneath her chin. He tipped her head ever so slightly and studied her with those beautiful eyes of his. She wondered why she hadn't lost consciousness.

125

"In fact," he drawled, "I'm wondering how I've endured life this far without having met you."

A tiny splinter of hurt pricked her. "You have," she corrected him, and her voice held neither smoke nor breathless excitement.

His look of disbelief was almost instantly displaced by one of charming self-reproach. The light danced over his fair hair as he shook his head. "I've heard about it happening, of course, but I never believed it could happen to me. But no one does, do they? I mean, who could believe going senile at my age?"

"You're not—"

"I must be. What other explanation can there be for forgetting someone like you? Though I'm half inclined to think you're making it up."

Her hurt faded. "No, I'm not. I'm Rhea Nichols."

"Rhea Nichols?" he echoed blankly, and her hurt galloped back.

"The librarian. Pat's sick today, so I'm filling in."

This time his look of disbelief lingered. He eyed her up and down. Slowly, recognition came into his gaze. "I do believe you are. But I was only gone two weeks—"

A harsh buzz interrupted. Rhea, uncertain of the various feelings flowing through her, reached to answer. Addison's slim hand caught hers in midair. "Not yet," he said quickly. "Not before you agree to have supper with me."

Elation, regret, even fear added themselves to the excitement over his attention, diminishing the small letdown over his failure to remember her. The buzzer sounded a second time. The light flashed. "I'm sorry, I'd love to, but I can't. I've already got a date for tonight."

"So break it," he said.

The impulse to call Steve and do just that had already flown through her. It had crashed in midflight. She shook her head. "I can't, really."

The console demanded her attention. Two lights were blinking. "If it's Stockard," began Addison when she broke in hastily, "It's not anyone from the firm. It's a very good *friend* I can't let down."

He caught the emphasis and smiled confidently. "Lunch tomorrow then."

"Lunch tomorrow," she agreed.

He released her hand and gracefully unfolded himself from the desk even as she pressed the first button. "I'll be waiting," he said, and she scarcely managed to speak into the phone.

Later, when the console was darkly quiet, she replayed the scene over and over in her mind, imagining how she'd relate it to Steve. Her triumphant elation grew. Wouldn't Steve be proud of her? Wouldn't he be thrilled? That Addison hadn't remembered her didn't matter. He'd been so insistent, so anxious to be with her, that's all that mattered. She simply couldn't wait to share her victory with Steve.

She threw open the door before he'd finished his first rap. "Oh, Steve, I've been waiting for you!"

He lowered his hand and smiled down at her. "So I can see. Is that lovely flush for me? What did I do right?"

"I thought you'd never get here," she said, paying no attention to his teasing.

"You're that hungry, huh? Haven't you been eating? Has somebody been keeping you on a diet or something?"

"I'm just hungry to tell you my news!"

Stroking his moustache, he eyed her speculatively. "You've inherited a million from a long-lost uncle? No? Then a grand from a great-aunt?"

"No, don't be—"

"You got a promotion, a raise, and your own private jet?"

She shook a finger at him. "Will you be serious?"

"Sure," he said agreeably. "That dress is pretty and even prettier with you in it."

She gave up. He obviously wasn't going to be serious. She ran her eyes over him, liking the deep blue shirt with the gray cords, the woven blue belt, and the brushed suede jacket. He looked pretty good himself. "Thanks, you don't look so bad yourself," she said. "And now that we've passed out the compliments, can I get on with my news?"

He chuckled and stood aside from the door. "Grab a jacket and let's get going. I'm hungry, even if you're not. In fact, I'm starving. I was down in the Springs all day, working at the Gresham house, and I missed my lunch. You can tell me your big news on the way."

"I don't know if I should. You don't seem too interested," she teased with an exaggerated pout. She donned a lightweight tan jacket and looped the fabric belt as she spoke. He didn't say anything. Worried that he'd thought she meant it, she quickly looked up, intending to reassure him. Her unspoken words shriveled on her tongue.

It had been weeks, months, a different year, since she'd seen that expression on his face. That intense resolution of a man who sees a woman he wants, a woman he means to have. The Steve who was her buddy, her jogging partner, her confidant, had vanished. This was a stranger, a man who obviously desired her as a woman. But it was a stranger she'd met once before . . . on Christmas Day.

The belt crumpled within her palm. Her fingernails dug into her skin. She licked her lips and saw his eyes follow the motion. "Uh, maybe, maybe we'd better go."

"Maybe we'd better," he agreed, the short statement rippling with meaning.

She stepped around him, stunned and unsure. Why had he looked at her like that? Why was she feeling so quivery? Which Steve was he now?

They walked to the parking lot in silence. Rhea didn't dare to so much as glance at him. She wasn't certain which disturbed her the more, the way he'd looked at her or the way she'd reacted, but she didn't intend to put it to another test to find out. At the MG, though, Steve opened the door and she was unable to resist peeking at him.

He smiled his friendly smile, the one that tilted his moustache and brought radiant lines beside his blue eyes. Her relief was tinged with an unwarranted regret she decided to ignore. She was, she told herself, glad to be back on the old, safe, familiar footing. He walked to his side and got in.

"So what's this news you were bursting to tell me?" he asked as he backed the car out of the lot.

"Are you sure you're interested?" she returned, infusing her voice with a teasing lilt.

"I thought you knew by now that I'm interested in everything about you."

It was a matter-of-fact statement, totally devoid of the earlier intimations, yet it had an even stronger effect on her. She couldn't understand her sudden tension, her sudden awareness of everything around her. It was as if her senses had come alive. The nutlike scent of his tobacco mingled with the suede of his jacket. The rhythm of his breath synchronized with the whirr of the motor. A chain of headlights strung a flashing necklace along the freeway as they whizzed toward the heart of town. The chill of the night air on her face contrasted sharply with the warmth of the heater blowing on her legs.

Most of all, she was attuned to the invisible pull of the man beside her.

"Hey, what is this? Are you turning into a tease? You get me all roused—" he threw her a quirking grin. "My curiosity, that is, and then don't deliver. Come on, spill. What's your big story?"

129

For some unfathomable reason her ecstatic excitement over Addison's invitation wasn't as great as it had first been, but she laughed lightly and said without looking at Steve, "It's not big, it's the biggest. Guess who got back from New York today? And guess who was in the right place when he got back? And guess who's taking whom out to lunch tomorrow?"

After a palpable pause, Steve said, "So that's what put that blush of excitement on your cheeks. Congratulations."

Her own pause stretched scarcely more than two heartbeats, but it was long enough for disappointment to settle heavily within her. What had remained of her victorious jubilation was crushed beneath the weight. "Are you sure you can spare so much enthusiasm?" she asked on a tart bite.

"What did you expect? Blowing horns and confetti?"

"I thought you might share my feelings of excitement a little," she muttered. It was absurd, she knew, to feel so let down just because he didn't share her elation. It was absurd, but she felt it nonetheless. She'd waited all afternoon to tell him, impatient to bask in the warmth of his pride and approval. She almost laughed at herself. For the kind of warmth he was providing, she might as well be in Siberia. He'd spoiled her moment of triumph and she resented him for it. Staring fixedly at the dabs of light punctuating the night, she snipped, "You might at least show some appreciation. After all, I did achieve what we've been working for."

"I congratulated you."

"In a voice deader than a doornail."

"All right, okay, you want enthusiasm, you got it." He hit the horn, which barked like a weary seal. *Ah-ooo-gah, ah-ooo-gah.* The last *ooo-gah* faded and Steve cheered, "Whoopee."

As this was said through clenched teeth, the effect was somewhat less than joyous. Rhea hunched into her seat, crossed her arms over her chest, and determined to ignore him.

"In actual fact," he said a few minutes later, "I'm surprised that you're even going out for supper with me."

She frowned at him. He glanced at her, then away. "I'm surprised you're not at home getting ready for the big luncheon with Attwood."

"Addison," she bit out. "Addison. You *know* his name is Addison. And come to think of it, that's a damn good idea. Why don't you take me home and save us both a wasted evening?"

"Fine, I'll do that," he barked, sounding rather like his car horn.

"Good," she snapped, and fell silent.

A solid silence reigned, a thick block of ice frozen between them for the ride home. The staccato of their shoes rang on the pavement as he walked with her back to her apartment. The click of the key magnified in the lock. Rhea stepped through, intending to slam the door shut on his face. Steve slid in behind her.

"What are you doing?" she croaked.

"This is a damn stupid argument, and I want to apologize."

She gaped a moment, then dropped her gaze to the floor. "You're right and so do I. I'm sorry."

He set his palms against her cheeks and lifted her head. She stared into blue eyes darkened with concern. "I'm glad you've gotten what you wanted, Rhea. I hope your Addison proves to be everything you've wanted him to be."

Bending forward, he gently kissed the light brown fringe of hair dusting her brow. Then he released her and stepped back.

"I—would you like to stay and have a sandwich or something?" she said quickly. "I feel bad that you didn't eat."

"No. I think I should be going." He started out, then stopped and looked over his shoulder. "Good luck, pal."

The door shut with an empty echo. It sounded as hollow as Rhea's victory suddenly felt.

CHAPTER TEN

Rhea stood shaking with indecision. Before her, the closet door gaped open, hangers and tumbles of discarded clothes dotted the floor, reminiscent of Laurey's habitual clutter but actually jumbled evidence of Rhea's morning jitters.

The click of the digital numerals changing position on her bedroom clock spurred her into action. Grabbing a nearly transparent ruffled dress, she darted down the hall and burst into Laurey's darkened bedroom. The lump beneath the satin eiderdown didn't stir. Rhea hit the switch, splaying the room with a harsh overhead light. The lump still didn't stir. She marched over and shook the sleeping form's shoulder.

"Laurey, wake up. I need some advice. Wake up."

"Mmmph," said Laurey, and burrowed deeper into her pillow.

"Please, Laurey! I've got an important lunch and I can't figure out what to wear. Please look and tell me if I should wear this dress."

Laurey propped open an eye, focused blearily on Rhea, then closed it again. "Nope," she mumbled.

After staring dumbfounded at the gauzy green dress in her hand, Rhea dumped it in a fluffy heap and shook the inert shoulder with renewed vigor. "Wake up, Laurey! Please! I need you to tell me what I should wear."

"I won't be able to tell you anything if you don't quit rattling my teeth."

Rhea backed away. "I'm sorry, Laurey, but this lunch is so important. I've just got to look my best."

Honey-blond hair spilled over slim white shoulders as Laurey sat up. She stretched, yawned, stretched again, and eventually rose. "This lunch of yours had better be damned important. Do you know what time it is? I didn't get in until after four."

"I know. I heard you. Was it Vincent?"

"Who? Oh, him. No, it wasn't Vincent," replied Laurey with unusual reticence. "Sorry I woke you," she added.

Rhea was too wound up in her own concerns to notice Laurey's uncharacteristic lack of animation about her new man, whoever he might be. "Oh, you didn't wake me," she said. "I was awake."

"Hmmm, this must be some humdinger of a lunch," said Laurey as she shuffled into a coral robe and slippers.

Rhea didn't bother to explain that her night's sleeplessness had been due more to agitation than anticipation. It had not been thoughts of Addison that kept her tossing from one side of her bed to the other, but thoughts of Steve.

Somewhere in the restless shifting of the night she'd realized she'd behaved childishly. It wasn't Steve's fault he hadn't reacted as she'd expected him to. She'd never understood just why Steve had wanted to help her capture Addison's attention, but she'd supposed it had something to do with the thrill of the chase, a sort of war game in the battle of the sexes with Steve as commander-in-chief. But her original opinion that he wasn't the sort to play emotional games was now reinforced. He must have done it simply because he'd wanted to help her. That didn't mean he shared her feelings about it. She would, she affirmed for what must have been the thousandth time since he'd left her with that gentle kiss, apologize as soon

134

as possible. She pushed aside thoughts of the other Steve—the Steve of Christmas Day . . . and yesterday. That was too confusing for her tired brain to deal with.

For now, she had work to do. She scurried off in Laurey's wake. Laurey floated past the discards scattered in front of Rhea's closet to riffle through the contents still on hangers. She selected a dress and almost instantly tossed it to the floor. Finally she pulled out a thinly striped navy dress dotted with red. She held it up. "This one," she said with decision.

"But that's so simple," protested Rhea. "The green has a low V-neck, and besides, it matches my eyes. Don't you think the green would—"

"If you want to wear the green, wear it. But this is the one you should wear. The blue will contrast with your peaches-and-cream coloring and the simplicity will make your figure stand out. Now I'm going back to bed." She thrust the dress into Rhea's hand and left. She was half-way down the hall when her words drifted back. "Don't you dare wake me again."

The soft silk sash swished against her knee. Rhea held the dress in front of her and studied her reflection in the mirror. It was a pretty dress, but not the kill-'em-dead sort of thing she'd wanted to wear. Even though it was silk, the scalloped neckline, puffed sleeves, and sashed waist looked to Rhea like something she'd wear to work, not to knock the socks off Addison Chambers. Still, if there was one thing Laurey knew, it was what to wear for what occasion.

She slipped the dress over her head, knotted the sash, and inspected the results. In her mind's eye she saw herself standing before another mirror examining this dress. And she saw Steve smiling and saying decisively, "Buy it. It suits you, really suits you. Gives you a sort of . . . smoldering innocence."

"How can innocence smolder?" she'd asked on a laugh, and he'd said, "I don't know, but you make it happen."

One of those odd surges of warm happiness had pulsed through her and she'd bought the dress.

The emptiness of the night before threatened to sweep over her once again. Spinning away from the mirror, Rhea forcibly brushed it away. She'd worry about whatever bug had gotten under Steve's skin later. She fully intended to patch it up with him, but for now she had to put the matter out of her mind. She wasn't about to let last night's tiff spoil the thrill of her day.

This was her day of triumph. Never before had such an attractive man paid attention to her and she was determined to look worthy of Addison's attention. After a long, hot shower she'd shampooed and styled her hair just as Terence had shown her. She'd powdered and perfumed and prepared herself, then fallen apart while trying to decide what to wear. Now the memory of Steve's urging coupled with Laurey's choosing decided her on the dotted navy dress, simple as it was. She donned transparent white hose, which brought out the thin white stripes of the dress, and red pumps that made her feel like clicking her heels together, then hunted up a bright red bangle bracelet and round red earrings to match. While she fluffed her hair and applied her makeup her exhilaration mounted. So did her trepidation.

Dropping the lipstick, she intently examined her reflection. The woman staring back at her was a far cry from the Rhea Marie she'd grown up with. The rounded face held no hint of plumpness, the freckles were expertly covered by cream and powder which served to enhance the peachy tone of her skin. Feathers of soft caramel hair brushed back from her face, flattering her features. No eyeglasses sat on the uptilted nose to hide the bright shine of excitement in her eyes. She studied herself, and her glossed lips parted on a breathy sigh. She couldn't deny that she looked all right.

But would that be enough? Addison Chambers was accustomed to a great deal more than "all right."

She tried out a soft, husky laugh, the kind that came to Janice naturally. On her it sounded like an old woman's death rasp. She tried again, pushing her lips out like she remembered Marilyn Monroe doing in all those old movies. Visualizing Laurey's animated swirl, she swished around the room, stumbled over the thick carpet, and decided maybe she'd better rely on the laugh.

Throughout the morning, whenever she found herself alone in the library, she practiced the laugh as well as imitations of Ilona Drake's polished mannerisms. Even when she wasn't alone, she was utterly preoccupied with her upcoming lunch date. Several times secretaries and attorneys had to clap their hands to gain her attention. As the lunch hour approached, even that failed to work. Her abstraction was complete. Her heart beat furiously to the rhythmic tick of the bulbous wall clock. Her mood swung wildly from exultation to despair. This was her dream come true, but would it turn into a nightmare?

Spectres of doubt rose up to haunt her. What if she failed to interest him? What if she wasn't sparkling enough, sophisticated enough, sexy enough? Just before noon her fears overcame her. She decided she'd go home "sick." It really wasn't such a lie. She *was* sick, sick at heart. She started for the door.

It veered open just as she reached it. Addison filled the frame with his golden radiance. His beauty blinded her. She stood staring in open admiration, her pulse throbbing out of control and her breath caught in her throat.

"Well, I didn't think it could be," he said as he ran his eyes over her, "but it was definitely worth the wait to see you again."

She blushed with pleasure and forgot the cosmopolitan greeting she'd rehearsed. "It's always worth it to see you," she said, and instantly longed to remove her tongue. She was acting like a schoolgirl! Addison, however, seemed to enjoy her flagrant adoration. He smiled his gorgeous smile and stepped aside to usher her out. As they walked together through the corridor, he lightly grazed her back with his palm. They passed several people and Rhea nodded and smiled, but couldn't have said to whom. Her whole being was concentrated on the brush of that palm against the silk of her dress.

He paused at the reception desk. "I'm out for lunch. A long lunch," he added, and Rhea saw Pat's eyebrows skyrocket as he led her out of the office.

"I hope," he said, "the library can do without you. I intend to keep you to myself for a good long while."

She wondered how she managed to walk on legs as suddenly insubstantial as hers.

"Uh, what about my coat?" she murmured when they waited by the elevator doors.

"You won't need it. I'm taking you up to the Rooftop."

No doubt about it, fantasies do come true. For as long as she'd worked there, Rhea had wanted to eat at the restaurant that dominated the top of the office building, but it wasn't the sort of eatery to fit into a working girl's budget. She'd have had to sell her car to merely taste the appetizers there. Now she had the Rooftop and Addison too. She decided that she really wouldn't mind dying now, so long as it was *after* lunch.

The mirrored elevator doors shimmered open. Every woman who stepped out cast her a look of envy mingled with admiration. It was heady stuff for Rhea. A warm sense of pleasure welled up within her. To be with a man who garnered such attention, whose single smile was a conquest, to be the woman other women envied, well, it simply intoxicated her. She entered the elevator with a confident swish of her hips and wondered what Steve would say when she told him.

Some of the fizz went out of her. After the way he'd

acted last night, she rather doubted he'd be interested in how those women had looked at her. Not, of course, she hastily reassured herself, that it mattered whether he was interested or not. Addison was interested, and that's all that counted.

She turned her attention to the man who mattered and felt a slight surprise bolt through her. He lounged in the gleaming glass-and-chrome corner, watching the lights race through the numerals above the doors. Rhea blinked. They were alone in the silently gliding elevator. She momentarily wondered if she'd put her contact lenses in the wrong eyes. Her vision was definitely impaired. This Addison was good-looking, yes, but not the sort of shining god to turn women's heads.

She was about to inquire if he wasn't feeling well when they slid to a motionless stop, the doors yawned open, and three smartly dressed women entered. Addison straightened with a lazy smile. The three newcomers each passed their eyes over him, regarding him with blatant interest. Rhea watched in amazement as the radiance returned to Addison in full glowing force. It was like seeing a puppet come to life. She wondered who was pulling the strings.

He glanced down, saw her gaping at him, and caught hold of her hand. As the other women observed with envy, he pressed a kiss upon the back of it.

The touch of his lips was cool on her skin, so cool that she shivered with relief when the elevator again stopped and he released her hand to guide her into the Rooftop. She didn't understand her relief. And why hadn't she melted into a puddle of gratification over that chivalrous kiss?

Because, answered a voice in her mind that sounded suspiciously like Steve's, *that gallant demonstration was all for effect, an actor's grand gesture for his audience.*

Though a crowd of people hovered in the small lounge, waiting for a table, Addison was greeted immediately by the effusive hostess, who led them directly into a world of rainbows. Prismatic chandeliers captured the sunlight pouring in from the outer wall of windows and released it in an iridescent array. Like velvet candle flames, roses in crystal vases glimmered over sparkling glass tabletops. A muted hush, a swiveling of heads, followed their progress. On one level Rhea enjoyed the attention, enjoyed being the woman with Addison, but on another, deeper level, she knew an inexplicable dissatisfaction. She shrugged it away and concentrated on her enjoyment.

They sat at a table overlooking the skyline of Denver and she remarked how breathtaking the view was. In the distance, beyond the city buildings, the sun spun gold threads over the mountain rim between puffs of grayish clouds. Addison glanced at it once, then asked what she'd have to drink. She had the feeling he was too busy keeping a tally of just how many pairs of eyes were fixed on them to pay heed to the view. She shoved the nagging thought away and ordered a Kahlúa and cream.

The waiter departed. Clouds arrived in a gray clump to obscure the sunshine. The beauty of the room dimmed, the rainbows disappeared, and an awkward silence filled the void. Addison tapped a long finger against his water glass. Each crystalline ping pierced Rhea's confidence. She shifted in her seat and struggled to think of something witty to say.

"So tell me about your trip to New York," she finally produced. Not exactly witty, but it was better than nothing. "You were there on the Newton case, weren't you?"

He flashed his perfect teeth at her. "Now, how did you know that? The Newton case is supposed to be strictly hush-hush. But I guess I should have expected it. The office gossip mill does love to grind."

Again she had the fleeting notion he'd just stopped short of saying *especially about me*. She didn't understand what was wrong with her. She should be on top of the

140

world, not nit-picking his every statement! She set an encouraging smile on her lips. He responded to it immediately.

"Aside from the work, New York was the proverbial great place to visit. It's always like that for me. At first I thrive on the constant hustle, the fluctuation of the city on the move, the sheer energy of New York, but after a while it gets tiresome, almost as enervating as it was uplifting."

"I know what you mean. My parents took me there when I was thirteen and I adored it for about two days, but then—"

"The fact is," cut in Addison without seeming to notice that he was being rude, "I don't think I care for any other place as much as I do Denver. The mellow, relaxed atmosphere suits my temperament. Actually I've been told I'm a lot like the climate here—you know, mild and sunny."

"Especially sunny," she said, right on cue.

His melodic laugh caught the attention of several diners nearby. He seemed to thrive on it, his physical charm enhanced by the reflection of it in others' eyes. "I was glad to get back, particularly when I saw what I'd been missing."

"The thin air?"

"I meant *you*," he said in a whispery tone that shivered down her spine, instantly erasing the small frustration over his failure to understand her humor.

She could, she thought, quite easily describe heaven to anyone who cared to listen. It was being the recipient of that tone, that smile, that beautiful gaze. She sat enraptured within the charm of his consideration.

The spell was broken by the appearance of the waiter with their drinks. "Now for lunch," said Addison, and Rhea cast him a questioning look. She was about to ask for a menu when the young waiter said, "Yes, sir, today's specialties include roast rack of lamb . . ."

At the end of his recital they chose their meals, Rhea

opting for Addison's recommendation and being reward-
ed with another of his special smiles. She leaned forward,
saying eagerly, "I can't thank you enough. I'm so thrilled
to be eating here. I've always wanted to, but it doesn't
exactly fit into my budget. I'd probably have to take out
a loan to pay for the drink!"

"I rather doubt that," he said with an unmistakable
patronizing note that effectively damped her pleasure. He
began talking about a recent palimony suit he'd success-
fully sued for, the details of which Rhea already knew
quite well. But she listened quietly, still feeling a tiny sting
of resentment toward him. As his resonant voice flowed,
she heard Steve's at the back of her mind saying with a
hint of contempt, *He's about as deep as his three-piece suit.*

Leaning an elbow on the table, Addison pushed his
jacket back and set his right hand on his hip. The stance
emphasized the tight hug of his dark blue vest on his trim
waist. The initialed gold link shone against his white-on-
white cuff. She watched the sunlight wink over it, sipped
her Kahlúa, and wondered what Steve was having for
lunch. Had he ever eaten at the Rooftop? She glanced
around, trying to select the words she'd use to describe it
to him if he hadn't.

A hand curled over hers and she jerked slightly. She
riveted her eyes on Addison, guiltily recognizing that
she'd been ignoring him. There was the faintest line of
irritation beside his mouth. A tiny jolt shook her as she
noticed how wide that mouth was. And really, now that
she looked, his nose was long and, well, too large for his
narrow face. The line deepened and the hand over hers
tightened. She realized he'd stopped speaking and was
expecting a response.

"Well, you, uh, you certainly handled that case magnificently," she said, and the line faded, the hand loosened its
grip.

142

"Not my best work this year, though, certainly not my best. I believe settling the Henderson affair—"

"Addison! Addison, you mean thing. How could you return and not let us know you were back?" A slim, striking brunette skimmed up to their table. She cast a single, dismissive glance toward Rhea before purring, "Why, you didn't even come to the Millers Saturday night."

All the luminescent glass in the restaurant paled beside Addison's sudden dazzling smile. "That's because I wasn't here on Saturday. I just got back."

"Only just?"

"Only just," he replied. He sketched a hand toward Rhea. "May I introduce Rhea Nichols? Rhea, Connie Feldman."

With a bare nod in her direction, Connie launched into a description of what Addison had missed at the Millers. They spoke of people Rhea didn't know, leaving her to silently observe. If anything, Addison shone more brightly than ever. It occurred to her that he was like a light bulb, switched on by anyone's attention, dimmed without it. She heard him repeat to Connie that he was like the Denver climate, mild and sunny, and knew it was one of his standard lines, and a pretty corny line at that. She imagined Steve's reaction to it and almost heard his warm laughter. How he'd laugh, too, when she told him that Connie'd responded precisely as she had by stressing the sunny. She couldn't wait to see the expression on his face.

She visualized Steve sitting across from her. He'd undoubtedly have shared the glories of the view with her and just as undoubtedly he'd have quirked his moustache at her over the rosebud and winked behind the ramrod stiff back of the young waiter. If Steve were with her, she'd be having a great deal more fun. She managed to stifle a sigh of regret that she wasn't, but before she could explore the source of this regret, their lunch arrived.

143

With a flick of her abundant black hair, Connie swept away as the waiter began serving. Rhea, at least, didn't miss her. She devoted her attention to her meal. The filet was unbelievably tender and she enjoyed it thoroughly. It was even, she thought dryly, almost worth listening to Addison's account of the Henderson affair. As she ate, something akin to boredom settled over her. It wasn't that Addison wasn't interesting. She knew he was a very sharp attorney, one of the best in the firm, and his cases were actually stimulating subjects. But Addison had only two topics of discussion, himself and his work. His interest in her didn't extend to Rhea, the person, but only to Rhea, the woman who was there to react to him. Her responses only mattered inasmuch as they reflected on him.

Long before the waiter rolled by with the dessert cart, from which she dug into a rich Black Forest chocolate cake, with mental excuses to Steve, she had understood why Addison was always with somebody new. For years she'd thought it was because he was so popular, such a sought-after bachelor, because so many women were dying to be with him. But she knew now it wasn't evidence of his charm, but of his ego. Even his seemingly admiring compliments were calculated to magnify her admiration of him. The only mystery left to Addison Chambers was how she'd remained so stupidly infatuated for so long.

She set down her fork with a foolish grin of gratification. The cake had been luxuriously rich, every bite absolutely wonderful. She thought it a good thing that Steve hadn't been there to see her eat it. What Steve didn't know wouldn't hurt him. Besides, she'd run it off. She giggled inwardly. Who was she kidding? She'd have to run all night to work that off.

Instantly she wondered if Steve would run with her. After last night he might not want to run with her anymore. The thought depressed her. The argument of the night before—and the apology—replayed slowly in her mind. She clearly saw Steve's somber face, clearly heard his parting, "Good luck, pal," and a new worry assailed her. There'd been a definite ring of finality in that farewell.

Addison spoke and she offered appropriate murmurings, but she didn't hear anything beyond those words of Steve's. Like a stuck record they repeated again and again in her mind. And as they did, worry turned to terror, to gut-gripping fear. What if he—? But he couldn't, he just couldn't! He couldn't mean to stop seeing her! She'd be lost without him. Her world would be so dull, so empty.

She stiffened in her chair. Comprehension flooded her, drowning her in the discovery. She should have seen it long ago. She should have known how much Steve meant to her. How could she have been so stupid, so blind? He was far more than a friend. He was the man she wanted to be with. He was the man she wanted.

She let that roll around her head, listening to it. It rang clear and true. She did want him. She wanted him as a friend and a companion and most of all, as a lover. She had wanted him for weeks, but she'd been too damn dumb to see it. She'd been blinded by her infatuation for Addison. The thought made her feel sick. Addison Chambers wasn't worth so much as a single hair on Steve Bradley's head.

She had to forcibly tamp down the urge to dash out of the restaurant, to run to him and fling herself bodily at him. Instead, she made herself calmly finish her coffee, nodding agreement with whatever Addison said, while telling herself over and over it wasn't too late, it wasn't too late. She'd make Steve see it wasn't.

CHAPTER ELEVEN

The thwack of the knocker faded into nothingness. Her racing heartbeat slowly did the same. After seconds that seemed like light-years, she curled her fingers around the cool brass and lifted it again. The door wrenched open. She flew forward, crashing into a very solid—and very bare—male chest.

"Collisions must be your specialty," said Steve with laughter in his voice as he steadied them both.

The soft tangle of hair on his chest tickled her cheek. She could have rested against the warmth of him forever, but he was already righting her on her feet. She reluctantly straightened. She looked him up and down and nearly collapsed again.

A black towel clung tenaciously to his hips. Nothing clung to the rest of his tapered, muscled body. She longed to press into the breadth of his shoulders, to run her hands down the flat plane of his stomach and over his slim hips, to twine her legs with the shapely length of his. The images that crowded into her mind dizzied her.

"But it appears you're more resilient than the MG," she joked, and wondered how she'd found enough breath to produce the words.

"Fortunately," he agreed.

A slight reserve had replaced the laughter in his voice. Behind her the open door gaped meaningfully. Fear closed in on her. She licked her lips. "You, um, you busy?"

"Well, I was about to take a shower. You need something?"

Her mouth went dry. He gave the impression he'd sooner welcome an invasion of cockroaches. She'd rehearsed what to say all afternoon, but couldn't remember a single word. "I, uh, just wanted to, er, talk."

"Maybe some other—"

"You go ahead and take your shower," she rushed in. "I'll wait. I don't mind waiting, honestly."

Steve leaned his weight on his right foot. The edge of the towel swayed gently. Rhea gawked at it and felt desire radiate from the center of her being.

"That what you wore today?" he asked.

She pulled her eyes away from the tantalizing towel. His face was set, not in an unfriendly manner, but certainly not friendly either. "Yes. Yes, it is."

"Nice dress. Did he like it?"

"Yes, I think he—"

"Is that what you want to talk about?"

"Yes, it is. You see—"

"I don't have a lot of time, I've got to be ready to leave at seven, but go ahead and wait." He reached over her head to shove the door shut, then turned on his heel. "I'll try not to keep you waiting too long."

"Leave?" she echoed.

"I'm going out for dinner."

"Dinner?"

"To the Normandy with Ilona," he said as he left the room.

Rhea could feel the blood draining from her face. Her fragile conviction that it wasn't too late crumbled to dust. She stumbled into the living room and sank into the umber depths of the Venus's-flytrap. She sat in a stupor. Steve and Ilona! She'd known it, deep down. She'd known it and that's why she hadn't been able to like Ilona.

She shouldn't have come. She'd let her opportunity to

deepen their relationship slip through her fingers. She felt like a fool, aching to throw herself at a man who wasn't interested. She couldn't bear to let him see just what a fool she was. She would leave, leave now.

Something brushed against her leg, startling her out of her depressed reverie. She looked down. Socrates fixed his wide yellow gaze on her. She blinked back her tears and shifted, intending to unfold herself from the couch. The cat grazed her legs once more, then leaped nimbly onto her lap. Her surprise kept her from getting up. Up to now Socrates had done his best to ignore her existence completely. He settled into the blue silk of her skirt as if prepared to stay a lifetime. He felt soft, warm, comforting. She relaxed into the cushions.

"Oh, Cat," she said sadly, lightly stroking the fluffy gray fur, "why do you want to be my friend now, when it's too late?"

A rumbling purr that vibrated up her fingertips was the cat's only reply. Rhea let her head droop back while her gaze roamed the room. It was so much like the man himself, vibrant yet cozy, stamped with his distinctive individuality. Carpet samples spattered a colorful patchwork over a stack of wallpaper books propped upright by the wallshelf. She focused on a diminutive wooden tribesman who'd fallen on his side, his long-handled spear piercing the cold cinders in a blue marble ashtray. It hurt to look at the outward symbols of Steve's personality. She closed her eyes against the ache.

"It seems to be your day for making conquests."

She jerked her eyes open and sucked in her breath. Steve strolled forward. The muted lamplight glistened darkly over his still-damp hair and glowed faintly over his strongly sculpted nose and jaw. It chased shadows within the folds of his mocha brown shirt and blackened the nut brown of his slacks. She knew an urge to trace the path of light with her fingertips.

Firmly suppressing her urgings, she manufactured a light laugh and said, "I'm not letting it go to my head. I'm assuming Socrates must be pretty hard up for attention. I know he'd never deign to notice me otherwise."

"Oh, I don't know. I think any male of any species would notice you in that dress. You look good, pal."

Elation over the off-handed compliment was overshadowed by the sinking of her spirits over that single, short "pal." That's all she was to him, a pal, a buddy, a friend. No way could she let him know of her desires. It would embarrass them both and probably ruin the friendship. It wasn't the relationship she wanted, but if it was all she could have, she'd take it.

"Thank you," she said somewhat lifelessly.

He sat beside her, though not closely, and leisurely stroked Socrates. The cat's purring hummed through the fabric of her dress. She was surprised his fur didn't crackle with electricity; her pulse certainly did.

"So you wanted to talk about your lunch? I take it it was a big success."

"Oh, yes," she bubbled with false froth, "it was the ultimate fantasy come true. Addison took me to the Rooftop, which is gorgeous—all crystal and roses and rainbows of light, and we had the most delicious meal, fabulous service, and all the while he dropped flattering compliments. It was wonderful, unbelieveable."

"So Addison lived up to your expectations?"

"Surpassed them. He was utterly—"

Steve's hand jerked. Socrates hissed in protest and dug his claws in her lap. With a sharp gasp, she broke off, but didn't really notice the pain. She was relieved. She felt as if she'd have choked on that lie. Steve reached over, lifted the cat from her lap, and dumped him unceremoniously on the rug. With a disgusted whisk of his tail, Socrates swaggered away.

"I'm sorry. Did he hurt you?"

"No, not really. I was more surprised than hurt."

"I hope he didn't snag your dress. You're sure you're okay?"

He rubbed his hand over her thigh. Rhea followed the motion with her eyes, unable to concentrate on anything but the silken rhythm of his touch. When he repeated the question, she shook herself into breathing, "Yes."

She instantly wished she'd replied in the negative, for he pulled his hand away, shifted on the couch, and said, "I've got to be getting ready to go. I'm glad for you, Rhea, really glad that Addison turned out to be everything you'd dreamed of."

"Only in my nightmares," she muttered before she could stop herself.

He glanced at her. His blue eyes reflected pinpoints of lamplight. "What?"

"Oh, Steve, Addison was utterly boring! You overrated him when you said he was as shallow as his suit. He doesn't go as deep as his vest. He's one gigantic walking ego. I couldn't wait for the lunch to end."

"You aren't in love with him?"

"He's so stuck on himself, he doesn't need my adulation."

"But you've wanted him for years."

"All that was an illusion. It wasn't Addison I wanted—" She stopped short from saying, *It was you.* She fiddled with the sash on her dress, unable to look his way, afraid he'd see the truth in her eyes. After a moment she went on. "Don't you see? He's so popular. I was infatuated with the idea of being the woman with Addison, not with Addison himself. And I've got to admit, it was thrilling to have all those women looking at me today with envy in their eyes. Me, Rhea Nichols, being the envy of other women! It was heady stuff, let me tell you. But it was a hollow thrill, a momentary boost to my ego, that's all."

A silence ticked away. Rhea felt empty, drained. She

imagined Steve laughing about this with Ilona and knew she had to leave before she burst into tears. She struggled to push herself up out of the spongy recesses of the couch. Steve's hand circled her wrist, tugging her back into place.

"Well, it certainly took you long enough," he said.

The tenderness of the smile playing beneath his moustache took her breath away. She didn't understand the keen look he was focusing on her, nor what he'd said. "Huh?" was all she managed to utter.

"I was about to run out of patience." The low huskiness of his words whispered along her neck as he bent toward her. He nibbled gently on her ear. "I've been waiting for you to wake up, but I never dared hope . . ."

"H-hope what?" She shivered to the deft flick of his tongue.

"That it'd take just one date. I thought I'd have to let you go out with Addlehead a couple of times. I'm glad I underestimated you, pal. The thought of you with him has been driving me crazy."

She turned to gape at him in amazement. "Crazy? What do you—mmmpht."

He muffled her exclamation with a hungry kiss, a kiss to devour her resistance. His lips probed hers and his tongue plumbed the depths of her mouth. He nibbled and tasted and tempted Rhea into responding without restraint.

She wrapped her hands around the column of his neck. His pulse beat against her palm, delighting her with its rapid drumming. She feverishly kissed his chin, jaw, mouth. A shudder of desire rippled through him, thrilling her. His desire for her was intoxicating, as stimulating as her own eager emotions.

A thousand questions hurdled somewhere at the back of her mind. She wondered why he was kissing her, why he'd said he'd been driven crazy, what exactly he'd been waiting for. But those questions were buried beneath the avalanche of sensations cascading through her.

The wiry wisp of his moustache tickled her lips. The curling ends of his hair feathered her fingertips. The fresh scent of soap and talc tingled her nostrils. The pounding of her heart roared in her ears, the pounding of his hammered against her breast. Her body thrummed to the rhythm of it all.

At some point she kicked off her shoes and slid under his hard frame. Swept away by a current of pleasure, she arched toward him, wanting him, needing him.

He skimmed kisses of exquisite brevity from her mouth to her ear, down her jawline to the hollow of her throat. His lips blazed a trail of need to the pit of her being and she burned to have him extinguish the flames.

He swirled his hands over her in a silken cadence, teasing from her shoulder to her breast to her hip. Her dress crinkled beneath his touch and she trembled to know the feel of his hands on her bare skin.

He stretched his shapely body over hers and gently pressed her deeper, deeper into the cushions. His need for her was obvious and she yearned to ease that need, to be his completely.

Each kiss, each caress, each sensuous movement, raised in Rhea a yearning so overpowering she thought she'd explode with the force of it. She hungered to be part of him, to have him within her. More, she needed to make him hers, hers in a way that transcended the physical bond. She pulsed with the potency of her need.

He slipped his hands beneath the hem of her dress. She raised her hips to help him. His fingers skated lightly over her thighs, exploring higher and higher. Every inch dizzied her. Perhaps, she thought, perhaps she'd already passed out and this was all a fantasy. Perhaps she'd better check it out. Her lids fluttered slowly open.

But it was not a fantasy. No fantasy could approach the

reality of the passion glazing his eyes, tightening his features. The stark intensity of his need almost frightened her, it was so savage, so fierce. Desire covered his face like one of the tribal masks decorating the wall. She glanced over his shoulder. The ferocious masks seemed to be eyeing her with hostility. She shivered a little and he tightened his hold, squeezing the breath from her.

"Chilly?" he asked on a rasp.

She buried her face in his shoulder, feeling more than a little foolish. She couldn't say, *Seeing how much you want me scares me.* She couldn't say, *My longing pales beside your intensity and it panics me.* Instead, she whispered, "It's *them.* The masks. They're watching us."

The warmth of his chuckle caressed her cheek. "If that's all, my sweet, it's easily taken care of."

Before she understood his intent, he'd lifted himself off her, then reached down to scoop her into his arms. He started down the hall.

"I—you—don't you have to be going?" she asked, not daring to hope he was heading where she thought he was heading.

He was.

He pushed open the door of his bedroom with his foot and carried her into the shadowed interior. "Nope."

"But your date with Ilona," she pointed out on a bare thread of sound.

"Haven't got one. I lied about that."

"Lied about it? But why?"

He dropped her onto the soft mound of blankets rumpling his bed. "Because I was too proud to let you know I'd been sitting around here moping about you. And I didn't want to stick around to listen to you rave about Attaboy. How was I to know you didn't intend to bore me with a recital of his sterling qualities? I had to say something, so I made up the dinner date with Ilona."

Whispery soft blankets enfolded her. Slivers of light

153

crept through the partially open door to cast his silhouette on the opposite wall. She watched the shadow flicker as he slowly removed his shirt. She heard the quiet rustling as it fell to the floor. The shadow bent, discarding the slacks, and Rhea closed her eyes.

She felt moist and quivery and wasn't sure whether it was from anticipation or fear. Her mouth was dry. Her throat constricted. Yet her nerves were very much alive, tingling from head to toe, and her heart thumped so wildly, it was a wonder it didn't thump right out of her chest. When had she ever wanted a man this way? When had she ever known such trembling excitement, such shivering doubt? The answer was simple. Never.

It was because she'd never felt this way that Rhea's fears began to outpace her desires. The bed sagged and she jerked upright. Peering at Steve's shaded features, she squeaked, "What did you mean, you've been waiting for me?"

The heat of his bare body sizzled over the silk of her dress. His hands sought the curve of her hips, the indentation of her waist. He removed her half-slip and hose. His legs felt both downy and rough against the smoothness of hers as he glided forward to unknot her sash. He tugged the hem upward. "Sweetheart, we've got more important things to do than talk."

"B-but we need to—to discuss this," she protested weakly, raising her arms as he lifted her dress over her head.

"Ummm, later," he hummed against the heated rise of her breasts. He unhooked and discarded her bra with ease, then seductively kissed his way down the smooth skin of her stomach to her lace panties. The lower his kisses tracked, the higher her temperature zoomed. She was so hot, she was certain she'd sear the sheets. The scrap of cream lace went the way of the bra.

And then he lay beside her.

The feel of his nakedness next to hers prompted one final attempt to reason. "I—" she said hoarsely. "I don't understand."

"Shut up and kiss me," he said. He pushed her into the pillows and she shut up and kissed him.

His lips were sweetly coaxing. His tongue was warmly insistent. His hands were deftly everywhere.

Doubt and fear disappeared, erased by his practiced assault on her senses. He explored her slowly, nuzzling from her mouth to her chin, down her throat, to the rapidly heaving swell of her breasts. His breath traced over the hardened buds, then the tip of his tongue, and finally, his mouth nurtured each in turn. He stroked downward, from the soft undersides to her belly, hips, buttocks. Leisurely, with great deliberation, he massaged the curves of each. He fondled and caressed her to a state of arousal unlike any Rhea had ever known.

She was stunned by the compelling excitement from his merest breath, his lightest touch, his briefest kiss. When he lingered over her, she thought she'd burst from the pleasure consuming her. What makes this difference? she wondered. What creates this joyous explosion within every cell?

He poised tautly above her and her questionings were forgotten in her shaking expectation. Gently he joined her, filling her soul with warm delight. He shifted with unhurried thrusts, a measured cadence that heightened her desire to give unreservedly of herself.

Sweat slicked their bodies. Heavy breaths merged raggedly. Straining muscles flexed to the same tempo. He moved faster and faster. She moved with him, rising up to take him farther within her. All of him, she wanted all of him. Just when she thought she'd shatter into splinters of satisfaction, he slowed, then stilled until he lay quietly within her, filling her, completing her.

He pressed a tender kiss into her neck. "Oh, Rhea," he

155

whispered, "I want to go on being part of you. I'd like to make this last. I'd like it to last forever."

The heat of his breath melted over her, scorching right down to her soul. And in that instant she became his. She didn't understand what was happening to her. She knew only that this moment of being his, this sharing of heartbeats and breaths and bodies, this was all she wanted. Now and forever.

"Forever," she agreed on a murmur, and he brought his mouth to hers on a low groan.

They kissed and touched and came to know each other all over again. Gradually the mattress swayed as they soared higher and higher. Passion mounted with the renewed fervor, surpassing all that had gone before.

"You feel . . . so good," he rasped. "No . . . better than good. Perfect. You . . . feel . . . perfect."

Then he was beyond words. She was beyond hearing them. They clenched tightly, carrying each other to release. When at last their interlocked bodies relaxed, they drifted together in a drowsy state of repletion. Time wafted by. Shadows shifted in the darkened room. With silent determination Socrates leaped amid the tangle of blankets, sheets, and bodies and curled into the curve of their bent knees.

"We've got company," observed Rhea sleepily.

"He knows," Steve said between nibbles on her lobe, "a good thing when he sees it."

"Did you mean it?" she asked.

"Mean what?"

"What you said about me. You know."

He chuckled at her embarrassment, then leaned over to gaze at her shadowed face. "Fishing for compliments, m'dear? Okay, I'm hooked. Yes, I meant it. You felt absolutely, utterly perfect."

"You did too," she said shyly.

"Thank you, sweetheart."

Happiness filled her. He rubbed his palm over her hip and she almost purred as loudly as the cat. She enjoyed the feel of his palm. In fact, she enjoyed everything about him. She always had, but she'd been too stubborn to acknowledge it.

"You know something?" she said.

"What?"

"It was you all along. I've been wanting you and wanting you. For weeks, ages."

His hand ceased to move over her hip. She could feel the surprise ripple through him. She looked worriedly over her shoulder and saw his teeth gleam in a smile.

"Well, you could've let me know," he said in mock disgust. "I wouldn't have wasted all that time *running*."

They laughed together and he pulled her closer against his warmth. "Stay the night, darling?"

The husky request took her by surprise. A slight indefinable panic rose within her. "Oh, I don't know—"

"Stay with me, Rhea," he interrupted, and this time it sounded more like a command.

Her panic increased. Part of her wanted to stay, wanted to stay a thousand nights. But part of her resisted with unnamed fear. "I don't think I should," she said weakly.

"Why not?"

She flinched from the harshness of his tone. "I—my contacts," she stumbled. "I don't have my case and—"

"Is that all?" he broke in with evident relief. He dropped a light kiss on her tumbled hair and rose. "Wait just a minute. I'll take care of it."

He left the room before she could add any further objections. She lay arguing with herself. What on earth was the matter with her? What difference would it make if she stayed or didn't stay? She'd already committed herself to him in the most elemental of ways.

And yet she knew she'd withheld a tiny, fiercely independent portion of herself. She heard the faint slam of

157

cupboards, the muted running of water, and wondered why she was reluctant to stay, reluctant to give up that tiny independence. Her mind and body were too sated to unravel the mystery. He returned before she could puzzle it out.

Setting something on the nightstand, he reached out and turned on the lamp. "Here you are," he said with all the flourish of a magician pulling the rabbit out of the hat.

Rhea blinked against the sudden glow of light. She focused blearily on two plastic tumblers, one cherry red, the other a dull green, half-filled with water. She turned her uncomprehending gaze to Steve's triumphant grin.

"Red for right and lime for left," he explained. "For your contacts. Put the right one in the red glass and the left in the green and they'll be safe and moist till morning."

After a moment's hesitation she gave in. She'd let her independence take care of itself. Right now she wanted only to lie again in his arms. She removed her contact lenses, saying, "Very clever of you."

"I'm inventive. Always said so on my school reports," he said smugly. He turned off the light and climbed back into bed. Objecting to the disturbance, Socrates jumped down and disappeared into the night. Rhea didn't miss him. She was cradled within Steve's arms, listening to him murmur, "Next time we'll prepare ahead and have your case and solutions ready."

Next time . . .

Rhea fell asleep wrapped within his warmth and his loving words.

Next time . . .

CHAPTER TWELVE

"Next time," Steve was saying, "you'll have to do the honors. This time, enjoy it."

Rhea pulled her surprised eyes from the white wicker tray he'd positioned over her lap. Engulfed in his sapphire velour robe, she felt unaccustomedly small and vulnerable. The whole morning seemed like some sort of fantastic dream, and she half wondered if she weren't actually still asleep.

"Next time?" she repeated, eyeing him a bit warily.

"I'm partial to pancakes swimming in syrup, but eggs will do. You can fry eggs, can't you?"

"What are you talking about?"

"Tomorrow morning," he replied, leering at her hopefully.

A wave of enigmatic panic crested through her. "Steve, I—"

He cut in with the calm authority that exemplified him in her mind. "If we talk all morning, your breakfast will get cold. Unappetizing things, cold eggs."

She didn't argue. She was too bemused to argue. Besides, she was hungry. The aroma of bacon wafted from the plate to stir her appetite. An egg and lightly buttered toast completed the plate. A cup of steaming coffee was on one side of the tray. A sprig of fern dangled from a vase on the other.

"God, this is great," she mumbled around a mouthful. "Waking up to this could easily become a habit."

The bed shook as he sat on the edge. He picked up a piece of toast and bit into it while grinning slyly at her. "It could be arranged—for the right price."

"Humph!" she said, and turned her attention back to her meal.

She ate in silence, trying not to let him see her hands shake as she did so. From her first instant of awareness when she'd gradually recognized that warm buzzing as Steve's lips nuzzling her ear, Rhea had been fighting the excitement he roused in her. It disturbed her. She wasn't altogether certain she wanted to be so excited by him. It was all so new, had happened so unexpectedly. She hadn't had time to think it through, to analyze what exactly had happened between them, to understand what she was feeling. So she resisted feeling anything at all.

Even as she strove not to be affected by him, heat licked through her veins. Without looking at him, she was vividly aware of just how broad his shoulders were in the tan-and-blue plaid shirt, just how slim his hips were in the khaki slacks. She couldn't resist stealing a glance at him over a sip of coffee. Bronze streaks glinted in his hair and his teeth gleamed in a friendly smile. How, she wondered in breathless agitation, had she ever thought of him as comfortable-looking? He was handsome, heart-stoppingly handsome. She forced her gaze back to the tray.

She pointed to the fern. "What's this?"

"Isn't a rosebud considered mandatory for breakfast in bed?"

"That's not a rosebud."

"Well, no, it's not, but I didn't have a rosebud. Where was I going to find a rosebud at this time of the morning?"

She laughed. The last shadow of her unknown anxiety faded in the glow of her pleasure. When he smiled at her like that, she couldn't feel anything but sheer joy. She resumed eating with relish. "This is delicious," she said at length. "I think maybe I'll hire you after all. What's the right price?"

"Well, pal, my services are available only on a full-time basis." He slid an inquisitive glance at her. "You interested in having me around full-time?"

Coffee sloshed over the rim of the cup. She managed to still her shaking hand enough to return it to the tray. "What did you say?"

"I just wondered if you wanted my services full-time," he answered lightly. He tapped a finger on the tip of her nose. "But from the look of horror on your face, I don't think I need to hear your reply."

"I'm not horrified," she protested, sounding horrified to her back teeth. "I'm just stunned. Steve, a night together is one thing, but—"

"But commitment's another," he supplied, smiling wryly.

"Don't you think that you're rushing things a little?"

"No, but then, it doesn't seem like a rush to me. I've already waited several months for you."

"You mean you meant all that stuff?" Her voice rose an octave and exasperation tugged his smile into a frown.

"Of course I meant it. Now, you'd better eat up and get your fanny off to your apartment or you'll never make it to work on time."

He stood up and strode out of the room. She watched him go with mixed emotions. Excitement battled with doubt over his insistence that he'd wanted her all these months. If he had wanted her before, why hadn't he ever said so? He'd waited until now, when she was several pounds lighter and a great deal more stylish, to say anything. As thrilled as she was to have his attention, she couldn't help believing that he was taken only with the new Rhea, not the Rhea she really was.

Furthermore, she couldn't help being panicked by the

way he was rushing things. Suggesting any sort of full-time arrangement after just one night seemed to her to be the height of folly. And at the same time, his desire for a commitment, his desire for her, made her tummy tingle more warmly than ten gallons of hot coffee ever could.

She finished eating, shed his bathrobe, and threw on her rumpled dress. She took the tray into the kitchen, where she rinsed her plate while trying vainly not to glance continually toward Steve. He sat at the dining table, his sleeves rolled up to his elbows as he sorted through a mound of wallpaper samples. He looked up, caught her eye, and motioned. "Come give me an opinion."

She came forward and he waved a hand over the array of selections. Wrinkling her nose, she shook her head. "You won't want my opinion. I'm not any good at this sort of thing. I've no flair for decorating."

"That's okay, I just want some input from someone other than myself. These are for the house we're redoing down in Colorado Springs. It's an authentic Victorian monstrosity, built in 1879, and what we're aiming for is to retain the flavor of the period while adding all today's conveniences. I'm trying to select the paper for the master bedroom. What do you think of these? Anything catch your eye?"

She studied the samples. One, a shell pink so pale as to be almost white, with tiny twigs of baby's breath patterned over it, really appealed to her. She pointed at it hesitantly. "I like this," she said doubtfully. "But it's not very masculine, is it? I mean, maybe it wouldn't work for the master bedroom. Maybe something like this would be better." She indicated a patch of russet with cream dots.

"Both of those caught my eye too," he said, and lifted the two from among those on the table. The gold glimmer of his watch struck Rhea's eye as he did so. She saw the time and yelped.

"I've got to dash or I won't have a job to be late for!"

162

"See you at the regular time tonight?"

"Sure," she agreed and ran for the door.

"Rhea?" he called, and she paused to look back at him.

"Yes?" she said impatiently. She really would lose her job at this rate. How could she explain her tardiness? *Sorry, Mr. Chambers, but I was eating breakfast in bed at a man's apartment and simply forgot the time?*

"You were worth waiting for."

She floated out on a cloud of happiness. It was without doubt the most wonderful compliment she'd ever received. The thrill of it carried her all the way to her own apartment. Her vague doubts about his motives and her feelings were as elusive as the wispy clouds that gave promise of a beautiful day. She couldn't chase them down and, to be honest, she didn't even try. The morning was far too fair to be plagued with insubstantial worries.

Throughout the morning she had a glow that radiated outwardly. More than one person wandering into the library remarked on how good she was looking; most attributed it to the summery lilac and violet dress that swirled over her. Rhea knew the dress had nothing to do with her sudden brilliance, but she made no attempt to correct the mistaken impression. Instead, her glow got brighter, and she hummed beneath her breath as she worked. She couldn't remember the last time she'd been this happy.

At noon Janice stuck her head into the library. "Want to take that sack lunch you brought and picnic outside? The sun's so gorgeous, I thought we'd get out and bask in it. But looking at you, I wonder if the effect wouldn't be just the same inside."

"What are you talking about?" asked Rhea, laughing.

"That shine of yours. Everyone's been telling me about it. I was skeptical, but for once, office gossip's turned out to be true."

Shaking her head at her friend's saucy teasing, Rhea

163

accepted the invitation. They stopped by the lounge to collect the paper bag containing Rhea's ham sandwich, apple, and carrot sticks. As they headed for the elevators, she queried, "What's there to gossip about? So I'm happy today. I don't understand the fuss. Am I that much of a grump normally?"

"Oh, come on, you can't be that obtuse. Of course everyone's all agog at your sudden transformation to chirping happiness." Rhea continued to gape at her blankly. Janice sighed heavily and explained in the voice of a teacher talking to a particularly dense student, "Everyone knows you went to lunch with Addison yesterday."

It was a darn good thing, thought Rhea, that she was leaning into the elevator wall or she'd have fallen down laughing. Addison! People actually thought she was ecstatic because of Addison! Her amusement was almost immediately dampened by dismay. How could anybody think her that brainless? When they got out into the marbled lobby, she gripped Janice's arm and pulled her out of the flow of traffic. "I simply can't believe you'd believe that, Janice. You know better. You've been out with Addison."

"Well, yes," she admitted with a knowing grin, "and the experience *was* eye-opening. But I also know you've been infatuated with him since day one."

Rhea's dismay deepened. "Does everyone else know that?"

"No, no, of course not. Come on, if we don't get out there, all the places to sit will be gone."

They moved outside. Bright sunlight bounced from office windows to strike the pavement. The clouds that had wisped through the morning sky faintly feathered the stunning royal blue of noon. Cars whooshed down the street. People whizzed down the sidewalk. A breeze skipped in their path, ruffling hair and playfully wrapping skirts around knees. Oblivious to the male admiration

164

following them, Janice purposefully led Rhea past windows with bikinied mannequins cavorting on cardboard beaches, to the end of the block, where a square of green shrubs was encased within a low concrete wall. Others with the same idea of enjoying the spring day sat at intervals along the wall. They slid into a vacant corner and settled down to their meal.

After swallowing a good hunk of her pastrami sandwich, Janice fixed a speculative eye on Rhea. "So you weren't dazzled by the Golden Boy. Or at least you say you weren't."

"Honestly, Janice!" she huffed indignantly. "You know I have more brains than that!"

"Oh, I know. But I also know that when it comes to love, brains don't count for pips. How many times have you heard about a perfectly charming woman who's run off with an unemployed artist who beats her every third day? You shake your head and think, hasn't she any sense? But that's just the point. Love is senseless."

"That's a pretty cynical attitude."

"I've been around the track enough times myself to know what I'm talking about. But you still haven't—" She broke off to greet an acquaintance who stopped to show off the contents of a bulging sack from Joslin's.

While Janice exclaimed over her friend's purchases, Rhea pondered what she'd said. Maybe it wasn't so cynical after all. She couldn't say Janice was right about love. She didn't know about love. She didn't think she'd ever really been in love. She hadn't loved Dave. He'd been more of a crutch propping up her flagging confidence. And she certainly hadn't loved Addison, though her experience there proved that infatuation, at least, had little to do with common sense.

The woman with the Joslin's sack ambled away and Janice returned her attention to Rhea. "You still haven't explained why you're walking on clouds today."

"Huh?" said Rhea, startled from her musings.

"You. You've been over the moon all morning and with the sort of gleam that can mean only one thing."

"Oh? And what's that?"

"A man," stated Janice with flat indisputability. "It's a man and you say it's not Addison . . ."

The name trailed off into a meaningful silence. Rhea tried to ignore the searching regard being focused on her. She attempted a shrug that was supposed to be nonchalant, but was simply crooked. "You missed your calling. You ought to be working in the courtroom instead of typing Stockard's documents. You've got a questioning technique any attorney would be eager to imitate."

Janice smiled at the sarcasm, calmly finished her sandwich, then dusted her fingers on a tissue. "Let's see," she murmured. "Who could it—" She snapped her fingers and grinned triumphantly. "That guy who took you to lunch a few weeks ago. The good-looking one with the moustache and super smile. Stu? Stan?"

"Steve."

Janice's grin grew to the size of Pikes Peak. "Well?"

"Yes," admitted Rhea with a sigh. It was useless to withhold information that Janice wanted. She had more tenacity than a case of that miracle glue always advertised on TV. "But it doesn't mean anything like what you're thinking, Janice," she added quickly, "so stop looking at me as if you're about to throw rice. He's just a nice guy who happens to be a good friend."

"And a better lover, hmmm?" deduced Janice, a teasing glint in her eye.

"Isn't it about time we got back to work? I was ten minutes late this morning, so I can't be late now."

Janice obligingly got up, but as they walked back to their office building, she said, "He seemed like a terrific guy. I wondered at the time why you were wasting all those sighs on Addison when you had him within reach."

"Believe me, our relationship isn't—"

"Like that. I know, I know," laughed Janice as they crowded into an already jammed elevator. "But if you were smart, you'd hang on to this *friend* of yours. He was something special."

"You figured out all that in one two-minute introduction?"

"No, I figured it out when I saw you today. Any man who can make you shine like you have been has got to be special. And men like that don't come around too often in this life."

They spilled out of the elevator and Janice sped away before Rhea could refute her assertion that Steve was special. Not that she could refute it. Steve was special. Nor could she deny that he'd made her shine. And not just this morning either. Over the past few months he'd made her happier, he'd made her prettier. Her steps slowed. A slight frown marred her brow.

The truth of the matter was he'd practically made her, period. Or rather, remade her. But then, remods were his business, weren't they?

Now you're sounding as cynical as Janice, she scolded herself as she hurried to her desk. But even as she tried to laugh it off, she couldn't rid herself of the notion that Steve had created the person she now appeared to be. It was this vague fear that had disturbed her last night. It was this fear that had panicked her this morning.

All this time she'd thought she was reshaping herself and changing her style to reach a personal goal—to capture Addison's interest. But her goal had turned out to be an illusion. Where did that leave her? Changed, but changed for whom? Herself? Or for Steve?

Once before she'd tried to change herself to suit someone else and it had been a disaster, not only ruining the relationship, but weakening her self-confidence as well. She'd danced to Dave's tune and had regretted it. She'd vowed afterward to be her own piper from then on. And she thought she had been, but had it actually been Steve blowing the pipes?

Now she remembered Steve saying he'd waited for her. Waited for what? For her to be remolded to his liking? For her to become the woman of his dreams?

Her glow was dimmed by these reflections. As she had when swamped within the folds of Steve's robe, she felt vulnerable. Worse, she felt confused. The only thing she knew for certain was that she couldn't allow him to rush her into anything not of her own choosing. She determined to lay down the rules as soon as she saw him.

But as soon as she saw him, he circled her with his arms and bent his head to kiss her. She interrupted by setting her fingertips against his mouth. "We have to talk," she said, aching to kiss him.

"Okay," he agreed, and loosened his hold.

She dropped her fingers. He swooped. His arms tightened around her waist. He kissed her with a resounding mastery that made her weak all over. It was exactly the sort of kiss she'd been longing for. She couldn't even pretend not to kiss him back.

"Ummm, you taste good," he murmured at the edge of her mouth.

"So do you, you rat," she sighed.

He chuckled and eased back. "Well, I'm relieved to know that my powers of distraction are still intact. Now, stop blushing, sweetheart, and tell me just what we have to talk about."

Corraling her bemused senses back into line, she stepped away from him. During the afternoon she'd worked out a little speech, but all she could remember of it was how reasonable it had sounded. She took a breath and said in what she hoped was a voice of supreme reason, "We have to talk about us."

"Good topic," he said.

"About what's happened between us," she persevered.

"Even better," he said with an innocent deadpan that managed to look more lascivious than a leer.

"Steve! This is serious. What happened last night took me by surprise—"

"Are you saying you regret it?"

She sensed as much as saw the abrupt tension within him and instantly softened. "No, that's not what I'm saying at all. I couldn't ever regret it. It was too special."

"You were special," he whispered, and she shivered from head to toe. Somehow, she continued, reciting a line from the speech she'd prepared.

"But our friendship is special, too, and I don't want our friendship ruined by false expectations."

"Such as?"

"Oh, I don't know! Such as you expecting me to be anyone other than who I am. Such as you expecting me to rush into anything. Or expecting more from our relationship."

"Aren't you assuming a great deal? Just what makes you think I'll have all these expectations?"

He had her there. She didn't have a single, solid reason for making this speech. She only had nagging doubts and wavering confidence. She felt like stamping her sneaker at him and shouting, "Forget reasons! Just listen, buddy! This is the way it is or else!" But she tried to think of something more rational to say to him, something that sounded as reasonable as her made-up speech once had.

Before she came up with anything, Steve slid close behind her, running his arms around her. "Look, Rhea, I understand more than you credit me with. I admit, I do expect more from our relationship. But that doesn't mean I want to browbeat you into anything. The last thing I'd want from a woman is blind obedience. What I want from our relationship is to deepen it, expand it, make it grow."

The way his breath curled over her neck with each word made it difficult for Rhea to think. None of this had gone quite the way she'd envisioned. She couldn't think of a way to regain control. She couldn't think beyond the way the undersides of her breasts nestled against the band of his arms. With each breath she drew, she felt the rigid warmth of him behind her. Breathing became increasingly difficult. Almost as tough as thinking.

"I, uh, we—are we friends or lovers?" she finally gasped.

His arms tightened convulsively. "Do they have to be divisions? I happen to think we could be both. Friends *and* lovers. Don't you think we could be both?"

This was the moment of decision. This was the moment when she had to make the choice. If she chose wrongly, she knew she'd end up hurt, and hurt badly. But if she chose correctly . . .

He gently spun her around in his grasp. "Can't we be both?" he repeated on a hoarse rasp.

"Yes," she said simply, and realized she'd never had a choice at all. She'd made her choice the night before.

Whether she got hurt or not in the long run didn't really matter to her now. All that mattered was how much she needed him. He made her happy. He made her shine. And she needed him.

"Yes," she repeated. "We *are* both."

The tension drained from him. She could feel his muscles relax, rippling down the length of him. She thought he'd take her in an impassioned kiss, but he surprised her by tenderly pressing her head into his broad shoulder. He held her, not speaking, making no physical demands. With his hand on her neck, he toyed leisurely with the short ends of her hair while nuzzling his lips along the fluff at top. Gradually Rhea, too, relaxed.

She let her cheek snuggle farther into the soft folds of his dove-gray T-shirt. Her eyelids drifted down. The steady thump of his heart sounded beneath her palm. His fingers worked their way more thoroughly into her hair to lightly massage her scalp. His lips slid downward, over her brow to the shell of her ear. She mewed with the pleasure of it.

"Hey, you," he said against her ear.

"Ummm?"

"Which is it now?"

"Huh?" She raised her lids. He was smiling at her softly, the ends of his moustache lifting in a loving curve.

"Which is it right now? Are we friends or lovers?"

"I thought," she murmured in voice of sleepy seduction, "you said they weren't divisions."

He groaned and this time showered her with the passion she'd expected earlier. He covered her face with intense little kisses that chased her drowsiness away. Soon her hands cradled his head as she returned kiss for kiss, passion for passion. Hip to hip, stomach to stomach, chest to chest, they pressed closer and closer until they swayed unsteadily. "I think we're falling," she pointed out breathlessly. "I think you're right," he agreed just as they toppled to one side.

She shrieked and he caught hold of the end of the couch, saving them from crashing to the floor. Bent over the couch, they laughed together. They stopped in the same breathless instant. His blue eyes blazed an unspoken question. Hers darkened as she nodded mute agreement.

And then they were on the couch, twined together, discovering each other with a savage joy.

He sought her mouth with fierce impatience. She sought his with fevered insistence. He explored the rigid line of her spine, the supple swell of her hips. She explored the hard bone of his shoulder, the rough wisps on his chest. Each kiss, each touch, spiraled them toward mind-shattering need.

There was none of the slow tenderness of the night

171

before. Rhea didn't miss it. This was a hunger so compelling, tenderness would have been torture, the least pause a punishment. She forgot her resolution not to be rushed into anything. She couldn't bear to hold back. If she didn't have him now, this instant, she'd die of the anticipation. She hurried him as he undressed her. She shuddered as she undressed him. When at long last he crashed into her, she cried out wildly, not even realizing it was her voice so hoarsely breaking into the harsh pattern of ragged breath.

Had she been capable of viewing herself, Rhea would have been shocked at her lack of restraint. Never had she given of herself so completely, so uninhibitedly. But she wasn't capable of it. She wasn't capable of anything beyond feeling, feeling the rigid flexure of his muscles shifting against hers, the downy scrape of his moustache grazing her cheek, the damp trickles of sweat slicking her breasts.

They strained against each other and fulfillment flooded her senses, drowning her in a momentary torrent. She lay in a haze, scarcely conscious of the man stretched atop her. Gradually she became dimly aware of his crushing weight and then of the solid lump pressing into her back. It occurred to her she'd probably be bruised there. But she made no attempt to be released from between the couch and Steve. Instead, she laced her hands in his hair and let the softness drift through her fingers.

"Steve?"

"Ummm?"

"Maybe we were wrong. Maybe there should be a division between friends and lovers."

He tensed. She bit lightly on his neck and blew a husky laugh in his ear. "The combination of the two is potentially a killer."

He relaxed, chuckled, and began fondling her all over again. "Yeah, but what a way to go, eh?"

"What a way to go," she agreed on a sigh.

172

Frosted lilies were etched into the oval glass. The knob was cut crystal. Rhea put her hand on it, then drew back. "This is almost too lovely to be a door."

"Go on, go in," urged Steve. "The door's only one of the treasures of this house."

They'd driven down to Colorado Springs to tour the house that was currently Steve's pet project. It was, as he'd once told her, a Victorian monstrosity, complete with a turret and a wide porch that seemed to ramble its way around the house. It was in the oldest section of the town, away from the four-lane freeways and modern shopping malls that ribboned the plains below Pikes Peak, and when Rhea crossed the wooden porch to the elegantly etched door, she could almost believe herself to be in another place, another time.

She opened the door and entered. Steve followed, carrying a large, lidded wicker basket that held their lunch. On the hour's drive he'd told her all the major renovations had been done. The kitchen and baths had been totally updated, while throughout the house wood floors and sills had been stripped and returned to their gleaming glory. Paint and paper had been diligently removed from walls. One room had had "seven layers of the most godawful paper you'd ever want to see," he'd explained with a laugh. The original walls had been repaired, plastered, painted, or papered anew.

"We've been lucky," he said now. "Most of the glass and fixtures in the house were originals, or dated close to original. The structure and foundation were basically sound. We did some shoring and replacing, but surprisingly little for a house this old. The old radiator system had already been replaced with central heating, though we updated the system and added air."

"It's lovely," said Rhea, enjoying his enthusiasm as much as she was the house.

And the house *was* lovely. Straight ahead from the entrance rose a staircase with beveled railings; off to one side was the dining room, off the other, the living room. Farther down the hall were kitchen, half-bath, and study/family room. Steve led her quickly through to the kitchen, where he set the basket on a tile counter and instantly began pointing. "Dishwasher, microwave, trash compacter, Jenn-aire with grill. Every convenience you could ask for." He looked at her expectantly.

She slowly turned, taking in the oak cupboards with brass handles, the sunflower mosaics on the counter tiles, the butcher block island centered in the room, and finally faced him. "I'm impressed," she said. "If I were a cook, I'd be drooling."

He beamed. "This one's strictly my baby. I did the design work for it, planned it as if I were planning my own kitchen."

From there they went back over the ground floor slowly, Rhea expressing more warmth than she might normally have done. It was obvious to her that this house meant more to Steve than a dozen other remods put together. Not that it was hard for her to admire the spacious rooms; all the modern conveniences had been added without losing any of the old-fashioned graciousness. Paints had been selected to enhance the size and light of the rooms, sand-tone browns, creamy beiges, and in the bath, a striking bright blue. Many of the doorknobs were crystal and the doors themselves warmly polished solid wood. The fireplace mantel was beautifully carved, but the highlight was a stained glass inset in the circular window dominating the living room. Like the etching on the front door, the stained glass showed a lily swaying gently in the wind. As she walked beside him, she could easily imagine a family filling the house with life.

She said as much as they climbed the stairs. "A happy family, with dogs and cats and goldfish."

"I agree. This is exactly the kind of house I'd like to raise my family in."

She glanced at him, but he didn't look as if he'd meant anything beyond the bare statement. She hoped not. She still wasn't ready for that, not when things were going so well for her. It was as if everything had suddenly gelled in her life. Her new looks, her job, her social life, all were brighter, more fulfilling. She'd recently been invited to join a select business women's group and was already serving on the program committee. It was the sort of thing Rhea had always envied other women for, getting out and becoming part of something without having to rely on a man for approval. At work, too, more attorneys and secretaries talked to her as a person, rather than treating her as part of the filing system. Janice held that it was because Rhea herself seemed warmer, more open, but she personally thought it had to do with her more approachable good looks. Whatever it was, she was feeling confident about herself and her own success, and as always, she was reluctant to consider changes of any sort, especially the sort of lifetime change she feared Steve wanted.

So she said brightly, "Have I mentioned I've been asked to give a speech at my women's group?"

"That's the problem with getting on the program committee," he said. "You become the program."

"*Now* you tell me. Wait'll you hear the topic. Keeping Fit Professionally."

They both laughed, then Steve asked, "What the hell does it mean?"

"I don't know, but I'm working on something to the effect of not letting your work get flabby."

"So what do you do, make it run two miles?"

"Oh, no, sit-ups," she replied with a sparkling grin, and passed through the door he'd just opened.

It was the last of the upstairs bedrooms, the master bedroom that extended the length of both the living room and study below. She entered, then halted. The walls were covered with paper of a pale shell pink patterned with baby's breath, the paper she'd chosen the morning after their first night together.

"Oh, Steve, it's lovely," she sighed.

A circular seat was cut beneath the window filling most of the upper portion of the turret. She went directly to it, leaned a knee on the seat, and gazed out through leaded glass. The glass was old, the view slightly distorted. At least, she told herself, it was the age of the glass and not any extra liquid passing over her contacts.

"With the right decor the paper won't seem feminine at all. The print is so small, the pink so nearly white, that it simply lit up this room. It made it airy." He came up behind her. "It certainly doesn't make me feel less masculine."

He pressed against her and she knew he was feeling very masculine indeed. "Steve," she whispered.

"Rhea." He imprinted the back of her neck with a kiss. Thoroughly, lovingly, he traced up to the back of her ear, then down to the lobe. "Do you like the house, Rhea?"

"I—yes, yes, I do."

"This room, you like it?" His mouth worked its way along her neck to her other ear.

"Ummm," she managed unsteadily.

Nudging her forward, he maneuvered her toward the center of the room, between the two square floor-to-ceiling windows. He remained closely nestled against her back every step of the way. When he pulled her to a stop, he tightened his embrace. "This is where the bed would be. A king-size bed."

"Y-yes," she said, surprised she could say anything at all. The only thing she could think about was the moist tenderness of his lips on her ear, her throat. Then the warm sensitivity of his hands on her waist, her ribs, the undersides of her breasts. "What—what are you doing?"

"Isn't it obvious?" He twirled her in his arms and rasped against her mouth, "I'm making love to you."

Any protest she might have uttered was swallowed up in his deftly diverting kisses. He'd smoked his pipe during the drive down and the tang of tobacco bit sharply with each kiss. Yet it wasn't unpleasant. Nothing about his kisses could ever be called unpleasant. His kisses were filled with warmth and comfort and exciting artistry.

He nibbled lightly at her lower lip, flicked his tongue teasingly between her teeth, tempted and tantalized until Rhea thrust her hands into his hair and held him still. Then she probed the secrets of his mouth with her tongue, pierced the sweetness of his lips with her own. She enticed, she roused, she transported them both to a state of pure sensation.

They were sinking, sinking into a rapturous spell. The solid wood flooring caught them, but gently as Steve lowered Rhea within his grasp. Westering sunlight sprinted through the unshaded windows to ricochet within the empty room. Enchantment seemed to dance with the dust whirling in the rays. It almost seemed to Rhea as if the hard floor softened to bed them. They lay in a toasty pool of light, bathed in the heat of the afternoon, drowning in each other's senses.

Goose bumps rose in shivering masses as his hands stroked lightly, quickly, beneath her blouse from her ribs to her breasts, then along her stomach as he loosened the madras button by button. Her nipples firmed in response to the caress of his breath as he traced the lacy edge of her bra with his lips. As the front clasp gave way, the fullness of her breasts spilled into his palms. He nestled his mouth in the valley between them and murmured her name, blowing moist warmth into her pores.

He set his hand at the zipper of her jeans and some last shred of sanity returned to her. She lay her hand atop his. "Here? In the middle of the afternoon?"

"Here, now, always," he said on a thickened note. "It's always good, always better."

How could it get better? she wondered. Yet she knew it would be. Every time he touched her, every time he kissed her, every time he completed the loving, it got better.

She removed her hand and let him unzip her jeans. She returned the favor and hastily raced through the buttons on his shirt as well. His skin seemed to scorch her fingertips; his nipples seemed hard as granite; the soft mat of curls seemed static with the electricity crackling between them.

Soon nothing but dusted sunshine covered them. A moment of embarrassment struck Rhea. She'd never been totally naked in the middle of the day, much less contemplated making love in a completely bare room at that time. All her discomfort disappeared before the fervent sincerity of Steve's hoarse, "My God, you're beautiful."

He leaned away from her. Intently he loved her with his impassioned gaze. "You're beautiful here," he said, and skimmed the dark areolas of her breasts with his fingertips. "And here." He slid his finger down over her belly to the darkly tangled triangle of hair. "Beautiful here," he said, gliding both hands from her buttocks up over her hips, waist, and on up to her shoulders. "And most of all, here. You're beautiful here," he whispered as he gently set his mouth to hers.

She knew then that there was nothing to be ashamed of in this. It was right, more than right, perfect. How could she have doubted for a second that it was perfect?

Opening her mouth fully to him, she sighed with pleasure as he darted his tongue within. Wreathing her arms about him, she nibbled as he kissed, kissed as he nibbled. His hands kneaded the roundness of her hips, then moved to rub her arms, her shoulders, the tips of her breasts. He seemed to know just where to stroke, how long to linger to make her body pulse with need.

But the game was not his alone. She felt his quivers when she flicked her tongue over the grainy texture of his nipple. She heard his shudders when she slid her hand between his thighs. She touched him and knew his need was as great as her own.

Need overpowered his playfulness. He shadowed her body with his, coming to her in a dizzying explosion of desire. She took him with the same frenzied desperation, as if she couldn't get enough of him, as if she couldn't give enough of herself. She dug her fingertips into the muscles of his hips and urged him to love her again and again and again.

The unbending floor slapped her back, but Rhea didn't care. There was no breeze within the closed room; the air was stifling, but Rhea didn't care. The warm pool of sunlight became a baking steambath, but Rhea didn't care. For her there was only the exhilarating pleasure of Steve rhythmically filling her. There was only the slick sheen on the muscles straining above her. There was only the passionate catch in the breath coating her breasts. There was only the heat rising from the skin beneath her fingertips. His evident excitement erased any discomfort she might have felt, erased it amid the power of unparalleled ecstasy.

Then even these senses were overwhelmed in the shattering delight that excluded all else. They tautly carried

179

each other beyond the mutual fulfillment, then lay, too exhausted to move, too satisfied to try.

Slowly, lazily, Steve came to life. He stretched over her, stirring her again with the sensual movement. He bent his head and kissed her jaw. "I love you," he said huskily into the arch of her neck.

Her hand clenched, digging into the small of his back. She said nothing. What could she say? She couldn't say she loved him. She didn't know if she loved him. She didn't know about love. She'd thought she loved Addison, and look how wrong she'd been. She wanted to say, *Please don't say you love me, it confuses me, it complicates things.* Their relationship was fine just the way it was, she didn't want love brought into it, not yet. But she couldn't say that either, so she lay still and silent and sad beneath him.

After a long silence that hung as heavy as the smothering air, he shifted away from her. Her little surge of panic was almost instantly eased when he rolled on his side, propped himself up on his elbow, and grinned at her. "Can I pick 'em or can I pick 'em?" he demanded rhetorically.

"Oh, you can pick 'em," she agreed, then spoiled it by asking, "Pick what?"

"The site of the future master bed."

"What if the people who buy this place don't put it here?"

"They have to. It's been christened—very properly, I might add." His grin widened and he tapped her nose. "I love it when you blush like that, sweetheart. Especially when you're not wearing a stitch and I can see just how much of you is blushing."

"Oh, you!" she gasped, but it was hard to sound like an outraged maiden, lying bare on a bare floor. She ended up settling for giggles instead.

"Besides, I'll let you in on a secret," he said. "I might have some say in where the bed goes. I'm thinking of buying it myself."

Her first thought was selfish. It wouldn't be the same at the apartment without him. Her second thought was curious. Why would he buy a house like this? She realized he was looking at her, waiting for some response. She said, "It's a bit large for a bachelor, isn't it?"

He shrugged. "I hope to change that."

Change was his specialty, she couldn't forget that. He changed houses, he changed people. She didn't like change. She sat up and began gathering up her clothes. Steve flopped onto his back and rested his head on his hands.

"You know," he drawled after a time, "I think I knew the first time I saw this place that I wanted it. Even with the peeling paint and sagging porch and patched flooring, even drab and disused, I wanted it. I remember turning to my head carpenter and saying, 'This house is special.'"

She hunted for her diamond-patterned knee-highs, then asked as she yanked them from under Steve, "Have you always had this craving to live in a gabled Victorian?"

"Oh, I don't know. Maybe not always. I had a chance to buy a rambling antique of a house several years ago, but Tammie wouldn't hear of it. I don't think I ever stopped resenting her for it. She'd hate this place. Everything had to be brand spanking new for Tammie. Her ideal house was one just thrown up in the newest development, mud yard and all."

Studying the bronze streaks meandering through his brown hair, she decided she was glad Tammie would have hated this house. Not, of course, she hastily amended, that it mattered one way or the other, but still . . . Rhea glanced over the room. The bonding of their lovemaking here seemed to have bonded this room to them. It seemed to be uniquely theirs, their special room. She tried to tamp down the embers of the warmth she felt. Looking back at Steve's profile, she wondered if he'd planned for her to feel these things.

"How about lunch?" she suggested. "I don't know about you, but I'm famished."

"Stirred up your appetite, did we?" he inquired with a leer.

"Ummm, *all* my appetites. But while some pangs were fully sated, my hunger pangs are getting louder."

"You. You're always hungry."

"That's because you're always starving me," she countered, and threw his shirt at him. "If you want to eat with me, you'd better get dressed. I'm going down now."

As she slipped out the door, he sat up and hollered, "Try not to eat the basket too!"

"It would serve you right if I did!" she called back, and whisked down the stairs.

By the time he joined her in the kitchen, she'd piled two paper plates with bulging turkey-on-wheat sandwiches, cole slaw, potato chips, and pickles. She had a cold beer ready for him, a diet soda for her, and apples with cheddar cheese waited for dessert. She handed him the beer and said, "Good thing you got here when you did, you almost missed out. The first four courses have already been finished."

"I wondered why you'd begun to waddle." He expertly avoided the slap she aimed at his rear end, lifted the grass green tablecloth she'd spread over the butcher block, and took it into the dining room where he shook it out over the floor. "We can't eat in the kitchen, my dear. The dining room is for dining, ergo, we shall dine in the dining room."

"A place for everything and everything in its place, is that it?"

"That's it."

They carried their meal onto the square patch of green and sat beneath a splendid chandelier of dangling cut glass. The light in this room facing east was muted, but still the glass teardrops caught stray sunshine and created tiny rainbows. A prismatic array twirled over them as they ate.

"It doesn't sound to me as if you and Tammie were very compatible," she remarked, then wanted to kick herself for having done so. The last thing she wanted to talk about was his former wife.

"We weren't, not at all. Well," he qualified, "we were quite compatible sexually, at first. It was, in fact, the whole reason for our marriage. But that soon paled and it didn't take me six months to realize my marriage was an enormous mockery. Next time around, I want a companion out of bed as well as in it."

"Oh," she said, and chewed vigorously. Why had she even brought this up?

"We're pretty compatible, don't you think?"

"Us? Oh, well, I don't know."

A shadow passed over him, but that might have been the wavering light, a cloud crossing outside. She didn't want to think it was a sign of hurt.

"You don't know, not after all this time?" he asked gently.

Beneath her fingers, the bread of her sandwich tore. She stared at it, frowning. He kept waiting for her to speak. Finally she said, "I know we're compatible on some levels —"

"Just some?"

"Well, I can't say about all. I just don't know. Why are you pushing me? I'm trying to tell you what I think, but you don't seem to want to hear it."

"I'm sorry. I do want to hear it."

When he used that low, understanding tone, she couldn't resist him, and he probably knew it. She set down her sandwich, swiped her fingers on her jeans, and said, "I know we get along. We have fun together, a lot of fun. We laugh at the same things. We both like animals. But

I don't know if we share the same goals, the same principles, the same outlook on issues."

"We don't have to see eye-to-eye on every issue. That would get awfully damn dull. So long as we can talk about our disagreements, that's the important thing."

She saw where this conversation was heading and didn't like it. She was happy with the way things were; she didn't want to ruin what they had by bringing talk of love—or anything like it—into it. So she manufactured a happy tone and said, "Yes, it's important for friends to be able to talk things out. You don't always have to understand your friends, but you should be able to accept them."

"Why is it I get the feeling you're saying more than you're saying?"

If she hadn't looked at him then, she might have carried it off, but she looked and saw the sadness in every line of his face. She saw the tight line of his mouth beneath his moustache, the grooves cut beside his eyes. To think that she had caused him sadness made her sad in turn. Tears threatened, and she fought to hold them back.

"Really, let's not talk about it anymore. Let's not spoil our picnic."

"We have to talk sometime, Rhea."

She shook her head in a vehement denial. It was a mistake. Her contact lens flew out of her watery eye. "Oh, damn!"

"What's wrong?" He was beside her immediately.

"My contact. It just fell out of my eye. At least I think it went out."

"Which eye?" he calmly asked.

"The right one." She lifted her lid and looked up, down, to the sides. "Can you see it in there? I can't always feel it if it goes off to the side or top."

"I don't see anything."

"Could you get my purse? In the kitchen? There's a

184

mirror in it and I could check myself. I know where to look."

He was up and out in an instant. He returned with the purse, and while she scattered the contents in her lap he knelt and began searching the area around where she sat cross-legged. "I didn't hear it hit the floor, so it must have landed on the cloth."

"Or in the food," she wailed.

"God, it's green, isn't it? Why didn't we do like every other picnicker in the world and have a red cloth?"

She held the mirror at the tip of her nose and lifted her eyelid, checking this way and that. "It's not in my eye," she announced in a voice of doom. "It's somewhere out here."

"Don't panic. We'll find it."

She tried to help him search the plates, the cloth, but it wasn't easy. The unshed tears had blurred the one contact she still had in and her vision was next to nothing. "It could have gone off the cloth. They fly surprisingly far sometimes. It may be gone forever."

"Do you lose them often?"

"No, not often. Just sometimes. Actually, I've never lost one. They've slid out, but I've always found them. Until now," she finished with a sniff of self-pity.

"It's in this room somewhere. We'll find it," he was saying, when suddenly he tensed, then pounced. "Ah, ha! What did I tell you?" He held his hand before her face. On the tip of his curled index finger lay the small green speck that was her sight. She took it from him gratefully.

"Oh, thank you, Steve. I don't know what I'd have done if you hadn't found it."

"Don't you have your glasses with you?"

"No, why should I?" she asked as she sped off to the half-bath. While there, she not only replaced her contact, but dampened her face with the cold water as well. Though the plumbing had been turned on, the hot water

185

heater wasn't lit, but Rhea didn't mind. Cold was exactly what she needed to splash some sense back into her. She came back to the dining room feeling refreshed and in control of herself.

"You ought to forget those damn contacts," he said the minute she appeared. "They're more trouble than they're worth."

"Don't be silly. It doesn't happen very often and, besides, don't you remember how I looked in my glasses? Like a magnified owl?"

"You looked great in glasses."

She threw him a look of utter disbelief. "I did not look great. I don't consider owl eyes appealing."

"You could always get a different, more stylish pair of glasses. The point is, you don't need to go through the hassle of contacts to look good. You've always looked good."

Her disbelief hardened to incredulity. "Oh, come on, Steve, I know what I looked like. I saw myself in the mirror every day. It wasn't such a great sight. What is this? You want to change me again?"

He sighed. "I don't want to change you. I like you just the way you are. Even if you are blind and bull-headed."

She stuck her tongue out at him and they laughed, but the discussion lingered to taunt her. Sure, he might like her just the way she was, *now*. He was mainly responsible for the way she was now. She looked just like he made her look. The real Rhea, the one who'd stared at her from her mirror all those years, that Rhea wouldn't have stood a chance with him.

The problem was, beneath this Rhea, the one he'd helped make, was that Rhea, the real Rhea, the Rhea he wouldn't look twice at.

Though she listened to his explanations of what he intended to do with the house if he bought it, and even murmured appropriate responses at the appropriate times,

186

it was as if she did so from a distance. She held herself in reserve. She wanted so very much to believe him, to believe that he cared for her as she was, flaws and all, but she didn't dare to. Even as a child she'd withdrawn from potential hurt, avoided the risk rather than chance the happiness. And her own innate, fixed vision of herself as dumpy, drab, and unappealing told her that sooner or later she'd get hurt by Steve.

So when they returned home, she thanked him hastily for the wonderful day and slipped into her apartment before he could bring up any more disturbing discussions.

CHAPTER FOURTEEN

Rhea stood with her arms akimbo and looked him up and down. "What are you trying to do, make me fat?"

Steve sighed heavily. He spoke sadly to the elaborately sculpted bunny cradled in his arms. "You see how it is? I can't win with her. Either I'm trying to starve her to death or I'm trying to fatten her up."

"But it's chocolate," she pointed out.

"Are you sure? Maybe you'd better take a bite and check it out."

She gaped at him in astonishment. "Is this the same man who's dictated every little bite to my mouth for months?"

"That was only for the initial weight loss. You don't have to be as strict for maintaining; in fact, you shouldn't be so strict." Frowning, he deliberately returned the head-to-toe appraisal she'd given him.

Beneath the pin tucks running down the ivory front of her Victorian-style dress, Rhea's breasts tautened. The high collar suddenly seemed constrictive. The full skirt swayed about rubbery knees. Her body responded this way whenever he looked at her, tightening and dissolving all at once.

"You're almost getting too thin," he pronounced at last. "I hope you're not getting carried away."

"Don't be absurd."

"You've gotten downright fanatical about this diet. You never were that overweight in the first place."

"You don't call twenty pounds overweight?"

"You looked fine to me. Now you look too thin."

There was real concern in both his voice and the level look he was giving her. She'd almost tossed out the old line about how you could never be too thin or too rich. Instead, realizing how much he really cared, she laughed lightly and said, "You really don't have to worry. No one who loves food as much as I could ever get too thin."

He held up the bunny and wiggled it. She shook her head. "You could have a little, you know. A little won't make you fat. Besides, we'll work it off later."

The intimate tone of his voice made clear just what sort of physical exercise he had in mind. Rhea flushed with pleasure. The fact that he still wanted her as much as she wanted him always brought that glowing flush to her skin. Their mutual desire had continued to blossom with the spring; she hadn't yet gotten over the wonder of it.

"It's a holiday," he added, and she gave in. She broke off the tip of the bunny's ear. "Happy Easter," she said as she popped the bit in her mouth.

"Happy Easter, pal." He lowered the bunny to the table and strolled on into her kitchen.

As he poured himself a cup of coffee, she pretended to examine the chocolate while surreptitiously watching him. In all the months they'd been seeing each other, she'd never seen him look as gorgeous as he did now. She'd always known he was good-looking, and lately she'd come to realize he was actually quite handsome. His body was in superb shape and his face had a calm strength that would catch any woman's eye. But seeing that beautiful body of his encased in a steel gray three-piece suit, the tailored kind of suit that hugged waist and hips and emphasized shoulders, well, that was enough to make Rhea

189

consider canceling brunch and get right down to working off the chocolate.

He smiled as he came out with a mug of coffee and sat, leaning his elbows on the table. She hurriedly busied herself with another piece of ear.

"You talk to your parents yet today?" he asked.

"Got them just before they left for church." She picked at the licorice buttons lining the bunny's protuberant belly. Without looking at him, she said, "Mom wanted to know when they'll get to meet you."

"And you told her . . . ?"

She shrugged. "That I didn't know."

"Don't you want me to meet them, Rhea?"

"Don't be absurd," she said for the second time that morning. But he wasn't being entirely absurd, and she knew they both knew it. The subject had come up before. And always she'd stalled with excuses that had little originality and less substance. *It's such a long drive. I've had a rough week at work. Summer would be a better time to go.* It wasn't that she thought her parents wouldn't like him—they'd be more likely to fall all over him. He was exactly the kind of man they'd want for her. Nor did she have any fear that he wouldn't be taken with the entire Nichols tribe. It was just her own personal fear. Introducing him to her family implied a commitment she didn't feel ready to admit, not yet. So she quickly changed the subject, asking, "Did you phone your grandmother?"

He paused long enough to let her feel his quiet disappointment. But when he spoke his tone was normal. "Yesterday."

"And?" she prompted.

"Oh, I'm sure the blisters will heal in a few days." He cupped his hand around his right ear and grinned crookedly.

"She didn't take it well?"

"Actually she took it with surprising calm. I'd called

190

her a couple of weeks ago and told her the way the wind was blowing, so she accepted my excuses with relative graciousness. My role in the Bradley family remains intact —for now."

"That has the ring of more yet to come," remarked Rhea, reaching for another chunk of chocolate.

"Don't you think that bunny should last you longer than the next hour?" he inquired pleasantly.

"But you said—"

"I said a little wouldn't hurt. I wasn't referring to the whole damn bunny."

"You've got the makings of a medieval torturer, you know that?" she huffed, plopping into the chair opposite his. "One who'd excel at his job too."

"Don't pout. Makes your freckles stand out. And I learned my technique from a pro, my grandmother. Now, there's a woman who can lob heads in the grand tradition of Elizabeth Regina." He quaked visibly on his chair and Rhea couldn't help laughing.

"Is she out to lob off yours?"

"No, not this time. I was given a reprieve. She grandly told me I have any time between now and Memorial Day to put in an appearance."

"Will you be caught up enough by then?"

"If I'm not, the work will have to wait. Grandmother won't. The truth of the matter is, I could've gone this week if I'd really wanted to. It's not work that kept me here." Taking a long sip of his coffee, he eyed her steadily over the rim. Her heart skittered as he slowly set the mug on the table and nearly stopped as he said, "I could've gone, but I wanted to stay with you instead."

There it was again, that sparkling delight that coursed through her blood like champagne whenever he looked at her like that, making her forget why she hesitated at all. Her confusion evaporated in the clear heat of her desire

191

for him. "I'm glad," she said, and her smoky tone said much more.

"You about ready to work off that chocolate?" He quirked his moustache meaningfully.

She glanced down the hall. Laurey's door was closed. The walls were pretty solid for apartment walls. But even so . . . "Laurey's here, sleeping," she said with heavy regret.

"She's here? Are you sure?"

"Of course I'm sure. She's never up this early, and anyway, her door's still shut."

With a shake of his head he observed, "I'd begun to think you'd made her up. You know, a phantom roommate to keep intrusive men out of your life."

"Well, if I had, it didn't work. It didn't keep you out, and you're as intrusive as they come."

"Lucky for you."

"Not only intrusive, conceited as well."

"But you know you go for Mr. Ego types."

Straightening in her chair, she fixed him with a haughty eye. "I don't go, Mr. Bradley, for a *type*."

"No?"

"No. I go for *you*."

Steve went utterly still. He stared. She waited. Time breathed between them. Finally he pushed back his chair and stood. Holding out a hand to her, he said, "Well, if we can't work out here, let's not stick around."

Anticipation tingled over her nerve endings. Already images were flying through her mind, images of his handsome body gleaming over hers in the morning light, images of her legs wrapping around his, images of their bodies swaying together in a cadence of love. Later, imagery would become reality. Later, they would kiss and touch and love. Just thinking of later made her mouth go dry. Trying not to tremble, she took his hand and rose.

Outside, a gusty wind whipped over her skirt and

flapped the ends of his suit jacket. Sunlight twined over them as they hurried to where his car sat waiting.

"The MG looks good as new," said Rhea as she slid into the seat, then added as he got in behind the wheel, "No thanks to me, huh? I bet you still shudder when you think of that day."

"Oh, I don't regret the smash-up."

"You don't?"

"Not one tiny bit. The MG was sacrificed in a good cause."

She looked at him quizzically. "Cause?"

"Our meeting," he explained with a tender smile.

Her body thrummed to the tune of the engine as they drove off. She wouldn't admit it, not even fully to herself, but she loved it when he tossed out compliments like that. She loved the way his eyes crinkled into slits and his moustache tilted above his fine lips whenever he smiled at her. He could make her feel so special with just a smile, a glance, a phrase.

And still, somewhere deep within her, Rhea doubted.
. . .

By the time they'd finished their brunch, the wind had ceased to gust, blowing gently into the early afternoon. The sun still shone, but was muted by bubbles of clouds floating through the sky. They stood beside the MG, enjoying the breeze and the light and each other.

"You want to go work out?" he asked, then saw her knowing look and amended, "I mean, really. We could go back home, change, and go over to Lou's gym."

Rhea turned her face toward the sun and let her mind drift with the clouds. She felt replete. Filled with delicious strawberry crepes, good coffee, and excellent conversation, she felt lazy and dreamy and happy.

"Un-uh," she finally said. "Let's skip the workout and

let our meal digest in peace. Let's drive up into the mountains and just enjoy the view."

"I'm enjoying the view here," he said, but opened the car door for her.

She leaned against the headrest and drowsily watched the Denver suburbs thin. The Interstate twisted into the mountains, where the sky seemed bluer, the clouds fluffier, the air sweeter. Steve turned off the highway, drove along a two-lane road and, eventually, pulled to the shoulder by a flat swatch of wild grass banked by a steeply rising slope. Small flowers cheerfully daubed the grass with flecks of white, purple, and yellow. Patches of mud lay in the shadow of the slope, reminders of the last spring rain. They got out. Rhea stretched lazily and braced against the front fender.

"This is fabulous. Sometimes I wonder what the heck I'm doing in crowded, noisy, smoggy Denver. But up here I remember why I took the job at Chambers. I liked the thought of being so close to the mountains."

"You're a mountain girl, eh?"

"Umm. More of a nature girl. Not that I get out and eat berries and all that, but I enjoy having a bit of it to come to, away from the madding crowd. It's rejuvenating."

"I know. I've never understood people like my brother Warren who thrive on the bustle of the big city, the noise, the crowds. I need the space and quiet and renewal of life found here."

"Me too," she said, and fell silent.

Steve shrugged out of his jacket and flung it into the back of the MG. He tossed his silver-on-black club tie in after it, then came round to prop on the fender beside her. They stood without speaking, just letting the wind slide over them, tousling their hair before whisking through the grasses. She could feel the light pressure of his thigh beside hers, the muscles of his arm flexing as he rolled back the sleeves of his pearl white shirt. Out of the corner of her eye she could see the snug fit of his vest down his ribs, over his trim waist. She remembered how the sight of Addison in a vested suit used to make her quiver and sigh and she almost laughed aloud. Steve in a suit made Addison look like goldspun fluff—insubstantial and worthless.

On impulse she rolled forward, pressed against his chest, and kissed him.

"What did I do to deserve this?" he asked when she'd tilted back her head.

She set her fingertips against his jaw. "Nothing. I'm just feeling happy. Happy to be here with you."

He turned his head slightly, enough to nibble her fingers. "I'm happy too," he said, and the softness of it whispered into her palm.

They kissed again quietly. She nestled within his hold and decided this was the nicest Easter she'd ever had. After a lingering kiss that was more pleasant than passionate and yet stirred her as all his kisses stirred her, she sighed and told him it was the best Easter of her life.

"They could get better in the future," he murmured against the shell of her ear.

"I don't see how," she breathed.

"We could work on it together. We'd be happy together, Rhea, really happy."

The shock traveled slowly, seeming to delay in delivering the message to her brain. She bent back her head and focused a blank, uncomprehending look on him. "What are you talking about?"

"Us. You and me. Together."

"What do you mean, together?" she repeated, unable to admit she knew what he was talking about.

It was obvious he hadn't missed the note of panic in her voice. Hurt clouded his blue eyes. But he managed a light tone as he said, "I've made a mess of it, haven't I? But then, the only practice I've had was when I was eighteen

195

and too young to know what I was doing. I'm asking you to marry me."

This time the shock didn't hesitate. It hit her in one fast, furious jolt. She pulled away from him and stared, open-mouthed. When she finally brought her lips together, she spoke with emphasis. "You don't know what you're saying."

"Of course I do."

"No, no, you don't. Why, we hardly know each other!"

"I wouldn't say hardly. I know every delicious inch of you intimately, right down to a certain unmentionable mole."

"That's not what I mean, and you know it. Spending a few nights together—"

"A few?"

"All right then, several. But many nights together still don't make us candidates for marriage."

"I don't want to marry you just for the nights. I want to marry you for the days, for the companionship, for the comfort and pleasure of being together."

She burrowed the toe of her white sandal into the dirt beneath the grass. She watched the dust rise over her foot. "I'm not the sort of person who could consider marriage lightly. Not, I know," she quickly said, glancing at his set face, "that you're asking me lightly. It's just that when I marry I want it to be for all time. You know, one of the grand old traditional marriages. Today people just jump into a marriage knowing that they can bail out anytime. You know what I was told on the day I hired on at Chambers, the very first day? One secretary said, 'You'll love the perks—they do all your divorces for free.' She's getting her fourth and nearly every other person there has had at least one divorce. I don't want that."

He didn't say anything for a long time, such a long time that Rhea wondered if he ever intended to speak to her again in this lifetime. But finally he straightened and held out a hand. Hesitating only briefly, she lay hers within it. He stroked the back of her hand with his thumb.

"I can understand that. Being a veteran of the divorce wars myself, I understand your fears. I can only tell you, emphatically, that I fully intend to make my next marriage my last. But while I understand your hesitation, I also think you can hem and haw only so long before you have to take the chance. Nothing's guaranteed."

"I know, I know. But you're rushing things."

He studied her for a while, then sighed. "That's the second time you've said that to me, and that was weeks ago. I've been trying not to push you, but Rhea, I'm thirty-five. If we want a family, we can't wait around forever to be certain things are going to work out."

Her stomach was clenched in fear, fear that he'd issue an ultimatum, *marry me or else,* and she knew it would have to be *or else.* She simply wasn't ready to leap into marriage. As deeply as she cared for him—and she no longer tried to probe the depths of it—she still didn't know if she loved him, loved him as a lifelong soulmate. Her major problem was that she didn't understand what she wanted, not from him, not from herself. She knew only what she didn't want. She didn't want to ruin the relationship they had and she didn't want to be pressed into changing it.

"Things have been going so well, why change it?" she asked, her voice rising in despair.

"Because things could be better."

"They could be worse too."

Releasing her hand, he spun away. He walked to the middle of the field and stood looking out beyond the road, over the ragged beginnings of the Rockies. The wind tufted his hair. Shadows chased over him as clouds glided above. Finally he came back to stand facing her.

"Look, maybe I have been precipitous; maybe you're right, and we're not ready for marriage. But how about moving in with me? We could test it out, see how we get along together on a day-to-day basis. If living together didn't work out, we'd be free to go our separate ways."

The fear that had gripped her stomach spread throughout her. While he'd been standing in the field she'd been debating with herself, trying to make some sense out of a senseless situation. Why did he have to shake things up? Everything had been so wonderful, and he wanted to change it. Just as he'd wanted to change her, she thought resentfully, knowing she was being unfair, knowing she'd been the one who wanted to change. But she remembered vividly how he'd offered his help, then completely taken over. He'd set up her diet, he'd directed her exercise, he'd picked out her clothes, he'd reshaped her head to toe. He'd remodeled her, and now he wanted to remold their relationship. Something in her rebelled at that.

"I don't know," she stalled. "There's Laurey—"

"Laurey doesn't need a roommate. She hardly needs a room. She's never there."

"That's not true. At least it's not as true as it once was. You've just not been there at the right times, that's all. Laurey's been staying home a lot more than she used to, and I think she needs me there."

"I need you. Or doesn't that matter to you?"

Tears gathered at the back of her eyes. "Of course it matters," she mumbled, trying not to let those tears loose.

"You could've fooled me," he said on a snap, and Rhea lost her battle with her tears.

Some women cry quietly, with dainty crystalline drops trickling from their eyes and some sob, yet maintain a dignity in the rivulets that course over their cheeks. Rhea didn't cry often, but when she did, she gushed. Great, huge torrents of tears splashed from her eyes, sticking in her lashes and spilling off the end of her chin to spot the front of her bosom. This time was no exception.

198

At the first outpouring Steve hauled her against him like a fisherman expertly reeling in a catch. At least, she thought at the back of her mind, he knew what he was in for. Then she buried her face in his shoulder, and gave herself up to her emotions. Fearing for her contacts, she squeezed her eyes tightly shut. She didn't have the least hope of stemming the tidal wave of tears, and she didn't. A steady stream washed from under her lashes, down her cheeks, over her chin, and onto his vest.

"Hey, hey, don't cry so hard, you'll smudge your freckles."

"Mmmmpphft," she sobbed into his neck.

"What?"

"I'mmmmpphft," she repeated.

After that he simply held her, rubbing her back with the flat of his hand. She eventually calmed, feeling like a fool as she did so. She'd brought all this on herself. She wanted to have her cake and eat it too. She wanted to keep Steve dangling while she sorted out her own needs, never mind his. She wanted to have the comfort of his shoulder forever. Yet when he asked her to make the same commitment to him, she reacted like a child denied a treat.

When she ceased to shudder against him, Steve lifted her head and kissed her brow, both cheeks, her nose, her chin, and, lastly, her mouth. Her lashes unstuck themselves and she peered at him with all the clarity of vision of viewing someone through a goldfish bowl.

"Now, what were you trying to tell me?" he asked.

"I'm sorry," she said, and sniffed.

"There's nothing for you to be sorry about."

"There is, there is," she whispered. "I didn't want to hurt you. I need you too."

She felt the shifting of his muscles, saw the reserve fade from his face. He offered a lopsided smile and said, "I'm relieved to hear that. As long as we don't want to hurt each other, as long as we need each other, we can straighten everything out."

Rhea wasn't as certain of that, but she let it pass, merely accepting it with a nod. She didn't intend to risk losing him, not yet. Life without him would be unbearably empty. So she kept silent and they returned to the car.

When Steve got in, however, he didn't start it up. He leaned on the wheel, looked at her sideways, and said, "I'll try not to push you, Rhea, but are you willing to meet me halfway?"

"I'm not sure I know what you mean."

"You've got to be willing to come out of your shell a little more. Even when we're making love, you hold back a little bit of yourself, and it's not fair to either of us or our relationship. If you make the effort to quit doubting me when I tell you I care about you—"

"I don't doubt you."

"Yes, you do. Deep down, you do. When you first lost the weight, I thought you were being modest when you turned away the compliments. Now I realize you honestly don't think you're thin. You still see yourself as fat."

She twisted her hands in the folds of her lap. It had always been incredibly difficult for her to open up to others; his probing and analyzing made her nervous. "Maybe so. I mean, it's hard to picture myself as someone people think pretty or whatever, but I don't get the connection to us."

"It's the same with you when I try to tell you I love you. You accept it, but inside you withdraw. Inside you don't believe me, and I don't know how to convince you, especially since you seem unwilling to let me show you I mean what I say. Having you doubt me, that's what hurts."

"I don't want to hurt you," she whispered. Her gaze raced from her knotted fingers to his darkened face and back again. She realized that he was asking for a commitment, perhaps one even harder to give than a legal one or even a physical one; he was asking for her to trust him enough to open up totally to him. She didn't know if she could do that, yet if she didn't try, their relationship would come to a screeching halt. The thought depressed her. She kept her eyes firmly on her lap and cleared her throat. "I don't know if I can, I don't know if I'm sure I even understand what you mean, but, Steve, I'll try, really I'll try."

"That's all I'm asking, Rhea," he said, and turned the key in the ignition. As the engine burst into action, she thought she heard him add, "For now," but she couldn't be certain.

Like the drive out, the ride back into Denver was silent, but it wasn't the soothing silence of companions. It was a strained silence of problems not fully resolved. To Rhea it seemed as if the small interior of the MG throbbed with tension. To her ears the engine droned fretfully; to her eyes the sky now had a drab grayish tinge to it. The clouds which had before been pretty puffs now looked like clumps; they looked, in fact, rather like she felt.

When they at last reached their apartment complex, Steve didn't pull into his parking slot. Instead, he stopped before the sidewalk nearest her building and said, "You won't mind if I don't see you up, will you? I've got some errands to run."

It had an ominous sound to it, and despite his earlier assurances, Rhea's old bugaboo, insecurity, curdled her blood. She set her hand to the latch, but didn't open the door. Instead, she gripped it till her knuckles whitened and said on a shrill rush, "Are you sure? About waiting, I mean. Waiting for me to work things out within myself. Are you willing to wait for me?"

He leaned over, cupped his hands around her head, and turned her face toward him. His eyes shone more deeply blue than she'd yet seen them. His smile held more love than she'd have thought possible in a single line. Less than a whisper away from her lips he said in his wonderfully soothing voice, "For you, I'll wait till doomsday."

And as she stumbled out of the car, she clearly heard, "But I hope like hell I don't have to."

She hoped like hell he didn't either.

CHAPTER FIFTEEN

The first thing she noticed when she walked in the door was the aroma permeating the hall. The warm blending of chicken and butter tantalized her nostrils and started juices in her stomach gurgling. The second thing she noticed was that she was, indeed, in her own apartment. She checked the number on the door to be certain. But as she entered the living room, Rhea began to doubt earnestly where she was.

The usual cheerful clutter that awaited her when she arrived home from work was suspiciously absent. Stray bits of clothing and shoes did not drape over the chairs, the couch, the tables, not even the carpet. The carpet was miraculously free of dirt, fluffed as only a freshly vacuumed carpet can be. Record albums reposed in a neat stack within the stereo stand. Magazines lay in one precise pile on the end of a dust-free table.

Rhea stared incredulously at this remarkable sight as her roommate whirled out of the kitchen and she received an even bigger jolt. Neither chiffon, silk, nor crepe hugged Laurey's slim, gazellelike figure. True, the vermilion blouse was definitely modish, and true, it was tucked into a tight pair of designer jeans, but still, the sight was unbelieveable. In over a year Rhea had never seen her in anything but dresses or skirts—swirly, slinky feminine kinds of things. The hair that was usually a cascade of honey was banded into a simple ponytail and the face that made men stop in the streets was completely free of make-up.

"Laurey?" said Rhea, testing it out.

"Am I ever glad you're home. Hurry and get changed, or dinner will be ruined."

"Dinner?" She glanced into the dining room and wondered if she could escape by backing out slowly. The table was arranged for two, place mats, plates, flatware, and all.

"It's a chicken and rice thing with a sauce. You'll love it. At least I think you will," Laurey said doubtfully. "Go get washed up while I get it on the table."

Rhea didn't move. "Dinner? *You* cooked dinner? For us?"

A sheepish look stole over Laurey's face. "Well, I just thought I'd give it a shot. You know, sorta see what it's like. I don't really know if it'll be any good or not. The first stick of butter got burned."

The oven timer burst into a cacophony of shrieks and Laurey yipped. "God! There it is! Hurry up, Rhea!" She dashed back to the kitchen, mumbling, "Potholders, where're the damn potholders?"

"Top drawer, left side of the stove," called out Rhea. She heard a screeched "Thanks" as she went down to the bathroom. She paused to kick off her shoes in her bedroom, all the while wondering what on earth had come over Laurey. Was she sick? This may be normal behavior for some people. For Laurey it was as abnormal as running naked through the streets. Rhea washed her hands and face, but didn't change out of the dotted pink dress she'd worn to work. She approached the dining room with caution.

Steam coiled from a rectangular baking dish set in the center of the table. Laurey was busily dishing broccoli spears onto the plates. She glanced up when she heard Rhea enter and said anxiously, "It smells good, doesn't it?"

"It smells heavenly," replied Rhea, taking her place and shaking out her napkin. "And looks terrific. How did you get the skin to crisp like that?"

"Oh, the wine. I forgot the wine. Go ahead and dish up, try it. Tell me what you think," she directed on a rush. She scooted out of her chair and into the kitchen.

Suspecting that nerves more than the wine were the cause of Laurey's abrupt exit, Rhea scooped a chicken breast covered in a creamy sauce with rice onto her plate. She hoped it tasted as good as it looked, because Laurey would be crushed if it didn't.

It did. Tender, creamy, and succulent. She swiveled in her seat to find Laurey eyeing her in trepidation. "It's marvelous, really delicious. Where did you get the recipe?"

A gigantic grin overwhelmed Laurey's narrow face. "Really? It's good? You're not just saying that?"

"Come, taste it yourself. It's absolutely delicious."

Swinging the wine bottle by the neck, she sauntered in. She filled Rhea's glass, then her own before sitting and sampling her food. Pleasure flooded her features.

"Not too bad, if I do say so myself."

"Pretty darn good actually. My compliments to the chef."

They clinked wineglasses and Laurey remarked, "It wasn't so hard. Except for the burned butter, I didn't really have any problems at all. Why do people think cooking is so hard?"

Rhea managed to smother her smile and asked, "What brought all this on anyway? When I first walked in, I thought I was in the wrong apartment."

"Oh, well." Laurey tried to pass it off with a nonchalant shrug.

"Really, this meal, the wine, the immaculate living room. I can't help wondering if you've had a lobotomy or have been possessed by an alien being or something. What gives?"

"It's no big deal. I just wanted to see what it was like, see if I could do it, that's all. How'd work go today?"

"Same old grind," answered Rhea, accepting that whatever her reasons for the sudden immersion into domesticity, Laurey didn't want to discuss it. She talked a bit about the latest gossip circling the office, then as Laurey dished up rainbow sherbet for dessert, inquired, "So who are you seeing these days? Who was the lucky man last night?"

A mound of rainbow sherbet landed with a plop on Rhea's lap. "Oh, God, I'm sorry!" Laurey exclaimed. "I'll clean it up."

Between them they got the sherbet off the dress, or, rather, Rhea got it off despite Laurey's flustered help. Her reassurances that neither she nor her dress had suffered any lasting damage eventually got through, and Laurey sagged into her chair with relief, saying one last time, "I'm sorry."

"Don't worry about it. Have some wine and relax. This guy you were with last night must have been pretty spectacular though. You came unglued faster than a kite in a high wind."

The ponytail swished as she shook her head. "I wasn't with anyone last night."

Rhea couldn't hide her surprise. "No one?"

"Nope. I stayed home. Which," said Laurey quickly, "you'd have known if you'd been here yourself. This Steve must be pretty spectacular himself."

One of these days, Rhea instantly promised herself, she'd learn how not to blush unless she wanted to blush. One of these days. At the moment she was flaming and she knew it. "Oh, he's okay. A nice guy."

"*Very* okay, judging by the shade of red you're turning. And here I was, beginning to wonder if he even really existed. All these months, and I've never even seen him."

"Funny, he's said the same thing about you. But it's little wonder that the two of you haven't met, you're hardly ever here. Or you weren't before . . ." She let that trail off significantly.

"Oh, well, it's gotten tiresome, always being on the go, constantly socializing. I've just thought I'd take it easy for a while, catch my breath."

"I can't imagine you without a date," said Rhea.

"There is this one guy I've seen a couple of times," Laurey said off-handedly. She immediately stood up and began stacking empty plates together. "So anyway, you never did tell me about your night, which apparently was a whole lot more exciting than mine."

"Nothing to tell; it wasn't what I'd call exciting."

"You mean you aren't going to cough up the details?" Rhea smiled and took the plates from Laurey's hands. "That's what I mean. Look, you cooked, let me do the cleaning up. It's only fair."

"I hope you weren't expecting an argument, 'cause you're not getting it. I've been dreaming of a long, hot bubble bath ever since I burned the butter. Have you ever smelled burning butter? Ugh!" With that, Laurey breezed out of the kitchen, leaving Rhea to rinse dishes and reflect about the night that she wouldn't call exciting.

In the weeks since Easter, Rhea had kept by her promise to try to open up to Steve. He'd kept by his not to pressure her. All in all, it had worked out well, at least from her point of view. She still had the relationship she liked, that of loving friends, without the demands of a more binding commitment. She felt more independent, more reliant on herself, and she found she liked it. In fact, she was discovering that she liked herself. That amazed her; she'd always lacked self-confidence, particularly in the past few years when Dave had left her feeling somehow unacceptable. The added weight and poor self-image hadn't bolstered her ego, and she was just now beginning to realize she really didn't look like she used to anymore.

She'd managed, awkwardly at first, to explain some of this to Steve. His calm acceptance, his continued reassurance that he cared for her, had helped her to see herself in this new light. For the first time in her life she felt sure of herself and of her appeal to a man.

Working a frothy lather of soap into the baking dish, Rhea thought about Steve and the previous night. She again decided she'd done the right thing. A slow, satisfied smile curved over her mouth. Yes, she'd definitely done the right thing last night.

He had appeared at the law firm just before closing time. He'd impressed Pat every bit as much as he'd once impressed Janice, and it was in a quite breathless voice that she called Rhea in the library to tell her he was waiting. The elation that had struck Rhea at being the object of envy when with Addison didn't even compare to the thrill she felt now. Like the man himself, her victory then had been hollow, unworthy. Now she felt warm and glowing with pride.

Steve was charming and very good-looking in a perfectly fitting dark blue suit that exactly matched the shade of his eyes when he was most passionately roused. The thought brought one of those rosy flushes to her face. She quickly introduced him to the receptionist, bid her good night, then giggled as she went out on Steve's arm.

"What's so amusing?"

Her blush deepened. She wasn't about to confess she was turned on by his suit and even less was she about to confess why! She managed to say casually, "Oh, I'm just thinking Pat'll probably never take another lunch break again. Look what she missed before!"

"Is there a compliment for me somewhere in that garbled bit of nonsense?"

Giving his arm a squeeze, she batted her eyelashes at him. "You bet there is, fella."

"I love you," he said, as if observing how warm the day was or how wet May had been, or something equally matter-of-fact. But his effect wasn't matter-of-fact at all. The tremors of happiness that surged through Rhea were extraordinary.

"What's the occasion? Why did you come pick me up?" she inquired, somehow achieving a normal tone.

"The occasion?" he echoed. The elevator pinged as he punched the down button. "How about the ten thousandth anniversary of the discovery of the wheel?"

"You always celebrate the discovery of the wheel?"

"Never miss it."

The elevator arrived with scarcely room left for them. They crammed in at the front, Steve putting his arm protectively about her shoulders. He bent his head and said in a voice for her alone, "I'm so glad, sweet, to know that you think my mere appearance constitutes a celebration."

She wrinkled her nose at him, feeling happier by the minute. When they emerged from the elevator, she hesitated, looking from one exit to another. "Where'd you park?"

"Ah, well, I meant to explain about that. I'm not exactly picking you up. It's more like you're picking me up. I need a ride home."

"Why? What happened? Did you have another accident?"

"I, my dear lady, have never had an accident," he informed her with exaggerated dignity. "Nothing's happened. But if we don't get out of the crush of outgoing traffic, something might. Now, where's your car parked?"

"It's a good thing for you I drove it today."

"You drive into work every day."

They walked the half block to the car park where Rhea always left her car. She extracted her keys from her purse and opened the passenger door first, holding it for him while he got in. As she took her place behind the wheel, he told her to turn in the direction opposite from the way toward home.

"I am now assuming," she said as she obeyed him, "that we are not going home."

"That's what I love about you, you're always right on top of the situation." He quirked his moustache over a suggestive grin and drawled, "Actually, I love it even more when you're right on top of me."

The image his words raised heated her blood to the boiling point. The fiery fermentation raced through her veins. She forced herself to concentrate on the rush-hour traffic jamming the streets. "Well, do you mind telling me just where we are going? It might help, seeing as how I'm doing the driving."

He complied, naming a popular restaurant featuring German, Swiss, and Austrian cuisine. She followed his instructions to get there, remarking dryly that it was kind of him to give her such advance warning about eating dinner out.

"There's got to be a few surprises in life, just to keep it interesting. Besides, I didn't know myself until a few hours ago. It was an impulse. You do know what they are, don't you?"

"But whenever I give in to them, I seem to end up regretting it. Don't you?"

"I never regret anything. It's a waste of time and energy." He led her into the restaurant. "It's disgustingly early for dinner out, but at least we'll beat the crowds."

"And have lots of time to work it off later," she pointed out, casting him a sultry look. "You know—exercise."

"Like I said, you're always right on top of things."

"Oh, not always. Sometimes I'm beneath too."

The headwaiter interrupted their banter. Following the tails of his tuxedo to a table, Rhea reviewed the conversation with a sense of amazement. Sexy banter was not her usual style by any means. She'd never considered herself sexy enough, nor wickedly witty enough to indulge in it. Somehow Steve just brought those things out in her.

Since meeting him, in fact, she'd changed a lot. Not just in her new figure and clothes, but in her attitudes, the way she responded to other people. Those changes had been more gradual, so gradual that she hadn't even realized they were taking place. She peeked at him from behind her menu. Maybe she'd been hesitating and resisting without reason. Her fears seemed groundless. Thus far, the changes appeared to have been for the best.

After ordering, Rhea leaned back in her chair and regarded him steadily. "Okay, give," she said. "There's something going on. This may have been an impulse, but something's behind it."

"Yes, yes, your perception, my dear, astounds me," he said in a terrible W.C. Fields imitation.

"Oh, that's awful."

"That bad, huh?"

"I'd hold my nose, but we're in public." She did, however, wag her finger at him. "But don't get off the point. What were you doing downtown anyway?"

"I had some business dealings to take care of, among them, this," he said, pulling a folded paper from his inside pocket. He handed it to her. "You're the first to know."

She unfolded the paper. It was a deed to a house. She didn't have to read the Colorado Springs address to know which house. "You bought it," she said.

"I did. I'm not sure if I'm crazy or not. But I couldn't let that house go up for sale. I bought it from my company."

"When are you moving?" she asked in a dead little voice.

"Hey, sweetheart, this isn't the reaction I expected."

She couldn't say anything. If she said anything, she

feared she'd burst into torrents of tears right there in the middle of the restaurant. Glasses clinked as he moved them out of the way to stretch his hand across to hers.

"I'm not moving for a long time to come, and if I were, it wouldn't be any reason for you to look like you've just lost your best friend."

"But you are my best friend," she said, her voice on the verge of being weepy.

"Rhea, you silly twit, I love you. Even if I move, it's not the end of our relationship. How could you think something so foolish?"

She stared down at the hand so warmly clasping hers, at the fine dark hairs dusting the back of it, at the lines etched in the knuckles, and knew a surge of emotions, the strongest of which was relief. "I guess," she said unsteadily, "because I'm a fool."

"Well, they say only fools fall in love, so maybe there's hope for me yet."

Her eyes leaped upward. He was smiling crookedly. Something in her softened, mellowed. Before she could seek it out to understand it, they were being served. He released her hand, commented easily that she'd be unable to find such authentic Alpine cuisine anywhere else in town, and the moment of her inner truth was irrevocably lost.

They talked lightly as they ate, decorating his house on an imaginary unlimited budget. The meal was, as he'd promised, outstanding. She had kassler ribbchen, a pork chop cooked in sauerkraut. He had jager schnitzel, a veal cutlet smothered in prepared vegetables. But once the plates were cleared away and both had ordered coffee in place of dessert, Steve reverted to the subject that had lain between them throughout.

"You could, you know," he said, "put all your fears to rest quite simply. When the time comes, you could move with me."

"It wouldn't be very practical, what with my job here in Denver and all."

"There would be other jobs in Colorado Springs."

"Now that's a chauvinist attitude. Let the little woman give up her job. After all, it's only a hobby, isn't it?"

He leaned an elbow on the table and tapped a fingernail against his coffee cup. "You know I don't think like that. I'm just saying you'll always come up with excuses, excuses that are only obstacles because you want them to be."

"Jobs for legal librarians aren't a dime a dozen, you know. Most firms don't have a separate librarian, only some of the larger, more prestigious firms."

He stared off into the distance. Rhea knew he wasn't admiring the old-fashioned ski equipment that provided the restaurant's decor. The bit of softness she'd felt earlier was gone, buried beneath the granite of her resentment. She dug the toe of her black pump into the carpet at her feet and wondered if it would always come back to this, the same old argument. Finally he skewed his gaze to her.

"All that talk of yours about fearing divorce, about needing to be certain, was just a blind. That's not the real problem, is it, Rhea?"

"I don't know. You seem to know so much, you tell me."

"The problem is your lack of confidence. Your inability to believe that someone can like you as you are, for the person you are. You're insecure and you're scared."

"Thank you for the analysis, *Herr Doktor.*"

"You're afraid of getting hurt, so you shut me out. I asked you to open up to me—"

"And I've tried very hard to do so."

"I know and I'm glad. It's helped me to know you, to understand you. But, Rhea, you've got to let me get closer, or we may drift completely apart."

"I don't see how we could get any closer," she muttered.

"Sometimes I wonder why I bother with you," he remarked with absolute calm.

It hurt her that he could say such a thing so calmly. Refusing to look at him, she burrowed her toe farther into the unseen carpet and curled her fingers around the handle of the coffee cup. "No one is forcing you to bother with me."

"No, and you're doing your damn level best to force me not to," he bit out.

This time she looked up at him. His face was set in anger. She realized he wasn't calm at all. He was just as angry, just as hurt as she was. Contrition instantly filled her. "Steve, I'm sorry. I'm being childish and rude and I don't want to fight with you. As little as I like to admit it, much of what you've said is true. I'm insecure. I find it hard to accept myself, though, honestly, it's not been so difficult lately. I do fear rejection. When I think I might get hurt, I withdraw. For that same reason I need to make my own decisions, to be in control of what happens in my life. I don't like to have decisions thrust on me; I've been through that before and it only made it harder for me to trust people."

Her breath and steam ran out all at once. She slumped slightly in her chair and fell silent. She felt exhausted. Revealing so much of herself in such an outpouring tired her. She heard the clatter as Steve replaced his cup in the saucer. She saw the shadows waver as he bent over the table toward her.

"All right, here's a decision to make all on your own. I'd like you to come to Chicago with me next week. Will you?"

"I—you mean, to meet your grandmother?"

He smiled at the patent panic throbbing in her voice. "Well, that, too, of course. But primarily to be with me, full-time, twenty-four hours a day for three days. To see just how compatible or incompatible we really are. And mainly to see if you can't get over this hesitation to let yourself love me."

She seized at that, would have seized anything to delay having to make the decision. "Let myself love you? Love isn't something you allow, is it? Doesn't love just happen, whether you want it to or not?"

"That may be true for some people, I don't know," he replied with an impatient shrug. "But I think for most people, and for myself, certainly, love is a decision. I knew I liked you, I was attracted to you, I decided to love you. And that's why I think we'd have a good chance of success together. I've decided to keep on loving you, so I'm going to work like hell to make it work. If you decided the same, we'd work together to solve any problems."

"That's an interesting view."

"And you've avoided the decision."

Sipping her coffee, she looked supremely tranquil while her mind pondered furiously what to do. Go or not go, she couldn't see clearly which was best.

"It's just a weekend, Rhea. No strings attached."

She smiled at that. "Hmmm. I think I've heard that line somewhere before."

He didn't smile. "Do you want to think on it, let me know in a couple of days?"

"No, I don't need to think on it," she said.

He flinched as if he'd been physically slapped and started to rise. "All right, then."

"I'll go with you," she gasped on an expulsion of pent-up breath. "I'll go with you to Chicago."

As if by magic, the mood reversed immediately. They left the restaurant laughing and touching with the eagerness of new lovers. The night had seemed filled with enchantment, their loving more special, a seal to an unspoken vow.

Rhea had made her decision and nothing could make her regret it.

CHAPTER SIXTEEN

Already Rhea was sorry she'd said she would go. She didn't enjoy traveling much at any time; she detested flying. The never-quite-ignored fear of crashing, the noise, the air pressure, the mind-boggling time it took, all wore her out. Even though it was only a couple of hours actual flight, it seemed to her as if she'd been trying to get to Chicago all her life. First there'd been the drive to the airport, then waiting around the airport, then finally the flight itself, and now, at long last, another airport to be got through, another drive. She felt frazzled to her last nerve.

"I can see we're not going to be traveling much. You look as if you're going to bark at babies and kick dogs," observed Steve with a low chuckle.

He, of course, looked as composed as ever. She glared at him, thinking with relish of plucking his moustache out hair by hair. His chuckle escalated into a laugh. A little of Rhea's hostility with the world in general was muted in the sound of it. She just wished she could get rid of her blasted headache.

It was raining when they stepped outside, their carry-on bags in hand. "We'll never get a taxi in this," said Rhea in a voice as dismal as the steady drizzle.

"Cheer up, pal, it's all arranged." Steve whisked her black case out of her hand and strode off into the heavy gray mist. Skipping around a puddle, she clutched her purse to her side and followed him. Head bent, muttering dire imprecations against the whole line of Bradleys, she didn't see that he'd stopped and she crashed into his back. He turned around, caught hold of her arm, shoved her forward, and the next thing she knew, she was seated on the plush burgundy upholstery of a private limousine.

"What's this?" she demanded when Steve slid in beside her.

"A limo," he answered.

"Don't play games with me, Bradley. Whose limo?"

"My grandmother's."

She'd already figured that out, of course, but her heart sank to hear it just the same. He hadn't warned her that they were going to visit a woman with limousines and capped chauffeurs at her disposal. The car pulled smoothly away, skirting the clogged traffic of O'Hare with expertise. Rhea slumped back against the seat and tried to prepare herself.

After hearing Steve's good-natured descriptions of the tyrannical matriarch, she hadn't expected a sweet, apple-cheeked grandmotherly type of woman. But his respect and affection for his grandmother always shone through his jokes, and Rhea had envisioned a bossy, but loving, buxom woman who'd constantly press food upon her. Feeling the velvety ribbing in the cushion beneath her, she threw that image out and decided the only thing she could do was hope for the best. There was no turning back now.

His hand found hers on the velvety seat and clasped it, offering her silent comfort. She took it gratefully. The weekend would go fine. After all, she had Steve there to support her. She gazed out the window, but couldn't see anything through the rain. which seemed to have gotten harder just since they'd landed. Occasionally lights snaked like bright oil over the streets, coronas shone around passing headlights, and then darkness would again obscure the world beyond the window.

They turned. She had the impression of stone or iron

towers. Wind flapped the leaves of the trees on both sides of the narrow road. The limo swung around a wide curve, then slowed to a stop. Her door was opened. A man stood waiting with an umbrella. She took the hand he offered and decided she would pluck out Steve's moustache after all. How dare he not prepare her for this! Smiling sweetly at the man with the umbrella, she gripped her purse tightly and mounted a series of semi-circular stone steps to a colonnaded portico. There Steve dismissed the man with a nod, took her arm, and led her through a pair of double doors that must have been built for kin of Goliath. She was still craning her neck back to look up to the lintel beam, when a discreet cough brought her head down with a snap.

A young, dark-featured man in plain black slacks and white shirt lifted her cotton raincoat from her shoulders. As he removed Steve's trench coat he said, "Mrs. B. is waiting for you in her private parlor."

"Thank you, Antonio," said Steve, once again taking Rhea's arm and propelling her along.

"Was that the butler?" she whispered on a hiss. "I thought butlers were supposed to be old."

Steve glanced down at her with a gleaming smile. "That's my grandmother's latest 'all-jobs' boy. She takes them on in their early teens and keeps them right on through college."

Rhea digested that. "You mean she pays for their education, that kind of thing?"

"Yup. They do errands, whatever, for her. She pays a salary, educates them, in a way becomes a surrogate parent. Many of them haven't had any parents. Or haven't wanted the ones they had."

The image of the buxom, bossy, loving lady came back, complete with apple-cheeks. Her relief was short-lived. The image crumpled as they passed through an open door. Flames leaped within a gray marble fireplace, chasing shadows from a wing chair and casting red-gold halos over hair that reminded Rhea of snow-angel wisps, like the hair of the angels at the top of the Christmas tree when she was a child. The figure within the chair was small, slight, as delicate as porcelain. Every feature was elegantly molded on her narrow face. Bluish veins traversed the hands she held out in greeting. She rose as they entered, and Rhea had to bite back a plea not to do so. The woman didn't look as if she had the strength to stay on her feet.

"So this, Stephen, is the child you remodeled," she said in a surprisingly strong voice for her frail body. "I can't properly say, of course, but it appears you did well enough."

There simply weren't words for Rhea to express what she was feeling. The shock, the outrage, the hurt, that Steve had told his grandmother about their agreement. A slim hope that somehow somebody else had in some fantastic way spread the story died as Steve replied, "Yes, Lollie, this is Rhea."

The pride in his voice was unmistakable. It shook Rhea badly. He was proud of his success in remaking her. He was proud of his big accomplishment. She smiled weakly at Mrs. Bradley and murmured, "Hello."

"You're the project that's had Stephen ignoring me. I knew it wasn't one of those houses of his, and it's plain to see I was right."

"Yes," said Rhea.

"I've been very anxious to meet you, my girl." She took her chair again and swirled her hand in Rhea's direction. "Now, turn around, let me look at you. How much weight did you say she'd lost, Stephen?"

Rhea turned, but she was gritting her teeth to keep from shouting at Steve. She felt like she was the object of attention at a session of Show-and-Tell. Her semi-full pinstripe skirt flared gently, then stilled as she came to a halt.

"Twenty pounds. She lost most of that the first two months," Steve said, sounding as if he were describing

Exhibit A to the court. "But I've had to watch her to make certain she's eating enough not to lose any more. She's been getting too thin."

"She looks fine to me," repeated Mrs. Bradley in a ringing tone of pronouncement. Steve beamed. Rhea barely refrained from snarling at them both. She wondered when she'd be ordered to open her mouth to let them check her teeth. "She looks strong and fit, not at all like poor Tamara."

"She's fit because we've been exercising together," explained Steve.

"Oh?"

Mrs. Bradley packed more into that single syllable than Rhea had crammed into her case. Rhea felt impelled to defend herself. "He means running, Mrs. Bradley. We've been *running* together."

"So you like running, do you, child?"

"I hate running," she bit out.

"She means, Lollie, that she hated it in the beginning."

"I hate it now," she insisted, and was thrown slightly off-balance by the sudden gleam in Lollie's pale blue eyes.

"My granddaughter Louisa exercises regularly," she remarked in a placid manner at odds with the light in her gaze. She lifted a tiny silver and crystal bell and rang it sharply. "Have you eaten, Stephen?"

"A snack on the flight."

"We shall dine at eight thirty then. Show them their rooms, Antonio, and see that Miss Nichols has a bath drawn."

Rhea glanced back as they were led out. Eyes closed, hands resting on her lap, Mrs. Bradley sat with her angel-fine hair crushed into the salmon-striped wing of the chair. She looked delicately fragile. Rhea thought she was about as fragile as a Mack truck.

Determined as she was not to gawk at anything else in the house—the only thing that had saved her from falling all over the antiques in the private parlor had been her anger; she'd been too upset to care about Louis XVI chairs or Sèvres figurines—Rhea simply couldn't help swiveling her eyes this way and that as they mounted a curving staircase. The parquet entry below was larger than her entire apartment back in Denver and more magnificently furnished in its few stands, scroll-back chairs, and grandfather clock than many museums.

With a flash of white teeth Antonio ushered her through a door on the second floor. Like the parlor, the bedroom was comfortably, if expensively decorated. A black lacquer secretaire, a marble-topped marquetry vanity, and a canopied four-poster were the outstanding features of the room. Her black case stood inside a walk-in closet. She could see her dresses were already hung. She wandered aimlessly, checked a door, and discovered an enormous bathroom with a sunken marble bath. She went back and sat on the edge of the bed. She knew she should be changing for dinner—wasn't that what they always did in the movies?—but she was still trying to sort out what was happening.

The scene downstairs with Steve and his grandmother had greatly upset her, upset her because to her view it proved what she'd feared for so long. It proved that her main appeal to Steve was the fact that he'd made her what she was. As with the house in Colorado Springs, he was proud of his accomplishment. A heavy sadness shrouded her spirit. Even her anger at him couldn't be sustained in the face of her depression.

There was a light tap on a door just beyond the door to the bath. She hadn't got that far in her tour. Hoping it wasn't a maid appearing to dress her, and disgusted at the tremulousness of her voice, she squeaked, "Yes? Come in?"

Steve stuck his head around the doorframe. "Is it safe? Are you going to throw things at me?"

221

As dejected and distressed as she was, Rhea couldn't help responding to the teasing grin and the sparkling eyes. There was simply no way she could remain angry at him, ever, no matter what he did, not when he smiled at her like that. She sighed heavily. "No, but you'd deserve it if I did."

"I know," he said as he came in.

"Why didn't you tell me about this? Why didn't you warn me what I was getting into?"

"I was afraid you wouldn't come."

"You're not afraid of anything, least of all me." She traced the golden fleur-de-lis in the royal blue bedspread at her fingertips. "It wasn't fair, bringing me into all this. I had no idea you had such wealth."

"It's not mine, it's my grandmother's. I know it wasn't fair, Rhea, but I really did think you'd back out. I figured you'd get some crazy notion about not being sophisticated enough or some such stupid thing and refuse to come. And I very much wanted you to come."

She wanted to ask why it meant so much, but asked instead, "What are you doing out in Denver remodeling old houses when you could be here, living in this?"

He slid onto the bed beside her. Without touching her hand, his fingers began outlining the flower behind hers. "This isn't my home, Rhea. Besides which, you should know by now I'm not the sort of man to live off another's pickings. I want to earn my way in life. That was another of those things about me that Tammie couldn't understand. She thought she'd reached Easy Street when she married me. But we've all earned our own way, Lou, Warren, Jennette and me. Even if we'd been inclined to live off our grandmother's fortune, Lollie doesn't take to parasites."

His fingers were inching closer to hers. She could feel the heat radiating from them. "Why do you call her Lollie? It's such an informal name. That surprised me, too, because you've always been so formal, calling her Grandmother."

His chuckle wafted remarkably close to her ear. "It's one of Lollie's iron edicts that we call her only Lollie here, in this house. To the world out there, she's Mrs. Bradley or Grandmother. She always said she had an image to protect."

"And Lollie?" she asked on a whisper. His fingers now grazed hers with each passing of the pattern on the spread.

"She always had lollipops in her pocket for the children. I'm told that as a baby, Lou would run to her, saying 'Lollie, lollie,' meaning the lollipop, but it got mixed in her mind to mean grandmother, too, and it stuck. We all called her that."

"What's her real name?"

"Elizabeth Louise." He put his hand over hers, stilling the motion of it. He pressed his mouth against the side of her neck. He nuzzled up to her ear and said hoarsely, "I didn't come in here to talk about my grandmother. I wanted to convince you to forgive me. To tell you I love you."

The susurration of his words curled down the rounded collar of her gray crepe blouse. She wanted to demand an explanation of the scene downstairs; she wanted to hear him explain his grandmother's devastating greeting, but that warm coil of breath winding down her neck distracted her. She turned her head, intending to tell him to stop it.

Never one to let opportunity pass him by, Steve swooped to take command of Rhea's lips. Sweet and coaxing, his mouth moved gently over hers. Like a drug pervading her blood, his kiss infused her with a dreamy euphoria. She forgot how insulted she'd felt. She forgot her hurt, her doubts. She opened her lips fully to his and remembered only the joy of his kisses.

Her hands slid up into his hair, tickling the nape of his

223

neck and the sensitive spot behind his ears. He groaned and his kiss was no longer sweet and coaxing. It was full-bodied, demanding, and utterly intoxicating. Tangled together in passion, mindful only of the scent, the feel, the taste of each other, they tumbled back onto the plump mattress.

A rapid rat-a-tat-tat was followed by a flinging of the door. "Tony says you might like a bath—oh, sorry!"

They sprang upright, gazing in bemused surprise at the intruder. Steve slowly smiled as Rhea flushed furiously. The young woman displayed a sparkling set of healthy teeth in a cheerful grin. "Bad timing, huh? You want me to come back later?"

Straightening, Steve said, "No, it's time we got ready. I'll leave you in Katy's hands, Rhea."

He was up and gone before Rhea had even assimilated what had happened. She focused on the pert pixie striding toward her, waves of nut-brown hair flying in mischievous disarray with each step. Was this a maid? Weren't maids silent and stiff? Or at least, not full of bubbly impudence?

"Next time I'll pause after knocking," Katy was saying with a knowing wink. "Now, would you like a bath? You look like you could use one, not that you look dirty, just worn out. I'll get it going. Anything else you'd like?" she called out from the cavern of the bathroom where the sound of splashing water was already echoing.

The aftereffect of the euphoria was setting in. Rather than feeling joyful, Rhea felt listlessly dull. And her head-ache was back in full force. "Aspirin," she said feebly. "Could I have some aspirin?"

Her empty soup bowl was replaced with a plate of thinly sliced prime beef covered in brown sauce, peas, and yellow rice. Rhea glanced at the man serving them. At least, she thought, he looked like her idea of a servant. He was tall, solemn, and silently efficient. He had a pinched-in mouth, and eyes that never saw anything they weren't supposed to.

"Stephen has purchased a house. Have you seen it, Rhea?"

She opened her mouth to reply, but Steve said first, "I took Rhea there before I bought it, Lollie. In fact, she helped me select the wallpaper for the master bedroom."

With unnecessary force, Rhea speared a forkful of beef. She thought longingly of spearing her fork into the man seated across from her. But fearing it wouldn't be considered proper etiquette to stick her fork into a dinner companion, she nobly refrained.

Within the enormous cavity of the formal dining room, they were grouped at one end of a table long enough to seat both Houses of Congress, Lollie at the head, with Steve to her right and Rhea to her left. But Rhea thought she might as well not have been present at all. Every time his grandmother addressed a question to her, Steve leaped in with the answer, as if he doubted Rhea's ability to speak without spitting food on the hand-embroidered linen. Dave had always done her speaking for her, too, and Rhea hated it. She could, she mentally insisted to herself, converse quite well when given the opportunity. Though she'd begun the meal in a better frame of mind, refreshed by the bath and change to her ruffled violet chiffon, the beneficial effects had long since worn off. Feeling her head begin to throb again, she jammed the beef into her mouth and chewed vigorously.

"Victorian, didn't you say, Stephen? And tell me, did you like the house, Rhea?"

"Yes, she—"

Rhea gulped and rushed in, "I did like it, Mrs. Bradley. I much admired the work Steve and his crew had done." Over the Baccarat wine decanter, she gleamed in triumph at him. He flashed a smile of approval, as much as saying

225

"well done" to a puppy. Rhea's blood pressure shot upward.

"Do you like old-fashioned houses, then? Tamara, of course, detested them. Although she admired my home a great deal."

"I can't say that I like this or that type of house. Like people, houses have individual personalities and I respond to houses with warm, loving personalities."

Those pale blue eyes shone brightly through the muted light of the branched, gold-leaf chandelier. After a moment, Lollie swerved her gaze to Steve. "She is quite charming, Stephen."

"I think so," he said, and there was that ringing pride again, the one that tolled in Rhea's ears like a death knell.

"Why haven't you taken her to meet Louisa? I think Louisa would like her very well. Has Stephen told you that Louisa once shoved Tamara fully clothed into a swimming pool? Louisa was seven months pregnant at the time too. I, of course, wasn't there to see it," she said a shade wistfully.

The hint of a genuine smile touched Rhea's lips. "No, he—"

"I don't really think Rhea wants to hear about Tammie, Grandmother," cut in Steve. He fiddled with his fork. It pinged sharply against the bone china. "That's ancient history and best forgotten."

Listening to that steady ping, ping, ping, a new doubt wormed its way into Rhea's mind. His harsh tone, his nervous gesture, indicated a depth of feeling toward Tammie she hadn't expected still existed. Was he still, deep down, in love with his former wife? She didn't really believe that, but he was behaving so unlike himself, she didn't know what to think.

"Tell me again how you met Rhea," commanded Lollie, and with a chuckle, he did so.

Rhea remained silent throughout the narrative, eating

226

her way determinedly through food she never tasted. Her doubts soon gave way to another charge of animosity. With mounting irritation she wondered why he'd been so insistent about her coming. He was talking about her now as if she weren't there. She wished she'd asked Katy for a dozen bottles of aspirin. She could see she was going to need them to make it through the next two days.

She dimly realized her companions were silent. She looked up. They were looking at her. "Um, pardon, I didn't hear what you said," she mumbled.

"Lollie asked if you'd brought your glasses, Rhea. She'd like to see how you look in them."

Her lips tightened in what she hoped passed for a smile. What was he, their translator? Deliberately turning her head to Lollie, she said, "Yes, I have my glasses with me."

"Stephen tells me he doesn't think you need the contact lenses."

"Well, as I've told Stephen," said Rhea sweetly, "I like them, and I'm going to continue to wear them."

"Blessed with perfect vision, it's difficult for someone like Stephen to fully understand the problems of poor sight. His concern for you might very well be misguided."

It was a gentle reproof, but a reproof nonetheless. Surprisingly, for she'd felt she was beginning to detest the older woman, with her probing questions and pronouncements, Rhea realized she didn't want Lollie to think badly of her. She shifted restlessly on her chair. Would this meal never end?

Through fruit compote and coffee, Rhea sat quietly. She allowed Steve to do her talking for her. She glued a stiff smile in place and secretly seethed. She yearned to get away from this table, to get alone with Steve, where she could give him a piece, a very large piece, of her mind.

But when at last Lollie signaled the end of the meal by rising from her chair, Rhea's elation was momentary. Instead of being allowed to escape to the privacy of their rooms upstairs, they returned to the parlor. Steve and Rhea sat side-by-side on a navy blue sofa bespattered with orchids the same shade of salmon pink as the wing chair Lollie again occupied. The conversation at first showed signs of improvement. Lollie inquired about Rhea's family, a question Steve couldn't properly answer for her, so she talked about her parents, her brother, her childhood and warmed toward Lollie as she interjected comments and questions that indicated a true interest in what she was saying. But gradually Steve and his grandmother began talking about their family, friends, people, and events Rhea didn't know, and she once again took the role of silent listener, feeling almost like an eavesdropper.

A yawn caught her by surprise. Seeing it, Steve chuckled tenderly. "Have we been that boring?"

"Don't tease her, Stephen. She's worn out with traveling and meeting an old inquisitive woman. Take her up to bed and let her get some rest."

"Oh, no, I—" Rhea protested automatically, wanting desperately to go on up to bed.

"Lollie's right. You don't need to keep yourself awake just to listen to us reminiscing. Excuse me a minute, Lollie."

He stood, grasped her hands, and lifted her to her feet. The ruffled hem of her dress rustled about her knees. His palm lay flat against the small of her back as he guided her toward the staircase. For once Rhea received neither comfort nor thrills from the warmth of his touch. All she could think about was how he was going to make her wait still longer to talk to him. At the foot of the stairs, she pulled away from him, saying flatly, "I don't need to be walked to my room, thank you."

"You're sure? You won't get lost?"

How she kept from screaming at him, Rhea didn't know. Had he always thought her this witless, or was he coming to feel this way only upon longer acquaintance with her? In a voice of deadly frost she assured him she would not get lost. She turned and set a foot on the first step.

"Rhea?"

She paused, but didn't look at him. "Yes?"

"You've been wonderful. Lollie's been utterly charmed."

"I'm so glad."

He was on the step beside her, frowning. "Are you okay? Is something wrong?"

Out of the corner of her eye she saw a figure move in the shadows and knew she couldn't confront him here. So she said on a sigh, "No, I'm tired and I've a bit of a headache, that's all."

"You're sure?" And when she again reassured him, he smiled, kissed her forehead lightly, and told her he'd be up very soon. "I just want to say good night to Lollie."

Upstairs, curled into a speck of the massive mattress, Rhea resolved to wait for him. She'd cracked open the connecting door so she'd see the light when he entered his room. There was so much she had to say, so many explanations she needed to hear. The room was opaquely dark and cloister quiet. She couldn't even hear the ticking of the ormolu clock that decorated the top of the vanity. And after a time, still waiting for Steve to appear, she couldn't even hear the sound of her own breathing.

CHAPTER SEVENTEEN

"Can I help you, miss?"

Rhea jumped and whirled. The stranger wore a rubberized olive apron and a friendly smile. Her heartbeat slowed and she said, "Yes, I—I was looking for the kitchen. To make a cup of coffee," she added quickly at his evident surprise.

"Ah, yes, I see," he said kindly. He tapped the top of his shiny pink bald head and told her to follow him. She did. She ended up in a small, airy dining room, with nothing like the stifling formality of the room they'd dined in the previous night. "Now, you just sit yourself and wait here," he instructed, then vanished.

A multipaned window looked out over a meticulously maintained lawn. Lushly leafed trees and bright sprays of flowers dotted the landscape. Through the gray sky, daubs of blue glimmered, giving hope of sunshine to come. She turned away from the view and sat at the cherrywood table with carved legs tipped in brass that in her home would have been in the formal dining room. Propping her chin on her fists, she tried not to think about Steve.

That, of course, was a fruitless goal. He'd been in her thoughts from the instant she'd awakened. Her eyes had opened, she'd seen the haze of light through the curtains, and she'd thought, *he didn't come.*

Now she thought of him, and a heavy sense of foreboding settled over her. Last night he'd revealed to her just how right she'd been to keep such tight reins on their relationship. He had shown her that he thought as little of her as Dave ever had. He had shown her that his main interest in her stemmed from the work he'd done in getting her in shape; a "project" his grandmother had called her and accurately compared her to one of his houses. Steve didn't love her, he loved his project. And the way she saw it, no matter how much they might be attracted to each other, their relationship was doomed to fail.

She was in the process of venting a gloomy sigh when the friendly little man with the apron and smile came in. He bore a tray with a silver coffee urn, china cups, and a plate of aromatic croissants. He set it down, saying cheerfully, "Here you are, miss. Now, tomorrow, just push that buzzer in the wall there by the buffet. They'll hear it in the kitchen and get you fixed up."

Even before her thanks were uttered, he was gone again. She discovered butter and an assortment of jams and jellies behind the urn. Although she wasn't the least bit hungry, it gave her something to do besides feel sorry for herself, so she broke off a crumbly section of croissant and buttered it. Then she found herself adding rhubarb preserves, and before she knew it, she was starting in on her second croissant.

You're eating out of depression, not hunger, Rhea Marie, and that's stupid, she scolded herself as she lavished butter on the pastry. *This is how you got fat in the first place.*

But it tasted soft and savory and since she'd buttered it, she reasoned that she might as well eat all of it. She was debating about a third when the door again opened and Steve sauntered in.

"Mornin', sweetheart. You have jam on your cheek," he said with, to her view, misplaced cheer.

She put her hand up to rub it off, but he caught it, saying, "Allow me." He bent to kiss her. She quickly averted her head and his mouth landed on the shell of her

231

ear. He shot her a puzzled look as he slowly straightened. She very deliberately wiped the jam from her cheek. "Good morning," she said coldly.

He moved to take the seat at her left. As he poured himself a cup of coffee, he commented, "I like that jumpsuit."

"You should. You picked it out."

The cup returned to its saucer with a crack. "Okay, let's have it. What's wrong? Are you still mad because I didn't warn you what to expect? I apolo—"

"You didn't come into my room last night," she said, and rather feared it had a childish ring to it.

The frown left him as suddenly as it'd appeared. "Of course I did. But you were sleeping so soundly I decided not to disturb you. I thought you needed your rest more than you needed me."

"Oh," she said.

"I promise next time I'll wake you," he offered, trying out a smile on her.

She stared at the strawberry vines twisting over her cup, took a deep breath, and exhaled it in a burst as a brass pedestal clock directly behind her chimed, jangling her eardrum and nerves equally.

"Oh, damn," muttered Steve, finishing his coffee on a gulp. "We've got to run. I didn't realize it was so close to ten."

"But, I—we, Steve, we need to talk," sputtered Rhea.

He was hauling her out of her chair and thrusting her toward the door. "We'll have to talk later. Lollie told me to be ready to leave no later than ten."

"Leave?" she repeated feebly. Was this how Alice had felt when she'd fallen into Wonderland?

"We're going out for some visits. In a more old-fashioned age, we'd be going on a round of morning calls. She wants to show us off to her friends."

"Oh, but—"

"You look fine. Brush your hair, dab on some makeup, and I'll be back to get you in about five minutes." He pushed her into her bedroom, then pulled her back out. "By the way, pal, I love you," he added with a smacking kiss that echoed long after he'd disappeared into his own room.

Sitting at the vanity, she obediently brushed her hair and dabbed on her makeup. She decided that overall, she was glad she'd been interrupted. She decided that maybe she hadn't been giving him a fair chance. She'd been edgy and tired the night before. He loved her; surely she cared enough for him to make an effort for their relationship.

So she greeted him with a real smile of welcome when he returned in the promised five minutes. He gathered her up in a hug and whispered, "I'm beginning to think we should let Lollie go without us."

"Oh? And what did you have in mind to fill the day?"

"I'm sure we could find a way to entertain ourselves. . . ."

They entertained themselves for a very breathless ten minutes and then had to spend another two straightening clothes and combing hair. Standing behind her as they hastily primped before the mirror, Steve asked with supreme casualness, "What do you think of Lollie? Do you like her?"

The reflection of her eyes met the reflection of his. She saw tiny pinpoints in the deep, deep blue. She also saw that her answer mattered to him very much. "Of course I like her. She's not at all what I pictured—"

"Which was?"

"Part army sergeant, part Mrs. Santa Claus," she said promptly, and he laughed.

Her hopes that he'd leave it at that were dashed as he tossed his comb on the vanity top and prodded her. "Tell me what you do think."

"I can't really say what I think of her after such a short

time, but it's obvious how deeply she cares about you. I think she's autocratic and perhaps a bit insensitive, and I don't think she'd be easy to understand. She's a very complex woman."

"That's the way I like my women," he said with a grin as he ruffled the hair she'd just brushed into place.

And Rhea silently vowed to keep him grinning like that all day.

Their tardy appearance in Lollie's parlor didn't pass by unnoticed.

"I believe I said, although I may be mistaken, of course, but I was nearly certain I'd said ten o'clock. Perhaps I said ten thirty?"

"You know quite well you said ten," said Steve, pressing a kiss on the papery cheek she proffered.

"I thought I had," she said with satisfaction. She looked past his broad shoulder to where Rhea stood nervously retying the sash belt on her sunflower-yellow jumpsuit. "Good morning, child, did you sleep well?"

"Yes, I did, thank you."

"Good," said Lollie, rising. She wore a simple black suit with a straight skirt and waist-length jacket, and a pleated-front white blouse that thinned her slender figure to a single frail reed. She paused to cover her wispy white hair with a black pillbox hat and to collect a black purse and gloves. "Come along," she directed as she passed out of the parlor. "We're late enough as it is."

Exchanging a mutually guilty smile, Steve and Rhea followed her out. Once in the limousine, Lollie commented, as if continuing last night's conversation without a pause, "You selected the wallpaper for the master bedroom of Steve's house; did you help with any of the other decorating?"

"No, I—"

"She didn't even realize she was making the selection that day, Lollie. I just asked her for an opinion and she

234

gave it. She claims she doesn't have a knack for decorating, but it was a good choice."

"I've often found that the very things people belittle themselves about are the things they're best at. Describe this paper to me."

Steve obliged her and went on to describe other papers that had been used in the old house to retain the Victorian flavor. After a time, Lollie murmured that it sounded like a home for a family, not a bachelor, then abruptly said, "Tell me, Rhea, have you ever thought of having a family?"

"Oh, well, I'm not married," she stumbled in reply.

"That doesn't mean you haven't given the matter thought. I've haven't died yet, but I think about it, I think about it."

"You'll be around forever, Lollie."

"Nothing lasts forever, Stephen."

"I don't really think I agree with that," he countered, and launched into a philosophical debate during which Rhea seemed to have been forgotten by the other occupants in the limousine.

The rest of the ride proceeded along much the same lines. More often than not, Steve would answer questions on her behalf or the pair of them would get into a discussion and Rhea would be left to stare out at the view. At least there was a view to stare at today. Primarily for her benefit, they drove along the lakefront, where the choppy waters of Lake Michigan melted into the blue-gray of the overcast sky. The closer they got to the heart of Chicago, the more there was to see, and both Steve and Lollie took turns pointing out items of interest. The Sears Tower, the tallest building in the world; Marshall Field's landmark department store, though Lollie insisted it wasn't the store it used to be; and, of course, all the outdoor sculptures by Picasso, Miró, Calder, and others that were an integral part of the city. Lollie indicated her disdain for such art with a slight sniff for each.

After this whirlwind auto tour, they went to the home of Lollie's oldest friend, Frieda Meyer, where they were greeted with exuberant squeezes and loud laughter.

"Ah, Stephen, you get more handsome every time I see you, which isn't often enough these days," declared the short, stout woman who utterly fulfilled Rhea's image of a grandmother. Her bosom and hips were expansive, her hair a gray uncontrollable frizz, her mouth generous and constantly moving. "And who's this?" she cried, catching Rhea in a bear hug. "Well, now I see why you keep yourself hidden out there in the mountains! You don't deserve her, Stephen, I see that at a glance."

"Don't give her ideas, Aunt Frieda. She's full of enough ideas as it is."

"And isn't that what you need? A woman with some ideas in her head and not empty space like that—"

"Rhea will be thinking we haven't any proper manners here in Chicago," interrupted Lollie. She made the formal introductions, then instructed Rhea to sit down in Frieda's not quite shabby living room while Steve poured lemonade and Frieda served cucumber sandwiches. Rhea fleetingly thought of disobeying to help serve, but mindful of her decision to make an effort for Steve, she sat in an armchair more comfortable than stylish.

The room and its furnishings were a lot like Frieda herself—overstuffed and charming. Though he'd called her "aunt," she wasn't a blood relation, she was more like a godparent, Steve explained during one of Frieda's infrequent pauses for breath.

"Ha! And lucky for you! I could've been your grandmother and if I was your grandmother there'd be an end to this dillydallying. Whoever heard of a healthy man like you unmarried at your age?"

"You can't say I haven't been married, Aunt Frieda."

"Ah, well, *that* marriage was hardly a marriage at all. That doesn't count, not like a real marriage with babies and a wife beside you. Now, that's a marriage, Stephen, and it's time you—"

"Rhea, refill my lemonade," ordered Lollie. "The kitchen is the second door to the left. Thank you, dear."

She wasn't disturbed by the abrupt command so much as she was by the fact that when she returned, Frieda was sitting quietly, looking somewhat abashed. After listening for a few minutes to Steve tell Frieda about his new house, Rhea grabbed the first opportunity to ask Frieda how she and Lollie had met. Frieda's round cheeks puffed out as her face lit up and she launched into an explanation. Within the next hour Rhea was charmed by a bubbly history of Frieda's life as well as a vivid description of Steve as a boy. "Mischievous," claimed Frieda, "always into something, that boy."

Gradually, though, Rhea began to feel resentment build as once again Steve responded to whatever Frieda asked of her. Worse, Lollie began to tell Frieda about Rhea's family, as if Rhea were incapable of doing so herself. By the end of the visit, her nerves were frayed, a jagged edge that ripped more and more as the day progressed.

From Frieda's they went to another friend's, then another's, and finally a third, where several women were lying in wait for them. "My garden club," said Lollie in an aside to Rhea as they entered the plushly decorated ultramodern home. The aggravating pattern had been repeated at each stop. But where Frieda had charmed Rhea into resolutely ignoring her fraying nerves, Lollie's other friends only exacerbated them.

Her irritation at being constantly interrupted and spoken for soon gave way to another, far more disturbing problem. She slowly realized she was being greeted not as a friend, not even as a girl friend. She was being greeted as a future member of the Bradley family. An imminent

237

wedding seemed to be a widespread assumption among Lollie's acquaintances, that much was plain in all the sidelong glances and knowing smiles Rhea received. Talk of a wedding, however, was conspicuously absent. She recalled how Frieda's talk of marriage had been interrupted and how quiet Frieda had been when she'd come back from the kitchen. Putting two and two together, Rhea came up seeing red.

Seizing the first opportunity, she confronted Steve about it. Seated together on the short end of a stiff L-shaped couch, teacups precariously balanced on their knees, she whispered under the cover of the noisy conversation surrounding them, "Will you please tell me what's been going on? Why do all these women seem to think we're engaged or something?"

"Nobody thinks anything of the sort," he replied.

"Well, they certainly don't think I'm your jogging partner," she snapped under her breath. "In case you hadn't noticed it, I've been squeezed more today than Mr. Whipple's Charmin."

He leaned close to her ear. "That's because you're so squeezably soft," he said.

"This isn't," she declared coldly, "funny."

"I wasn't being funny. I was being truthful. You are squeezably soft. Especially in certain unmentionable places."

She was not amused. She was tired of being told what to do, of having someone else answer questions addressed to her, and most of all, of being the object of sly looks and subdued whispers. She had a headache. She also had a big fear that between them, Lollie and Steve were trying to run roughshod over her, that she was being pressured into a situation she didn't want. It all made her rather testy. She glared at him over her teacup. He sighed and set his cup aside.

"I don't see what you expect me to do." He spoke

238

calmly, unhurriedly. From a distance, it probably looked as if they were discussing the weather. "It's only natural for them to conjecture such things when you fly all the way from Denver with me. I can't exactly stand up and announce that you and I are just sleeping together."

Her cup rattled in its saucer as she shook with anger. She was about to tell him that was precisely what she expected him to do when Lollie loomed before them, wraithlike and pale.

"I'm sorry, my dears, but we must be going. It's bothersome, but at my age if I don't get a nap before evening, I can't last through dinner."

He removed Rhea's clattering cup from her hands and, taking her hand within one of his, rose to leave in Lollie's graceful wake. She could feel his distress in his palm, and once again her confused emotions blurred into an indistinct tangle. Early this morning she'd been certain he didn't, he couldn't, really love her, but as soon as he'd said he did, she'd wavered. It was the same now. Her conviction that he'd been deliberately trying to pressure her was obscured in the rigid anxiety of his clasp. She no longer knew what to think and so, unable to fight her way through the muddle, she simply pushed it all out of her mind and gave herself up to her headache.

By the time they got home, her head was bursting with pain. Even if she'd felt like unraveling any of her problems, she wouldn't have been able to through the headache. So when Lollie went to her room for her late-day nap, Rhea did the same. Steve immediately followed her.

"Are you really meaning to take a nap, or are you just doing this to avoid me?" he demanded quietly.

"I'm really, truly going to nap. My head is killing me." She rubbed her temples and tried to focus on him through her pain. "I'd talk to you if I could, Steve. I've been wanting to talk to you all day, but I can't, I really can't."

He must have believed her, for the next thing she knew

she was being lifted and carried to the bed. He lay her down gently, then walked away. She hurt too much to see where he'd gone. Suddenly he was beside her again.

"Sit up, Rhea," he commanded softly.

She groggily sat up. He held her contact lens case and she removed her lenses. He handed her aspirin with a glass of water and she swallowed. He nudged her and she toppled backward. She heard the swishing as he closed the drapes, felt soothing darkness steal over the room. She was dozing to the sound of his footsteps when she felt a cool, damp cloth on her forehead. She opened her eyes and fuzzily saw the gleam of a rueful smile.

"Poor Rhea. This trip has been a disaster for you."

"Un-uh," she started to object, but he firmly shushed her. This was one order she didn't mind obeying. She closed her eyes and let the moist coolness seep through her brow.

The knot in her belt was loosened, her shoes removed. The bed sagged with Steve's weight as he sat beside her. His fingers rhythmically massaged her temple, comforting, easing, lulling her to a relaxed state. She murmured her thanks, but he demurred.

"No need to thank me. I feel it's partially my fault for getting you into it. But I honestly didn't realize what we were in for, or I'd never have let Lollie drag us all over town like that. I could've cheerfully throttled her by the time we arrived at the damn garden club party. I really just wanted you to meet Frieda."

"I liked her . . ." she mumbled sleepily. His fingers felt so good.

"She liked you too. I'll probably be hearing a catalogue of your sterling qualities for the next decade. In fact, everybody liked you. I don't know about Peoria, but you sure were a hit in Chicago, pal."

I don't see how, she thought, but never managed to get it uttered. *Nobody talked to me, nobody heard me talk.*

"Lollie was very proud of you, did you know that? Every time one of her friends said what a nice girl you were, she puffed up and splayed more feathers than a peacock on parade. After you'd gone up to bed last night, she told me she was looking forward to showing you off today, that you were more than she'd hoped for."

A vague worry pulsed somewhere between her headache and her drowsiness. What was it?

"Hoped for?" she asked on a faint echo.

There was a hesitation, a shuffling, as he moved restlessly. Finally Steve said, "I thought you'd dozed off. Go to sleep and don't mind me." He bent down and kissed her on both eyelids. He started to rise, but she clenched at his wrist and said weakly, "Don't go," so he sank again to the edge of the bed.

"You'd do better just to sleep," he said after a minute.

"Please stay."

"Of course I'll stay." His whisper was rough with feelings Rhea couldn't define.

"Talk to me," she requested, so he began again to speak about how she'd wowed 'em in the Windy City.

"Even if you did begin to feel like a roll of abused tissue paper, it had to have been a great feeling to be such a star for the day. I was so proud of you, pal. You looked so pretty and fashionable in that jumpsuit. And I couldn't help thinking how ironic it was that you worked so hard to look so good for that idiot Addlebrain and here I'd reaped the benefits."

Rhea tried to rouse herself from her sinking state of unconsciousness to demand an explanation. Instead, she fell deeper, carrying with her the echo of his words.

I'd reaped the benefits . . . reaped the benefits. . . .

CHAPTER EIGHTEEN

"Steve, this hasn't worked out. I don't mean just the visit. I mean us. Our relationship."

There. She'd said it. Now if she could only say it to Steve instead of her own unhappy reflection.

She walked away from that woman with the sad eyes and down-turned lips and listlessly riffled through her carry-on for the third time. She knew full well she hadn't forgotten a single item. But she needed something to keep her busy, something to keep herself from dissolving into thundering sobs.

For the second morning in a row, Rhea had wakened to a single thought. *I'd reaped the benefits,* he'd said. It knocked within her head like a battering ram. She was glad then that she'd slept straight through from her "nap" to early morning. She needed the extra rest to deal with the ramifications of that statement.

As she rose from the beautiful bed, wondering when someone had tucked her neatly under the covers; as she shook free of the wrinkled and creased, once bright jumpsuit; as she bathed and dressed in her smoke pinstripe traveling suit, Rhea worked through everything that had happened since leaving Denver on Friday, everything that had culminated in Steve's statement.

And for the second morning in a row she came to the same conclusion. Steve's affection for her was delusive, not actually a love for her, but for what he'd made of her. He'd been acting like a man proud of a pet who's performed unexpectedly well. In front of his family and friends he'd shown that he didn't trust her to speak for herself, that he believed she had to be told what to do and when. But, then, he'd always been dictatorial. She'd just gone along with it, thinking it for her own benefit.

Wrong again, Rhea Marie, she thought with a dejected sigh. All along he'd been ordering her about, telling her what to do, what to eat, what to wear, expecting to eventually reap the benefits. She remembered Christmas Day and the underlying tension, the attraction that had unconsciously pulsed between them. At least it had been unconscious on her part. Now she realized it had been very much on Steve's mind. He'd been attracted to her, but she wasn't quite the woman he wanted, and thus his immersion into "her" improvement project. At long last she understood his motivation in so "selflessly" helping her. He'd told her as much himself when he'd admitted waiting for her, when he'd said he'd just about run out of patience.

She marveled at how pathetically blind she'd been. Several times, she'd come close to seeing the truth, but always something had blurred it, muddled it into an unrecognizable snarl before she'd been able to grasp it. No, not something, she amended, *someone.* Steve. She'd been hopelessly confused by her own very real attraction to him. And now she had to decide just what it was she wanted.

Did she want to give in and be whatever Steve wanted her to be? Her past experience told her that if she tried to be Steve's woman rather than her own, the relationship would fail. No matter how strong her feelings or his, it would fail. To work, she had to be loved for herself. Slim or pudgy, fashionable or frumpy, pretty or plain, Rhea needed to be loved for herself. But after these past few months she wasn't at all certain just who she really was. The only thing she was certain of was that she had to find out.

And that meant ending her relationship with Steve.

It would have ended anyway, sooner or later, because his supposed love for her was as much an illusion as her sighing adoration for Addison Chambers had been. But she couldn't find out who she was or what she wanted with Steve directing her life.

So Rhea came to the same conclusion she'd reached the day before. Only this time it was set in concrete. This time no teasing smile, no loving whisper, no heart-stopping kiss, was going to unsettle it.

Suffering the sorrow that comes with the ending of anything, recalling in unexpected flashes all the laughter and good times, Rhea thought her heart just might crack in two, like they always did in cartoons. Without wanting to, she saw in her mind's eye Steve trotting beside her, imitating a tough drill sergeant, "Hup, two, three, fahhhr," as he spurred her to run; she saw him pouring over blueprints, smoking his pipe, unconsciously stroking her thigh; she saw him loving her, filling her, being fulfilled. And she ached.

Yet, in a way, the painful memories helped stiffen her resolve. If that was the kind of relationship she could have when everything was wrong, think of what she could have when it was right, when she knew who she was and what she wanted, when she found a man who liked her just for herself, without expecting changes.

So she packed her bag and practiced her speech and propped up her sagging confidence with the old refrain, *it's for the best, it's for the best.*

When it was late enough for her to do so, she went downstairs to the small dining room. She pressed the buzzer set into the wall, then sat down to wait. Within minutes Katy popped into the room and popped out again with Rhea's order. "You're leaving today, aren't you?" she asked when she returned with coffee and toast. And when Rhea replied in the affirmative, she added, "Well,

244

good-bye then. We're all looking forward to seeing you when you come again."

I won't be coming again, she thought, but aloud, she politely thanked her. Katy whizzed cheerfully out and Rhea mechanically ate her toast. Even though she'd missed her dinner the night before, she wasn't hungry. She ate to fortify herself. She wished Steve would appear before her courage gave out. She feared he'd appear before her courage gave out.

And then he was there, grinning at her, tilting his moustache in just the way that affected her most. She looked down into her coffee. "Good morning," she said levelly.

"Morning. I peeked into your room and saw that you've already packed. You must've been up a long while."

"Yes. I woke early, which isn't surprising when you consider what time I went to sleep."

"Did you sleep well? Is the headache gone?" At her nod, he gently fluffed the top of her hair and said, "I felt so badly, putting you through such a strain. I checked in on you several times last night. You were out for the count, so I left you alone, but I'm sorry you missed your dinner. Did you eat any breakfast?"

"I've had toast."

"Doesn't sound like enough." He sat down and poured a cup, giving her the time she needed to gather together her breath. If he'd remained standing so close to her, ruffling her hair, a second longer, she'd have thrown out the whole damn speech. As it was, she inhaled deeply and began.

"Steve, we really have to talk," she said, and was amazed at how calmly she'd said it.

He glanced up, smiling. "You sound so serious."

"I am," she affirmed. His smile slowly faded. She forced herself to go on. "This hasn't worked out. *We* haven't worked out. Please, let me finish. If you interrupt me, I won't get it said, and it needs to be said. I don't think a

245

relationship between us can work. You have an image of me in your head that's not the real me. It's this image you love, Steve, not me. Any relationship founded on an illusion like that is doomed to fail."

Not a muscle in his face seemed to move, yet through wooden lips he asked, "Just what are you leading up to?"

"That—that it would be best if we ended it before it got deeper."

He blew out a pent-up breath, then propped his elbow on the table. Pressing his fist into his jaw, he stroked his moustache with his index finger. The silence stretched until Rhea thought she could have used it for a slingshot. Finally, almost as if speaking to himself, he mused, "I wonder how I can convince you that you're wrong."

"I have been convinced, don't you see that? This whole weekend has convinced me! This weekend I've realized that you don't really think me capable of thinking for myself."

"Where did you get a crazy idea like that? Of course I know you can think for yourself."

"You have an odd way of showing it. Every time Lollie or one of her friends asked me a question, *you* did my answering for me. You were afraid I'd say the wrong things, so you spoke for me."

Straightening, he leaned toward her and spoke with a low urgency. "That's not true. I was nervous, Rhea, afraid you wouldn't like Lollie, that Lollie wouldn't like you— and don't look at me like that! It's not because I don't think you're perfectly adorable. As far as I'm concerned, the world should tumble at your feet, but I was nervous about this, so I jumped in, eager to impress them with you. I'm sorry you misunderstood it. I wasn't speaking for you, but of you. I'm so proud of you the way you are—"

"Yes, you are, you're proud of the way you've changed me."

He threw up his hands and gazed at her as if thrashing

246

her would give him the greatest pleasure of his life. She squirmed under the force of that gaze, then threw out in defensive accusation, "Between you, you and Lollie have tried to ramrod me into accepting that I'm part of this family!"

"I'll admit we'd both be pleased if you did accept that and I'll admit I'd hoped this trip might convince you that you could be part of my family, but we weren't trying to pressure you into anything."

"No? Then what was all that putting me on display for yesterday? Letting me see just what everyone expects of me? Of us? Wasn't that a form of emotional blackmail?"

"I think it was more a misjudgment on the part of some hopeful old women. They'd all love nothing better than to see me happily married off; they liked you, they started believing what they wanted to believe." He shrugged and added sadly, "I guess it's what I wanted to believe too."

"That's just it!" she pounced. "You've been wanting to believe what you wanted to believe all along. You've wanted to believe that I'm pretty and stylish and—"

"And you are."

"Only because you and Ilona Drake saw to it that I was. I'd never have chosen something like that jumpsuit I had on yesterday. *You* chose it for me."

"I thought you liked it."

"That's not the point. The point is that on my own, I wouldn't wear stuff like that and you wouldn't like the stuff I'd wear. The point is, you wouldn't like the real me."

"So, okay, I give up. Tell me, who is the real you?"

Her face crumpled. Her shoulders slumped. "I don't know. After all these months, I don't know. All my life I've been letting other people tell me what to do, what to think. First my folks and my brother and later Dave. The only time I was left to fend for myself, to make decisions on my own, I was a mess. I was miserable. Then you took over, you remade me—"

"You wanted that, Rhea. You. Not me. I would've been happy with you just as you were the day we met."

She looked skeptical. "Sure. Tell me you wouldn't have been pestering me to start running. Tell me you wouldn't have been pestering me to watch my diet."

"Maybe I would," he conceded, but defended himself stoutly. "But only for your health, not to change you."

"Whatever rationale you use, the result is the same. You'd have remodeled me the same way you reconstruct houses. The same way you *have* changed me."

Another silence draped over them. The weight of it was stifling. Steve shifted in his chair. "Nothing I say will convince you, will it?"

"I don't think so. Steve, I need to find out who I really am and what I really want before I let myself get involved with someone."

"You're thinking of that a little late, aren't you?" he snapped.

"Oh, Steve, I didn't want to end it like this." She twisted her hands together in agitation. She looked at him pleadingly. He met that look with an unsympathetic scowl.

"No? How did you want to end it? Politely? Please, Mr. Bradley, get lost. Yes, I will, thank you, Miss Nichols. Well, damn it, there's no polite way to hurt someone."

No, there was no polite way to hurt. Or to be hurt. Rhea sat aching and feeling very alone as he glared at her. Abruptly he ran his hands through his hair and exhaled roughly.

"All right. Whatever your reasons, it's obvious you've decided you can't care enough for me to make a relationship work. It's obvious that what I feel for you is immaterial. I'll just have to accept that you don't return my feelings and get on with my life."

She bent her head, unable to bear the hostility in his eyes, his voice. She heard the harsh scrape as he thrust back his chair and stood.

"I'll go pack," he bit out. "Do you want to say good-bye to Lollie before we leave?"

"Yes," she whispered, and he slammed out of the room. The brass clock behind her began chiming, a nerve-rattling clamor that Rhea didn't even hear.

She'd thought she'd settled it all in her own mind. She'd thought she'd prepared herself thoroughly. She'd thought he'd accept her decision with his usual composure, his usual understanding. She'd thought wrong.

It had all hurt far more than she'd ever imagined. She hurt far more. That she'd inflicted the pain for her own good, and his, too, didn't assuage it. Aching, numb with the pain, Rhea went back to her room. There she steeled herself for the long trip back to Denver in the company of a man who probably hoped she'd get airsick on the way.

Once again he surprised her. "You ready?" he asked when he came to get her. He lifted her suitcase, then paused. "Have you stocked up on aspirin for the return trip?"

Despite the normalcy of his voice, despite the joke, there was a new undefinable distance, as if he'd withdrawn from her inwardly. She tried to pinpoint exactly what was missing. The spark in his eye when he looked at her. A certain lift to his moustache. A warm intimacy she hadn't even been aware existed, until now, when it was no longer there.

She responded to him as cheerfully as she could. She found it was amazingly difficult to sound light and airy when one's spirit dragged leadenly.

They went down to say good-bye to Lollie. Rhea knew the instant she entered the parlor that Steve had already spoken with his grandmother. As she had the night of their arrival, Lollie rose and watched them, appraising, measuring them as they crossed to greet her. But in place of shining inquisitiveness, the pale blue eyes were dulled with sadness. She took hold of Rhea's hand and squeezed gently.

"I'm sorry to see you go, Rhea, my dear. More sorry than I can possibly say."

"I've been so glad I got to meet you, Mrs. Bradley," said Rhea, hoping very much she wasn't going to cry.

"Lollie. All my children call me Lollie."

Rhea's hand jerked in distress. The old woman retained her grip with astonishing strength. She scrutinized Rhea's face steadily, then smiled and loosened her glasp.

"I do consider you one of my children, and it's got nothing to do with my grandson. Stephen, quit glowering at us and go take the bags out to the car."

"Lollie . . ." he said, his tone a warning.

"The bags, Stephen."

There was a perceptible pause, then a rather forceful closing of the door. Lollie immediately led Rhea to the sofa where they sat side by side.

"Now, I wish to give you my apologies, child."

"Mrs. Brad—Lollie, you don't have to—"

"Yes, I do. I'm an overbearing old woman. Yes, I am, so don't shake your head at me. I've had my way for so long that far too often I don't take time to consider what others may be feeling. I simply charge ahead, expecting everyone else to fall into line with what I want. I may have pried too much, been too insensitive to your feelings this weekend, Rhea, and for that I'm sorry. But I've never meant to cause you to feel bad."

"Oh, no, I've never thought—"

"Of course you didn't. You're far too sweet to think such thoughts. But I'm not sweet. At my age, you don't have to be, thank goodness." She patted Rhea's hand comfortingly.

"I'm sorry, too, if anything I've done has hurt you," said Rhea on an agitated rush.

250

"Ah, well, it's not my feelings that concern me. Stephen is the one who's hurting."

Not wanting to discuss it, not knowing how to tell Lollie that, knowing it wouldn't matter if she did tell Lollie that, Rhea fluttered her hands and looked as if she longed to escape. Lollie ignored her blatant distress signals.

"My dear, I cannot let you leave without saying a few things for you to mull over in the days to come. I don't know the details of your relationship with my grandson, and quite frankly, I don't care to. That's your private business. But I know enough to tell you this. Stephen loves you."

"No, he—"

"Yes, Rhea, he does. Very much," insisted Lollie in her strongest voice. "He's needed a woman like you for years. He's not the sort of man to be fulfilled as a bachelor. He needs a wife and family to be truly happy."

"Yes, but I'm not the right woman. Can't you see that?"

"Honestly, no, I can't see that. Stephen certainly doesn't see it and that's what matters. Besides which, this family could use a woman like you. Louisa's far too much like me, Warren's wife is a scold, and Jennette's a dreamer. There's a solid core to you underneath all your hesitation and insecurity. I think if you'd let yourself, you'd realize that you love Stephen too."

"I'm sorry, Lollie, but I'm not in love with him. I care for him a great deal, but I don't love him."

"Well, dear, only you can say what's in your heart. But I think you should consider examining your heart very closely before you make an irrevocable decision. And while you're examining it, bear in mind that Stephen loves you. His love should be worth a lot to any woman."

She stood briskly. "Now, there's a few things for you to think over. And Rhea, remember you'll always be welcome in my home, whatever happens."

"Thank you," she said, and received a lined cheek to

kiss. She obediently pressed a kiss upon it, and then they walked outside to where Steve prowled the length of the portico.

"I wish I could come with you to the airport, children, but it's far too tiresome. After as much activity as I've had this weekend, I don't think I could bear up under it."

Rhea privately thought Elizabeth Bradley could bear up under anything, but all she said was "Good-bye." Rhea then went down the stone steps and got into the limousine while Steve remained for a private farewell.

Then he was climbing in beside her and they were pulling away, arching down the curved drive and onto the narrow, treelined road. Rhea twisted to look back through the window. The tiny, frail figure dwarfed by the huge colonnades lifted a hand and waved a final good-bye. She shifted back around, uncomfortably aware of the man beside her.

Although they sat in opposite corners of a very lengthy seat, she felt as if she were oppressed by his nearness. Across the burgundy expanse she could feel the anger throbbing in him. Without coming close to touching him, she could feel the tension radiate from him; she could feel the strain in his muscles. She knew that in another, less controlled man such rage would have exploded in violence by now. She scrunched tightly into her corner and hoped he'd forget she was there.

It was a vain hope.

"I hope you don't think," he bit out through thinned lips, "that I put Lollie up to whatever she had to say to you. I had nothing to do with that."

"No, I didn't think you had," she assured him in a fainthearted voice.

"Good," he growled, and that was the last of their conversation.

If Rhea had thought the flight to Chicago was long and tiring, it was a joyride compared to the trip home. She was fatigued in both body and spirit by the never-ending nightmare. Worst of all, of course, was the remote manner in which Steve treated her. While she supposed it was better than the hostility she'd expected, and far more cordial than she deserved, it hurt nonetheless to receive distant politeness from a man who'd imprinted her body from head to toe with passionate kisses. Continual reminders that she'd chosen for it to be this way, that she'd done it for the best, did nothing at all to make it feel any better. It exhausted her.

While waiting for their flight they talked, but it was limited to things like, "Did you want the aisle seat?" and "I'll go check on the departure time." It nearly drove Rhea to swallowing her entire supply of aspirin.

During the flight Steve buried his nose in a magazine. Rhea fiddled with her seat belt and tried not to think. For once it wasn't her fear of crashing she was working so hard to suppress. It was that last conversation with Lollie. As the old woman had intended, Rhea unwillingly mulled over what she'd said. She heard over and over again that strong voice saying firmly, "Stephen loves you." Lollie had stated it as an irrefutable fact, the kind of fact that withstood all denials.

Under the pretense of reading the safety information card tucked in the pocket at her knees, Rhea studied him surreptitiously. His jaw was set, his eyes fixed resolutely on the magazine. As she straightened, dropping the card back into the pocket, she noted that he'd been on the same page since the flight began. It was certain that he was hurting badly.

She looked away, unable to bear knowing she was the cause of his pain. He was so good, such a good friend. She had no wish to hurt him. But if she didn't hurt him now, wouldn't it be worse in time to come?

The more they were together, the more attached they became to each other. But Steve was attached to the woman he'd helped make; if she wasn't really that woman at all, sooner or later, the facade of their relationship would crumble and they'd both be hurt much more. She couldn't continue to see him, not even as a close friend. Under his dominant personality she'd never have an opportunity to find out just how much of that woman she really was. She reaffirmed her decision to find herself, even at the cost of losing Steve, put her head back, and closed her eyes.

CHAPTER NINETEEN

She missed him in ways she hadn't thought possible.

She missed him when she woke in the morning and knew it would be another day without him.

She missed him whenever something amused or interested or provoked her and he wasn't there to share it.

She missed him when in those last conscious moments before falling asleep at night, she ached to have him holding her.

At first she expected that it would soon get better, that soon she'd not think of him with every other breath, that soon she'd think of him only occasionally and then only fondly. But she didn't think of Steve Bradley fondly. She thought of him longingly, miserably, and constantly.

Nothing, no one, seemed to help her forget. In an odd role-reversal that in other circumstances would have amused her greatly, Rhea took up the social whirl Laurey had discarded. Now it was Rhea who whisked in at hours too late to be anything but early while Laurey stayed home reading, cooking, once even attempting to knit, but only once.

But despite the active social calendar, despite the dining and dancing, the picnics and the movies, and the shopping expeditions, Rhea wasn't enjoying herself. It was all like a glass of champagne that had lost its fizz. The whirl became more and more unappealing. It seemed to her as if she'd simply been going round and round in a revolving door with a series of indistinguishable men, men she had trouble remembering as soon as she said good night. In fact, every man she saw was compared unconsciously and invariably unfavorably to Steve. The dances and dinners and movies and men were all the same. Flat.

She wasn't certain she'd attained her goal of finding herself, but she did learn a few things about herself during the long days of summer. She learned she was a creature of habit. She continued to exercise and run every day, though she discovered she didn't enjoy it as much as she had before. She learned that even if she could afford to, she wouldn't throw out any of the clothes Steve and Ilona had helped her select. She liked them. She learned she liked doing her hair and makeup when the occasion called for it and leaving it alone when it didn't. And whether she did it or left it be didn't make any difference to who she was. She learned that making her own decisions wasn't as important as having someone who cared what she decided. Most of all, she learned she missed Steve; she missed him unbearably.

By the end of July, Rhea might have been willing to admit to Steve that she'd made a mistake. But it was too late. This time it really was too late.

Steve had moved out of the apartment complex.

She'd found out at the beginning of the month when she'd gone to pay her rent. Gladys had taken her check, blinking her dark lavender lids over it once before rearranging her rouged cheeks in what was, for her, a smile.

"By the way, Miss Nichols, if you know anyone who's looking for an apartment, we've got a new one available."

"Oh, um, no, I don't," mumbled Rhea disinterestedly.

She was already walking out when Gladys added, "Yes, three forty-six is vacant as of yesterday."

Screeching to a halt in her tracks, Rhea pivoted slowly. She could feel the color draining from her face. "Did you say three forty-six? Isn't that S-Steve Bradley's apartment?"

"Yes, it *was* Steve Bradley's apartment. He vacated yesterday. If you know of anyone . . ."

Rhea never heard the rest. She dashed over to the third building, second floor. She wasn't even granted the comforting reprieve of waiting, hoping for him to answer the door. The door was wide open, the smell of fresh paint clinging to the hall as workers applied a new coat of white to all the walls.

She'd stumbled out, dazed and empty. Slowly, insidiously, images had risen to fill the void. Taunting images of Steve in all his moods. Steve, laughing at her attempts to do a push-up. Steve, seriously explaining his stand on a political issue she'd mentioned. Steve, sensually contemplating the depth of her belly button. She saw continual images of him, but most of all, her mind filled with the memories of the night they'd returned from Chicago.

She remembered the long, silent drive home from Stapleton Airport, the equally silent walk up to her apartment. But when they'd reached the door and she'd put the key into the lock, he'd set his hand over hers, keeping her from turning it.

"Wait a minute," he requested.

She didn't think she could take another minute of this torture. She shook her head and tried to turn her key. "I'd better get inside."

"Rhea, I'm not going to say anything to try to convince you to change your mind. I've done my level best for six months to make you see how much I love you, and I've failed. Another minute won't make a difference."

She said nothing, did nothing. All her efforts were concentrated on not breaking down into streams of tears.

"I just want you to remember that I love you. Not the clothes you wear or the way you do your hair, just you. When you forget everything else, remember that."

257

The tears were dangerously close. She mutely nodded.

"I guess this is good-bye then, Rhea," he said, his voice a bit unsteady.

"I guess it is," she agreed, her own voice trembling madly.

Then he swiftly kissed the top of her bent head and left. And two months later the memory of it still pierced Rhea's heart.

She dutifully used her Sunday morning to catch up on her correspondence, but the letter she was writing was so dull, she was falling asleep writing it. She had nothing of interest to say. She'd refused all invitations to go out this week, and although she'd needed to get her laundry done, it didn't make for thrilling news. She hoped her mom would be content with seeing her signature at the bottom of the page, regardless of the boring contents.

The click of the front door sounded as loudly as a cavalry charge. Glad to be rescued from another minute with her letter, Rhea bounded out toward the living room, saying, "Laurey, let's go out for an ice cream or something. I've got to get out—"

She slid to a stop like a runner going into home plate. "My God!" she screeched. "Laurey! What happened? Are you okay? Was anybody hurt?"

"Hurt?" echoed Laurey in bewilderment. She saw Rhea's eyes travel anxiously over her and looked down. An impish grin danced over her mouth. "Oh, all this. This is just some grease."

What she termed "just some grease" was smeared from the top of the blue bandanna tied in a triangle over her hair to the toe of her once white sneakers. As far as Rhea could tell, beneath the grease was a pair of frayed and tattered blue jeans and a too large man's workshirt carelessly knotted under Laurey's breasts. Her usually flawless skin looked as if it were in the final stages of decay.

"I thought there'd been an accident," said Rhea. "You look like you've been bathing in grease—or worse. What have you been doing, trying out for a part as a hobo?"

"Nothing like that. I was learning about cars. You know, the engines and transmissions and all. Most of this" —she sketched her hand down her lanky figure—"came when I was under the car and accidentally drained the oil on myself."

She giggled at the memory. Rhea gawked. This was not the woman she'd shared an apartment with for almost two years. This was not the Laurey Wellman she knew. She cast an eye to the phone, decided she could call for help if she had to, and demanded an instant, full explanation.

"What on earth has come over you, Laurey? First the cooking and staying at home, and now this. I mean, are you all right? Have you been indoctrinated by some mysterious cult that worships carburetors?"

To Rhea's surprise, Laurey didn't receive this with the expected guffaw. Instead, she blushed beneath the grease and said rather sheepishly, "Well, sort of. Only it's not a cult, it's just Garland. You could almost say he worships carbs. He's really into cars. He's a mechanic."

"Garland? A mechanic?"

"Yes," said Laurey happily, as if that explained everything.

She started toward her bedroom. Rhea chased after her. "Wait a minute. Who is this Garland? Are you saying you let yourself be tarred for this guy? Is he the reason for your sudden interest in cooking and your sudden disinterest in dating?"

"Yes," she said again, then added with a totally uncharacteristic shyness, "we're getting married."

After a stunned moment, Rhea managed to close her gaping mouth and say, "Congratulations."

"We haven't really made plans, but we're thinking of

October. I'd like you to be my maid of honor, I mean, if that's okay with you."

"Okay? I'd be thrilled and you know it. Just name the day and I'll be there, bag of rice in hand."

Laurey clapped her hands together, then said, "Ugh! I'm a real mess. Come on, if you don't mind watching me clean up, I'll tell you all about it." She was spinning now, looking like her old self if you ignored the grease and old clothes and shabby hairdo. "He just asked me a couple nights ago, so we haven't settled anything, but I'll let you know as soon as we do. The thing is, Garland's got to get a job. He's got a couple of hopeful prospects right now, so keep your fingers crossed."

She really thought she should be used to the jolts now, she'd suffered so many little shocks right in a row, but this one really threw Rhea. As long as she'd known Laurey, the young woman had run through money almost as rapidly as through men. And the men she'd run through had all carried a large part of the tab. Laurey had less money sense than she did house sense. She continually forgot her share of the rent money, the grocery money, and so on. If this Garland of hers didn't even have a dime, there was no way they were going to be able to get along. She chewed on her lower lip as she trailed behind Laurey, trying to decide whether to say something or not.

While Laurey discarded her clothes and drew a steamy bath, she chattered breezily about Garland's virtues, which were apparently numerous, and their plans together. Rhea sat on the edge of the bathroom vanity, swinging a foot as she listened. But when Laurey announced that Garland wanted at least five kids, Rhea's foot banged into the vanity and stopped. This was not, she could see, a marriage meant to last.

"Uh, Laurey," she began tentatively. "Are you sure about all this? I mean, how can you be sure that it's the right guy?"

"I knew when I first met him, it was like the tilt sign on a pinball machine lighting up. At first I didn't want to believe it. In fact, I resented him for it. I didn't think I was ready and certainly not for someone like Garland, not for the old-fashioned macho man who'd expect me to settle down and have babies. But no matter how hard I resisted, I kept being drawn back to him. I wanted to be with him all the time. Finally I just had to admit it. I love him. It's the plain truth. I love him."

"Love doesn't always solve all the problems," said Rhea, thinking that nothing short of a miracle would solve the problems facing such a star-crossed pair.

"No. But if you love somebody enough, you'll try to work out the problems." Laurey lathered an arm and studied the soap foaming on her skin. "Are you trying to tell me you think Garland and I are going to have problems?"

"Well . . . you have to admit he doesn't seem to be your type of man. I mean, it doesn't sound as if he'll be able to give you all the glamor and excitement you're used to. Do you think you'll be able to accept that?"

"I already have accepted it. Besides, I never wanted the glamor and flash to last forever. It's boring in the long run. I just wanted to enjoy it while I could, while I was young and carefree. Now I want to share my life with Garland, to take care of him and have him take care of me."

"But, Laurey, you're changing yourself to suit him. Don't you think that one of these days you're going to resent that? That one of these days you're going to dislike him for making you stay at home and cook and clean when you'd rather be dancing?"

Laurey dropped the soap in the dish, curled up in a ball, and gave the matter serious consideration. After a time, she said on an unusual somber note, "I see what you're saying, of course, but I don't think you've got it right. It's like you're looking at the picture through a bit of warped glass, so what you see is distorted. You think because I've changed, it's a bad thing—an omen or something. But, Rhea, people aren't static. We're always changing, all of us. We change with circumstances, age, the people we meet. The only time it's a problem is when the change isn't growth, when it's a step backward. Otherwise, it's normal and healthy to change."

Plucking an imaginary bit of lint from the front of her aqua scoop-necked T-shirt, Rhea voiced her own fears. "Yes, but those changes are voluntary, or, at least, changes you accept. But when you deliberately change yourself to please someone else, well, isn't that like a living lie? Doesn't that eventually lead to trouble because it wasn't a true change?"

"Garland's never asked me to change," said Laurey with a hint of defensiveness. "He liked me right from the beginning. But I could see that what he needed was a more domestic type of person. I wanted to be what he needed, what appealed to him, Rhea. He didn't demand it, so I don't feel any resentment toward him. I wanted to please him in my own way. And I honestly feel happier, not only because he's happy, but with myself. This is a part of me I wasn't aware existed until now."

"Somehow I just can't see you at home with five kids," said Rhea, but teasing now, grinning at her.

"Lordy, do you think I can? Wait'll my parents hear about it! They'll pass out from the shock. But I don't think I'll ever win any awards for homemaker of the year, no matter what."

They laughed, remembering a few of the recent efforts that had caused Laurey to rethink her initial opinion that cooking was a snap. Later, as she was wrapping a short, fluffy bathrobe around her scrubbed body, Laurey returned to the earlier discussion, saying, "Some of the changes we're talking about are only superficial, Rhea. I haven't really changed. It's like when you wanted that attorney, what's his name—"

"Addison."

"Yeah, well, all you changed was the way you appeared. It made you happy and being happy changed you a little too. But you didn't regret doing it, even after you no longer wanted that guy. You're still the same person, just in a different way. I'm still the same me, just showing you different facets of myself."

"You're showing them and how," said Rhea with a low whistle. "Whoever's responsible for the new you, I like it."

"I've thought the same about you these past few months. Or I did before you took that trip to Chicago."

Rhea hastily switched the subject, inquiring if Laurey's family had any idea that she'd gotten herself engaged. But she listened only abstractedly as Laurey explained how she and Garland planned to break the news to everyone over the weekend. Like a ball bouncing wildly in the recesses of her mind, the thought of Chicago was resounding from one corner of Rhea's being to the other.

Long after Laurey had changed and gone to fix something for Garland to eat, Rhea thought about all that she'd said. She'd always thought Laurey rather flighty, but that seemed to have been another bit of personality that changed with circumstance. She'd been flighty because she hadn't had to be otherwise. Now she was showing a truer, deeper side of herself.

It didn't take much ingenuity to take the points of discussion and apply them to herself. She thought of how Dave had told her to do something and she'd done it. But like Garland, Steve had never demanded a change of her. When she'd said she wanted to do something, he'd helped her to achieve it. But she'd been so uncertain of being able to hold his interest on her own, she'd used the changes as an excuse, a ready point of blame, should their relationship fail.

Since the trip at the end of May, Rhea had realized only a portion of her goal of finding herself and what she wanted. Now, sitting coiled in a tight spring in one of her U-shaped chairs, she discovered the answer to one of the most important questions. What did she want?

She wanted Steve Bradley. She wanted to be with him, to share with him, to love with him. She wanted to make him happy and, in turn, be made happy.

Another realization followed on the heels of the first, almost knocking Rhea from her chair.

She loved Steve.

Yes, she loved him, pure and simple, just as Lollie had said. Dear, wise Lollie. The thought of Lollie brought back all the old memories, and for a time, Rhea got stuck in a morass of self-pity. She'd had her chance and she'd missed it.

But gradually a seed of hope sprouted within her. Why not go find him and tell him how she felt? The sprout grew with the rapidity of a dandelion. The worst he could do was tell her to buzz off. It was a chance, slim, maybe, but a slim chance was better than no chance at all.

Rhea vaulted to her feet in a world-record speed. She rushed to do it before she had any stupid second thoughts. She thrust her feet into a pair of leather clogs and slung her purse over the shoulder of her T-shirt. She raced out, then ran back in to scribble a note to Laurey which read, "Gone. Be back, Rhea," and finally clattered down the stairs and out into the parking lot.

There was only one place for her to look. Since he'd moved out of his apartment, she could assume only that he'd moved to the house in Colorado Springs. She headed for the Interstate with a tingly excitement working its way through her system, from the toes pressing the gas pedal harder than they should, up past the quivering knees and

264

butterfly-filled tummy, past the wildly thundering heart to the refrain in her mind singing, *Steve, Steve, Steve.*

She made the hour's drive in record time. Beyond actually arriving and throwing herself at him, she had no clear idea what she meant to do when she got there. Somehow, in some vague way, she meant to beg his forgiveness, to make him understand she loved him, to make him love her. That was the plan, as far as it went.

As she neared the block with his house in it, her foot eased off the gas pedal. Her mouth went dry. The butterflies in her stomach flapped with leaden wings. What if he turned her away? What if he refused to talk to her? What if he'd realized that he hadn't really loved her at all?

From out of nowhere she heard Lollie's firm *Stephen loves you,* and her courage returned. She turned into the driveway and pulled to a halt.

It looked the same as when she'd seen it last, yet different. But not different as she'd expected it to look, with that unaccountably warmer aura that only a lived-in house can have. It didn't look lived-in at all. No curtains flapped at open windows, no cars were parked on the drive. A profusion of weeds and tall grass indicated that the lawn hadn't been attended to for quite some time.

Feeling something in her sag, Rhea got out and mounted the porch to the lovely etched door. The sight of it stirred the memories of that day, of the unrestrained loving upstairs, the picnic downstairs, of his enthusiasm and her happiness. She recalled how she'd lost her contact and how Steve had insisted he liked her in glasses. . . .

She tamped down her panic and knocked sharply. The rap echoed into stillness, as it did a few seconds later when she knocked again harder. After five minutes and several attempts, Rhea had to admit that no one was there. Peering in through the oval glass, she'd been able to see the empty hall, the coating of dust on everything. Shoulders slumping, she turned and went down the stairs.

265

That was when she saw it. The sign posted in the yard that read FOR SALE.

A gut-wrenching depression smote her. It was ridiculous, but when she'd first stopped seeing him, just knowing he was in the same apartment complex had comforted her. Just knowing he was within reach had made it seem as if she could be with him whenever she really wanted to. After he'd left the complex, she'd comforted herself with the thought that she knew where to find him, that the Springs was only an hour down the Interstate. Now she had nothing left to comfort her.

The drive home had none of the tingles of the drive there. She didn't think she'd ever feel another tingle again as long as she lived. It could be a horror story, "The Day the Tingles Died," she thought, without enjoying her own humor.

It was her own fault. She'd waited too long to wake up. That didn't make it better and it certainly couldn't make it worse; nothing could make it worse, it was just a fact for her to chew over as she drove. She'd waited too long and she had only herself to blame for it. What good were these contacts when she was still so foolishly blind?

She fell into a zombielike reverie, thinking back, as she so often had, on everything they'd done together. As always, she ended by again replaying the trip to Chicago and in the midst of it, wondered if she dared to call Lollie and inquire about Steve. Maybe she could write a letter. Or a short, newsy note, ending, "By the by, have you heard from Steve lately?"

By the time she reached the complex, she'd written a half dozen letters and made twice as many calls. Deep down, she didn't think she'd do it. Without the impetus of a wild impulse, once she'd had time to reflect and let all her insecurities and doubts rise up, she'd never be able to reach out to Steve, least of all through his grandmother. She sighed the kind of sigh that hissed around the interior of her car, the kind of sigh that said, *Life's not really worth living, is it?*

Feeling a surge of hostility at the unfairness of it all, she stomped on the gas pedal, whipped into the parking lot, and plowed directly into another fender. All in one horrifying sequence, she jerked against the taut strap of her seat belt, her hands gripped the steering wheel, her foot stamped on the brake. Her ears filled with the squealing of rubber on the pavement, the crashing of glass, the crumpling of metal. Her eyes blurred with the dizzying flash of colors, trees, buildings, and other cars and people stopping to stare.

Then it was over, and Rhea was sitting, rigidly gripping the wheel and feeling a sense of déjà vu.

Her feeling of having been through this once before deepened as she turned off the engine, undid her seat belt, and opened the door. She heard crunching footsteps approach and looked up to meet Steve's tender, concerned gaze.

CHAPTER TWENTY

"My dear, we can't go on meeting like this," he said, smiling crookedly.

Rhea stared at him. She saw the lopsided lift to his moustache, the crinkles embedded beside his sparkling blue eyes, the kindness and goodness and desirability in every line of his face, and spouted a geyser of tears.

He tugged her to her feet and enfolded her in his arms. She pressed into the curve of his shoulder, reveling in the feel of firm muscle and hard bone beneath the azure cotton of his shirt. How she'd missed the comfort of this shoulder!

"Shhh, sweetheart, it's only a car," he murmured into her ear. "Better my bumper than some stranger's."

She continued sobbing. After all, she'd stored up over two months worth of tears for this. She was going to cry till she was wrung dry of every single drop. The longer she cried, the longer he'd be holding on to her. She shuddered with the force of her emotion and his hands automatically pressed into her back. She shuddered again, though this time from an entirely different cause. He began rubbing her back, all the while murmuring in that lulling voice of his. She wanted this to go on forever and ever.

But eventually even Rhea's tears had to diminish in force and quantity and this time was no exception. As she squeezed out the last possible trickle, he set her aside and asked, "Are you going to be all right now?"

At her reluctant nod of assent, he briskly told her to wait, then with the help of a bystander who'd witnessed the crash, he moved her Chevette out of the way of traffic.

She watched his every movement with eager eyes. She watched the way his back strained against his shirt as he arched against the trunk of her car. She watched the way the muscles in his legs tensed within the tan slacks as he pushed. She watched the way he flexed and stretched his arms once her car was in a slot. She watched, and hungered as she watched.

He quickly drove his own MG back into the slot from which he'd just backed out and then came back to where she waited. He was smiling when he returned, but there was a palpable hesitation to his smile now. "Ever get that feeling you've gone through all this before?"

"Déjà vu. I felt it the instant we hit, only then I didn't realize I'd actually hit you again."

"I think maybe it's more kismet than déjà vu."

He had taken hold of her arm and was already steering her down a sidewalk. She slid a glance at him. Kismet, he'd called it. What did he mean by that? The blossom of hope that had wilted in Colorado Springs now revived, flowering radiantly within her soul. "What's kismet?" she asked with studied casualness. "Fate or something, isn't it?"

"Fate, doom, predestined fortune," he confirmed.

She was less than thrilled with his definition. *Doom* didn't have a very encouraging ring to it. The radiant flower drooped a little, but didn't die. As long as they were together, she had hope. All she had to do was fall back on her earlier plan to open her heart to him.

"Where are we going?" she asked.

"Up to your place. I don't live here anymore."

"I know."

His gaze riveted to her. "You do?"

"Gladys told me when I paid the rent."

"Oh, I see."

Did she imagine it or did he actually shift slightly away from her? "I went over to look for myself then, and sure enough, you'd gone."

She wanted to ask, where? Where are you? But she swallowed back the questions. Her old insecurities were creeping up again, filling her with uncertainty. She doubted he wanted her to know where he now lived. If he wanted her to know, he'd tell her.

He obviously didn't want her to know. Instead of following up on her comment, he remarked casually, "Pretty top. I like it. Is it new?"

"Ummm. I got it on sale at May D and F."

"You still have the same insurance agent?"

"Yes."

"Well, you'd better give me the name and number again."

"Sure," she chirped, striving not to let hope wither at the evident reserve in his persistently polite manner. "I'll take care of it as soon as we get up to my place."

They walked the short distance quickly, Rhea hoping and praying every step of the way that Laurey was still out and would be out for the next hundred years. She was in luck. The apartment was just as she'd left it when she'd dashed out on her wild-goose chase to find Steve.

Well, she'd found him, but not quite as she'd expected to.

"I'll get my agent's number for you. Boy, he won't believe it. I can't believe it, can you? I mean, who'd believe it?" She knew she was babbling like a nervous brook, but she couldn't seem to stem the flow. "My rates are gonna skyrocket. All these years without a single accident and now I have two within a year and both within my very own parking lot."

"Not to mention both into my very own MG," he said dryly.

She skidded to a stop on her way to her room. She came slowly back to where he stood in the center of her living room, looking curiously about him as if he'd never seen the place before. Her heart plummeted and hope was crushed beneath the dead weight of it. How could she open up to this courteously remote man? This man who instead of reacting with honest emotion to having his car smashed, made dry jokes and avoided her gaze? She couldn't, she simply couldn't.

Digging her sandaled toes into the carpet, she said with true contrition, "God, I am sorry about this, Steve."

His gaze skewed to her and rested there. "What happened? I saw you careening around that turn and then you seemed to deliberately hit the accelerator."

"I did," she confessed sheepishly.

He was visibly taken aback. "My God, Rhea! I knew you weren't too pleased with me at the end, but I always thought we were friends."

"We are! I was! What are you talking about?"

"About why you deliberately rammed into me."

"But I didn't! I never meant to hit you. I never meant to hit anyone."

"You just said that you accelerated deliberately," he accused her. "You came around the corner, saw me, and hit the pedal."

"No, no, I never saw you. Not until it was all over. Oh, Steve, how could you think such a thing of me? I'd never hurt you for the world! I love you!"

The vehement declaration bounded from wall to wall, resounding like a tribal drum message in Rhea's ears. What on earth had she done? She'd declared her love for a man who had good reason not to like her in the least. A man who was simply standing there staring at her as if she'd grown a pair of extra heads. She longed to take back the words.

"You love me?" asked Steve. Suspicion mingled with outright disbelief. "*You . . . love . . . me?*"

Well, put like that, it did sound rather ridiculous. Rhea had hoped for some other reaction. Like exultation or exuberant declarations in return. What was she supposed to say or do to get out of this gracefully? She opted for flippancy, "Well, you know what they say. If you can't be with the one you love, love the one you're with."

"What the hell does that mean?"

He was scowling at her now in a manner reminiscent of the night they'd returned from Chicago. All the old pain welled up, hurting until she couldn't hold it back. Before she could help herself, she burst out, "I don't know! I just said it! I didn't want to tell you the truth. I didn't want to tell you that I do love you. I know my timing couldn't be worse, but I meant to tell you today anyway, so maybe it's kismet, after all. It isn't déjà vu because this isn't how we ended up last time and—"

"Show me you mean that, Rhea," he cut in on a rasp. "Show me you love me."

She gaped at him blankly. She saw the desire in his taut stance, the dread in the tight line of his mouth. Slowly she realized the twin of her own doubts and hopes were mirrored in his eyes. She realized he was afraid to believe her, as afraid as she'd been to tell him. In that instant all her hesitation fled. Only one thing mattered—to erase his doubts and fears, to replace them with the contented certainty of love.

She went to him. Touching the tips of her fingers to the hard plane of his cheek, she felt the mixtures of rough and smooth skin along his jaw. Lightly, then, she darted her fingertips over every feature, saying, "I love you. I love the way lines crease right here beside your eyes when you're laughing. I love the way these brows come together when you're angry. I love the way the ends of this moustache tilt when you're speaking. And I love, I really love, the feel of these lips on mine."

Standing on tiptoe, she kissed him gently, softly, slowly. For a fraction of a heartbeat he passively accepted her kiss. Then with a low groan he was holding her tightly, his hands feverishly sweeping everywhere, his mouth consuming hers with a fervor that rocked them both.

Tremors of excitement raced from her body to his. He squeezed the pliant swell of her hip, pressing her closer, closer into the hardness of his body, as if he couldn't get her close enough to him. He couldn't get her close enough to suit Rhea. She responded with quivering eagerness, swaying into his embrace.

Sighs of pleasure escaped her, twining with his husky gasps. They kissed and touched and rediscovered each other. And Rhea discovered a new joy in all of it. She'd always responded to him, but now she responded completely, lovingly, without holding anything back. The love within her response heightened each sensation she received from him; the delight of his mouth tracing the arch of her neck was fierce, the arousal of his palm on her breast was dizzying, the satisfaction of his body rippling with shudders against hers was boundless.

"I've missed you, I've missed holding you like this," she told him on a breathless whisper.

He tensed, then pulled back. She looked up at him in bemused surprise. His eyes were glazed with passion; his face was filled with wonderment. He touched her hair, her nose, her cheekbones. "Is this real? Are you really here, telling me you love me?"

"Yes, yes," she sighed on a happy laugh. "It's real. I'm here. I love you."

"I've been wanting this for so long, I can't believe it." He shook his head and looked at her again, as if just focusing on her for the first time. "What happened, Rhea? Why have you changed your mind?"

"I haven't changed it," she corrected him.

He flinched. She took hold of his hands and drew him to the couch. They sat. She lay her palm over his, splaying them finger to finger, and applied light pressure as she spoke. "I didn't change my mind, not really. I just finally figured it all out. I finally figured out that I've loved you for ages."

"It's taken you ages to figure it out."

She grinned at that. "It's taken me a while, hasn't it? I'm a slow learner."

He lifted her hand to his lips and nipped at her fingertips. "Not in some departments."

"I respond well to a good teacher," she retorted.

"I'll just have to put that to the test," he murmured as he again brought his lips to hers.

It was sweet, so sweet. How could she have let such sweetness go? Flicking her tongue over his, she vowed not to be so crazy again. "I'm never," she whispered at the edge of his mouth, "never letting you out of my sight again."

"I don't know what's changed you while I've been gone, but I like it, I like it." He settled back against the cushions, pulled her into his arms. He blew her bangs away from her temple and placed a kiss there. "I guess it was worth all the anguish of the past few months, after all, to have you fully mine, to have you loving me without doubt."

There was a thread of anxiety, a question he didn't want to ask. Rhea answered it anyway. "I don't know if I'll ever think anything was worth the agony of this summer, but, dearest, I do love you without a single shred of doubt. Loving you is the best thing that's ever happened to me. It's changed me for the better."

"I don't want you to change, sweetheart. Not for me."

"No, I won't change for you. I'll change with you. We'll grow old and gray and wrinkly together. Would you like that?"

274

"Rhea . . ." he moaned, and then they were prone on the couch, tangling together. He caressed her as he never had before, as if she were fragile, as if to cherish her.

His hand was inching delicately upward beneath her T-shirt, when Rhea remembered the house and bolted upright.

"The house! Steve, you've got our house up for sale!"

His perplexity turned to pleased understanding. "*Our* house? Do you really mean that?"

"You can't sell it," she said, sticking to the point. "If any kind of deal's gone through on it, you'll have to find a way to back out."

"It hasn't been sold."

She sagged back on his chest with relief. "Lucky for you."

"How did you know about that anyway?"

"When you moved out of here," she said, undoing the shirt button at her fingertips, "I naturally assumed you moved in there. So when I wanted to find you"—moving to the next button—"I drove down there. But you"—and to the next—"weren't there. There was just that awful sign."

"Yeah, well, I did that in a fit of depression. I don't think I'd have ever really sold it. I've had two offers, but I found excuses to refuse them both. Why did you want to find me?"

"To tell you I love you."

"I'm sorry I wasn't home."

Playfully plucking at the hairs now exposed to her busy fingers, she kissed his jaw and asked, "Where were you?"

"Lollie's. Poor Grandmother! I was such an ill-mannered guest, she was literally shoving me out the door by the time I left." He caught his breath as she blew playfully at his hard flat nipple. "Do that again," he sighed.

She blew, then trailed her breath with a little flick of her tongue. He inhaled sharply. She rested her chin on his

275

chest and mused, "I think you're right. It was kismet. It was fated that we run into each other—"

"You have such a way with words, my dear."

"No, I mean it. See, I'd been trying to talk myself into contacting Lollie to see if I could find where you'd gone. But I realized I probably wouldn't have the guts to do it, got mad at myself, and stomped on the gas. And whammo! There you were. Kismet."

He laughed. The vibration of it rumbled beneath Rhea. "Kismet got a little assistance from one Elizabeth Bradley. She got sick and tired of having me mope around her house and told me plainly that if I didn't come to see you, she'd call you up and make you come get me out of her hair. After I thought it over, I realized she was right. I wasn't doing anything constructive and, well, I missed you. So I came to see you."

"Is that what you were doing here? When I first looked up and saw you, I thought I was hallucinating. That I'd been thinking of you so hard, I was seeing your image. It scared me and I started crying and then you held me and I couldn't believe how much I'd missed being held by you."

He held her tightly and toyed with the short ends of hair at her nape, with the bone along her spine. "I'd thought you deliberately hit me. I didn't know whether it was the surprise of seeing me or anger toward me or what. When you started crying, I decided it was just an accident after all, and oddly felt deflated."

"If I had seen you, maybe I would've done it." She giggled at the thought. "I was that desperate to get you back into my life."

"Oh, Rhea, Rhea." He tousled her hair, then kissed her with tantalizing thoroughness before saying, "That's why I came. I wanted you in my life. I thought if nothing else, we could still be friends. I missed our friendship, Rhea."

"Me too," she said simply. "You really and truly are the

best friend I've ever had. I missed being able to tell you little things as much as I missed being able to . . . well, as much as I missed the rest of you."

"Care to go into details on that, madam?"

"Well, let's see. I think I left off *here,*" she laughed breathily, and slithered down to kiss him lightly on the chest. She spread his unbuttoned shirt wide and darted her tongue over his nipple. It hardened to her tongue's caress. She felt him tense beneath her. She heard his breath deepen, saw the passion darken his eyes. And excitement began to pulse wildly within her.

With deliberate sensuality she shifted over him, rousing herself as much as she roused him. She methodically began to nibble and kiss down past his ribs, over his taut stomach. Her fingers fumbled with his belt. His stomach sucked in on a sharp breath. His chest rose and fell in rough gasps.

"Rhea . . ." he whispered hoarsely.

The warmth of his whisper laced over her hair. She raised her head and met his heated breath with her own. "Touch me. Touch all of me."

He immediately slid his hands beneath her shirt and followed the line of her spine. This time he didn't touch her as if she were fragile. He touched her with short, brief strokes that spoke of his need to know all of her as quickly as possible. He touched her with hands that were hot and hungry, with hands that tantalized wherever they touched.

It had been so long since she'd known the delight of his touch, his kiss, his body swaying with hers. Rhea hadn't even known how much she'd missed the joy of it until now. She hadn't known how much she needed it. The need to have all of him was overwhelming. She almost cried out with her need.

As if he heard her silent plea, Steve swept her T-shirt over her head, then removed her bra with hands that shook. He cupped his hands over her breasts and gently kneaded them within his palms. She did cry out then, softly, with pleasure. He rubbed his thumbs over her puckered nipples and she trembled eagerly, with passionate urgency.

Patience evaporated. They broke apart and hastily flung off their remaining clothing, then tumbled back onto the couch and came together with the compelling insistence of uncontrollable desire. His firm, shapely body pressed against hers, and Rhea thought she'd faint with the ecstasy of it. She finally understood that the intensity of her passion sprang from the love they shared. She locked herself about him and gave herself up to the thrill of loving and being loved, completely.

Their muscles rippled together; their breaths misted together. Their skin seemed to melt together as perspiration slicked their bodies. Together. Rhea heard the word echo faintly to the cadence of their love. It grew in volume as they spiraled toward fulfillment until it burst from her lips, a low moan of sheer satisfaction.

She lay wrapped within his arms, trying to steady her breath and ease her clamoring heartbeat while listening to the thundering of his. He fluffed her hair with his fingertips. "What was that you said, sweetheart?"

A slight shyness overcame her. It embarrassed her to think of crying out like that. But she nestled closer against him and said, "Together. I said together. It's how we were, how we'll always be. Isn't it?"

"Do you really need to ask?" His voice was husky, filled with love. "But if you have any doubts, let me show you how together we're going to be."

She caught his hand in midair and kissed the fingertips. "I have no doubts."

"There's more to me than fingertips," he said helpfully.

She laughed, a throaty laugh ripe with understanding. "As much as I'd love to go on kissing every inch of your quite magnificent body, I fear I must point out that we are sprawling stark naked over the couch in the living room where at any moment now my roommate could come waltzing in."

"You're sure she's not a phantom?" he asked.

"I'm sure. Though at the moment, I wish she were. But if we're lucky, she's sprawling on a couch with her Garland and won't be home for a long, long time. Which brings me to a thought. What do you think about October?"

Looking at her slightly askance, he said, "Well, it's okay as far as months go, as long as you're not superstitious."

"I mean, for our wedding."

He lay so perfectly still for so long that had Rhea not been in a position to know intimately well that his heart was still pumping, she'd have feared for his life. "Steve? Are you okay? Don't you want a wedding in October?"

"Rhea, if you ever spring a shock like that on me again, I'll make you run ten miles every day before breakfast."

"You don't want to get married," she concluded on a flat note. She sat up and felt rather sorry that she'd used up her full quota of tears. She'd have enjoyed a good gush right now.

"And if you're this aggravatingly dense," he muttered, pulling her back into his arms, "I'll make you run twenty. Of course I want to marry you. Damn it, I've wanted to marry you for months! I just didn't know you had it on your mind, and when you sprang it on me like that, I thought my ears had malfunctioned. Now, why October, you silly twit?"

She sighed happily and snuggled into his warmth. "That's when Garland and Laurey are getting married. It'd be the perfect time for me to move out. I wouldn't be leaving her stranded or anything."

"Sure you want to wait that long?"

"It'd give us two months to make arrangements. Two months should be enough time, don't you think?"

"I think it's too much time to suit me."

"And," she presented her conclusive argument, "I'm not superstitious. What do you say?"

"I say it's the best proposal I've ever received."

"The best?"

"Well, the only. But still the best. I accept."

"Good thing too."

"And why is that?"

"Now I have a perfect reason for turning down Addison the next time he asks me out."

Some of the playfulness left Steve's face. "Have you been seeing that jerk?"

"Oh, once or twice," she replied off-handedly.

Steve unexpectedly sat up. Rhea tumbled backward and lay, staring up at him in amazement. "Did you enjoy yourself? Were you the talk of the town?"

"I just went out with him to keep busy," she explained. He continued to look at her as if she were a spider who'd encroached on his path. She tried again. "I didn't enjoy myself at all. You know I don't like him. He's boring and stuck on himself and—"

"And I don't want to hear you speak about him. Ever."

"Steve, you can't be jealous! Not of Addison! Not when I've told you how awful he is!"

"*I* always knew how awful he is," he said with pointed emphasis.

"Well, okay, so I was a bit blind at first—"

"A bit? That's a true understatement."

"I don't like him at all. And I never think about him, except how to avoid him when he hunts me down at work. What's gotten into you?"

He ruffled his hair. "Don't you have any idea what you put me through when we first met? Don't you realize I liked you, really liked you right from the beginning? The day you lost your key in the mailbox, I thought, great, here's my chance to get to know her. Then you spend the entire time in my apartment telling me how much you love another man."

The disgust in his voice had a hint of hurt in it too. Rhea sat stunned, scarcely able to believe what she was hearing, yet knowing, and finally accepting the truth. "You really were attracted to me then. Glasses, weight, and all."

"I really was." He smiled then, tenderly. "But you never believed that. You're damned obstinate, you know that? When you get an idea in that head of yours, it's cemented in place."

"Well, now I've got this idea that I love you," she drawled provocatively.

He refused to be sidetracked. "You were too busy mooning over that conceited buffoon to look twice at me. I thought if we could be together, you'd see what a terrific fellow I was—"

"You talk about Addison's ego! And I didn't moon."

He merely rolled his eyes. "But no matter how much we were together, you wouldn't see me as anything but a friend. It was damned frustrating."

"I didn't think your motives could be so altruistic," she said with the satisfaction of having been proved right.

He sat for a time, stroking his moustache. It felt good just to have him beside her. "No, I wasn't being altruistic. I wanted you, but you were all wrapped up in Atterboy and I was eaten up with jealousy. I didn't quite know how to handle it. I'd never been that way about Tammie. She could've gone out with the Broncos' backfield and I wouldn't have cared. So these things were new to me and I made mistakes along the way."

"I never meant to hurt you, Steve," she murmured.

"I know, I know. It was within me. But you don't know how difficult it was to see you getting prettier and brighter and all for *him*. To listen to you sigh over a smile of his and be completely unaffected by my kisses."

"Oh, I wouldn't say I wasn't affected. You're a pretty good kisser, you know."

"You'd better be careful. Effusive compliments like that go straight to my head."

"Well, as you've said, I go for men with big heads." She slipped back into his arms and added, "But only if they're good kissers."

"Isn't Addleton a good kisser?"

"Don't know. Don't care."

"He never got to kissing, huh?" asked Steve, sounding highly pleased.

"Never got to hand-holding. I have my standards, you know." She cuddled closer and kissed his jaw. "Steve?"

He was busily nuzzling his way down her neck. "Ummm?"

"What do you think of naming our first girl Elizabeth?"

For the second time he went utterly still. At length, he said, "Fifteen."

"What?"

"You're running fifteen miles before breakfast," he said firmly before showing her just what a good idea he thought it.

Journey across 19th century Europe with lovers whose deepest passions are ignited, whose loftiest destinies are fulfilled.

The Heiress Series

Roberta Gellis

Desert Hostage

Diane Dunaway

Behind her is England and her first innocent encounter with love. Before her is a mysterious land of forbidding majesty. Kidnapped, swept across the deserts of Araby, Juliette Barclay sees her past vanish in the endless, shifting sands. Desperate and defiant, she seeks escape only to find harrowing danger, to discover her one hope in the arms of her captor, the Shiek of El Abadan. Fearless and proud, he alone can tame her. She alone can possess his soul. Between them lies the secret that will bind her to him forever, a woman possessed, a slave of love.   **$3.95**